Blood of a Stranger

To Bill and Joan Sullivan
With best wishes,

Bill Booth
12/31/07

Bill Booth, MD

authorHOUSE®

AuthorHouse™
1663 Liberty Drive, Suite 200
Bloomington, IN 47403
www.authorhouse.com
Phone: 1-800-839-8640

This book is a work of fiction. People, places, events, and situations are the product of the author's imagination. Any resemblance to actual persons, living or dead, or historical events, is purely coincidental.

First published by AuthorHouse 8/16/2007

ISBN: 978-1-4343-2234-0 (sc)
ISBN: 978-1-4343-2235-7 (hc)

Printed in the United States of America
Bloomington, Indiana

This book is printed on acid-free paper.

This book is dedicated to my wife and best friend

Cherry

ACKNOWLEDGMENTS

To the numerous individuals without whose help this novel would not have been completed, I am forever grateful.

Those who read the complete novel at various stages and offered opinions and helpful advice include Ken Reynolds, Alan Beske, Barbara Schneider, Audrey Williams, Becky Nickens, and especially Cherry, my wife of 45 years who read not only the original version but several revisions.

Members of the Big Canoe Writers' Group read portions of the book and provided additional assistance with their critiques.

Without the enthusiasm and commitment of a small group of would-be novelists in Baton Rouge, Louisiana, the book probably never would have been started.

Heartfelt thanks to all of you.

WVB

BLOOD OF A STRANGER

Prologue

Well past midnight the dark figure of a man slipped down a dim hospital corridor, his soft-soled shoes almost silent on the tile floor. Because he might be recognized if seen, the man preferred to go unnoticed. He congratulated himself on timing as he made his way down the deserted hallway to the clinical laboratory and entered through a door where a sign read "pick up and drop off".

The laboratory consisted of a circular central core with separate suites for various departments and offices around the periphery. The man stood on the edge of the room and allowed his eyes to adjust to the low light. A faint chemical smell hung in the air.

He tiptoed to the door of the on-call room, which was illuminated by a night light near the floor. A young man, the tech on call, slept on a narrow cot in a corner of the small cubicle. For a few seconds the man watched the tech's rhythmic breathing. When he heard soft snoring, he proceeded.

He crossed to the serology section of the lab where a large refrigerator holding tubes of serum stood against the wall. The light through the glass refrigerator door cast a dull, yellow glow on his face as he looked in and located the object of his search. He opened the door and lifted a rack of labeled tubes to the front of the shelf.

Eyes now adjusted to the light, he scanned names until he found the one he wanted. But just as he reached for it, he heard the sound of a door opening from the hallway. His breath came in short gasps as he glided into the shadow of the refrigerator, trying both to hide and to keep the refrigerator door open. He knew if he let the door close a loud snap would result.

A light came on in the core. He heard muffled voices then the sound of another refrigerator door opening. Seconds later he heard the door snap shut, followed by the scrape of a chair and muted conversation.

The man's heart thudded against his chest as he melted deeper into the shadows. His left hand remained between the frame and the refrigerator door, and he watched cold mist creep into the room through the opening.

Someone stifled a yawn, and another person laughed. The chair scraped again.

Rustling papers suggested records being completed. Agonizing moments later, he heard the sound of footsteps leaving.

A hallway door opened then closed.

The light went out.

The cot in the on-call room creaked as the tech went back to bed.

The man exhaled a deep breath he had been holding and waited until his fingers were numb inside the refrigerator before he moved again. Once more, he opened the door.

Although he could breathe at a normal rate now and his heart no longer pounded, he found it necessary to wipe sweaty palms on his trousers. He opened and closed his hands a few times to limber the fingers then slid a tube of serum from the rack and replaced it with another, labeled with the same name and date, that he took from his pocket.

Mission accomplished, he crept out of the lab and left the hospital. He felt confident there had been no witnesses and there was no evidence that he had even been there that night.

Chapter 1

Dawn approached, and the operating room team at Graham Memorial Hospital was tired. Conversation lagged, eyes grew red and thoughts turned to morning schedules.

On the side of an instrument tray positioned over the patient's thighs, a large, curved surgical needle lay cocked upward in the jaws of a needle holder. Dr. Brent Dalton yawned and stretched his back as Mary, the scrub nurse, turned for a moment to do something on the back table. Dalton asked for sponge forceps, looked at Mary's back then reached across the instrument tray to retrieve the forceps himself.

"Jesus!" he exclaimed, jerking the hand back. The needle holder followed and clattered to the floor with the large needle still clamped in its jaws.

Mary whirled around. "What...?"

Dalton stared at a rip in the palm of his right glove and watched his own blood drip onto the floor. The room became silent except for Harry Connick's mellow voice coming from the CD player in one corner.

A bucket at the head of the table held multiple empty blood bags, and paper wrappers lay scattered around an overfilled hamper. The surgeon and his assistant had been summoned from their sleep at one o'clock on this cool, November morning. The clock on the wall now read six-twenty. On the street in front of the hospital, traffic in Houston's Texas Medical Center grew congested.

1

Dalton held out his hand for the circulating nurse to remove the torn glove. "What happened is I just cut the hell out of myself with that damned liver needle you left on the front of the Mayo stand. Why didn't you put it away?"

The circulator pulled Dalton's ruined glove from his hand and poured some alcohol over his injury.

"Damn, that burns!"

Mary looked at the surgeon through watery eyes and blinked away the moisture. "I'm sorry, Dr. Dalton! We were just so busy, I -- I should have moved it." She held out a new glove, and he jammed his hand into it. "I'm sorry," she repeated.

"Oh, it's not your fault," Dalton said, calmer now. "I shouldn't have reached across your stand like that. It's just a small cut. Now let's finish this case and get some breakfast."

They worked on in relative silence for a few minutes before Jeff Bingham, anesthesiologist, looked across the drapes at the young surgeon who assisted Dalton. "Do you have that nice, warm glow yet, Morgan?" he asked over the rhythmic whoosh of the ventilator.

Gary Morgan flicked his blue eyes up toward the head of the table while his fingers tied a knot in a stitch just placed by his chief. "Glow? What glow is that, Jeff?"

Bingham, dark circles under both eyes, glanced back at the fifth year resident and winked. "You know. That satisfying glow you get from saving a piece of shit like this. Just makes you feel good all over, don't it?" Bingham chuckled and shook his head. "What a save."

Morgan shifted his weight to the other foot and rolled his eyes toward his chief. "Oh, yeah. That warm glow. You bet."

Dalton, the senior surgeon, grunted as though about to respond then turned toward the scrub nurse. "Give us some number one Vicryl, Mary, and let's get out of here."

Dalton paused, waiting for the stitch. He looked toward the head of the table where Bingham chuckled to himself. The surgeon stood up straight and did not speak for a moment, his lean frame emphasizing his six-foot height.

"Listen, Jeff, just cool it. You don't know anything about this man. He might be a graduate student in astrophysics for all we know."

Dalton's flashing, brown eyes and graying but still dark hair lent authority to his deep voice.

Bingham snorted. "Yeah, maybe he's the Mayor's son -- with needle tracks on both arms and shot two times in the belly. Looks like someone from a good family all right. Hell, we might even get paid for stayin' up all night!"

"Okay, Bingham, that's enough," Dalton said. "Somebody had to take care of this guy, and we were in the barrel last night."

Bingham mumbled something incomprehensible to the others. He sat down again on the stool at the head of the OR table and worked on the anesthesia record in silence.

All three of the doctors and both of the nurses working in the room were aware of the serious potential of a needle stick. It was a hazard they all faced on a regular basis, and at one time or another, all of them had been victims. But to the best of their knowledge, none of them had ever been stuck with a needle that had been used on a patient who had HIV. The patient tonight appeared to be a drug user -- many patients with gunshot wounds were, and the needle tracks confirmed it. This fact made him high risk for harboring any number of blood-transmitted diseases, including HIV.

Gary Morgan pulled back on a retractor to allow Brent the visibility he needed for a last inspection for any persistant bleeding or sponges that might have been overlooked. "Everything looks good," Brent said. "Let's close."

Brent began the closure, starting with the deeper, first layer of sutures at the top of the long incision.

"The first sponge count is correct, Doctor," the circulator informed him minutes later.

"Dr. Dalton, I'm sorry about your hand. I know I should have put that needle away," Mary said, reaching over to touch the sleeve of his gown with her gloved hand.

"No problem, Mary. Let's just forget about it," Brent responded, his composure restored. "I'm sure it won't amount to anything." He handed the needle holder back to her and paused, looking at Morgan.

"Gary, if you wouldn't mind finishing up, I'll go out and talk to the family." He peeled off his gown and gloves and dropped them into a red plastic bag marked "CONTAMINATED -- BIOMEDICAL HAZARD". The heel of his right hand was bloody, and he wiped it on a clean towel, preparing to leave the room.

"Sure," Morgan said, holding out his hand for the suture Mary held.

Brent paused at the door. "Do we have a name for this guy yet?"

Bingham glanced at the chart. "Yeah. Andy Simmons."

Brent walked through the swinging door from the OR and down the corridor to the doctors' lounge. The lounge was a medium sized, rectangular room furnished with several chairs and sofas that could best be described as Danish Modern. A couple of the chairs were recliners, covered in leather. Pictures of hunting dogs and other outdoor pastorals adorned the beige walls. A bathroom adjoined the lounge on one side, and a door to a locker room with racks of scrub clothes was near the bathroom.

Brent went into the bathroom and washed his hands with disinfectant soap. He squinted at the wound on the heel of his hand. It was more of a laceration than a puncture, not large enough to require a stitch, and it had almost stopped bleeding. In his locker he found an adhesive dressing to cover it. The base of his thumb had begun to swell a bit, and it started to throb just before he left the OR. Brent guessed from this appearance that the needle had gone into the muscle of his thumb.

***

The family waiting area near the operating rooms had begun to fill with relatives of patients scheduled for surgery that morning. Brent had a Pink Lady page the family of Andy Simmons.

Two people stood and came to the desk where Brent waited. Both were women, one much older than the other. Brent invited them with a gesture of his hand to step into the hallway, and he followed them out the door and into a private alcove where they could sit and talk.

Brent assumed that the older woman was his patient's mother. She was short and a little plump but neat-appearing with gray hair. She wore a blue dress with a floral print and a light blue jacket.

The younger woman appeared thin to the point of looking malnourished. Her straight, brown hair was pulled back in a ponytail. She wore faded jeans with a thin, beige sweater and a pair of Nikes. Her lipstick, rouge and eye shadow were all thick and dark, and it was obvious she wore no bra. She introduced herself as "just a friend".

As soon as introductions ended, Brent assured the women that Andy was stable, and everything was under control. They both breathed sighs of relief and thanked him. He then proceeded to tell them the extent of Andy's injuries and what he had done to fix things. "He'll be in the Recovery Room for a couple of hours then we'll move him to the Surgical ICU," he said. After answering a few questions, Brent stood to leave the room but paused.

"By the way, does Andy have any, uh -- chronic health problems as far as either of you knows?" he asked.

The two women exchanged glances before the younger one spoke again. "It's possible. He's had problems with drugs in the past, and he's lost a lot of weight in the last few months. We don't know why."

Brent thanked the women and went back to the surgery lounge. It was now seven-fifteen, and he had been up since one o'clock with Andy Simmons.

A padded chair in the corner of the lounge beckoned him, but Brent resisted. Changing into a fresh pair of scrubs made him feel a little better before he walked down the long corridor toward the emergency room. He needed to go there and fill out an incident report concerning his needle-stick injury. Brent also would have a blood sample drawn in order to document his current status relative to hepatitis and HIV, or the AIDS virus.

The emergency room had been remodeled about a year ago and was state of the art. It was circular, with twenty small, private cubicles around the periphery of a spacious nurses' station. Trauma bays and fracture rooms were labeled as such, and there was even a separate isolation room on the far side. Nurses, aides, and orderlies clustered around the center of the large, well-lit room.

Tim Richey was the doctor on duty. Brent found him leaning on a counter, cradling a cup of coffee at the nurses' station and enjoying a slight lull in the morning patient flow.

5

"This happens all the time," Richey said after Brent explained the reason for his visit. "We have to fill out incident reports two or three times a month for accidental needle sticks. I have yet to see any of them develop any problems." He took a swig of coffee. "Care for a cup? You look like you could use it."

"Thanks, I'd like one, and that's good news about the odds," Brent said, feeling a little better. He glanced at his watch. "So, what do we need to do while I'm down here?"

Richey held his cup in the air and got the attention of one of the aides then pointed to Brent. The young lady nodded in understanding.

"We'll document what happened to you in an incident report and then draw a blood sample for an ELISA and a hepatitis profile. It'll be run tomorrow morning, so you can get the results after that. Of course, you'll be negative at this point – unless you already have hepatitis or an HIV infection."

The young aide placed a Styrofoam cup full of black coffee on the counter in front of Brent. "Sugar or cream?" she asked, smiling at him.

"No thanks, Miss. And thank you for the coffee."

"You're welcome," she replied with a broad smile.

Brent looked down into his coffee and chuckled. He had grown accustomed to this kind of attention from the younger female employees and tried to ignore it.

"To get back to your comments, Tim, no, I don't have HIV, and I pray never to get it. And I've had hepatitis B vaccine, so you don't need to check for that."

He rubbed his chin for a second. "By the way, what does ELISA stand for?"

Richey scratched his head. "I haven't thought about that in quite awhile. Step over here to the lab area while I try to remember." They moved to the side of the room, and Brent took a seat, extending his arm on a cloth-covered board adjacent to the chair in which he sat.

Richey gathered a couple of blood tubes and the equipment needed to draw a sample of blood.

"I think ELISA's an acronym for 'enzyme-linked immune – no, immunosorbent – assay'. It's not specific, just used for screening."

He proceeded to prep Brent's arm in preparation for drawing the sample. "It can sometimes give false positive results if you have some other acute viral infection. Had any recent illness?"

"No, but I had a cold a couple months ago. Does that count?"

"Shouldn't have any effect." Richey inserted the needle into a vein near the bend of Brent's arm and drew a tube of blood. Then he released the tourniquet, put a cotton ball over the puncture site and folded Brent's arm. "There, that should take care of it."

"Thanks, Tim. I'll check with the lab in the morning. Who gets the incident report?"

"It goes to the Risk Control Committee, and yours truly just happens to be a member of that Committee. Believe me, this will be just a routine matter as far as they're concerned." He put his hand on Brent's shoulder. "In other words, don't lose any sleep over it."

Chapter 2

Brent left the ER and went back to the surgery wing where he called the lab and ordered an ELISA and a hepatitis profile on Andy Simmons under the "exposure protocol". In circumstances such as this, the protocol allowed testing of a patient's blood, off the record and at no expense to the patient, using samples already in the lab.

After a shower and another change of clothes, Brent made rounds on a few of his other patients. Then, breakfast forgotten, he returned to the surgery lounge. He would have to finish rounds between cases later that morning, since it was now after eight o'clock and time to start his first case for the day. Gary Morgan waited for him in the lounge, and Brent's pager had started buzzing over an hour ago.

"Morning," Gary said when Brent walked into the lounge and poured himself another cup of black coffee. "How's the hand?"

"Hello again," Brent said, taking a seat. "The hand is fine, just a needle stick -- one of the hazards of the profession. You know, 'goes with the turf' and all that sort of stuff," he said between sips of coffee. "Any calls from ICU?"

"No, but I passed by there a few minutes ago. Looks like our warrior is pretty stable. Blood pressure is good, but his pulse is still a little fast -- one twenty."

"How's his urine output?"

"A little on the low side -- twenty cc's last hour."

"Sounds like his tank's not full yet. Has the CBC come back?"

9

"Yeah, his `crit's just twenty seven."

"How about giving his nurse a call and order two more units of packed red cells. Tell her to bolus him with five hundred of Ringers and let us know if that doesn't bring his output up.

"Sure," Gary said, heading for a phone.

Brent's elective cases that morning began with a laparoscopic gallbladder removal, followed by a liver resection for cancer. He had a special interest in surgery of the liver and bile ducts and enjoyed a busy practice. He also lectured on occasion and had published several articles on these topics. The cases proceeded without any problems, and they were finished shortly after noon.

The appointment schedule in Brent's office that afternoon was full, and Gary had patients of his own to see in the residents' clinic. After a quick sandwich together, the two agreed to meet the next morning for rounds at seven in the ICU. The incident with the needle had been forgotten -- almost.

Brent's last patient that afternoon was Raymond Atkins, a post-op from last week. Raymond was a forty year old accountant who had AIDS. Brent had been asked by Raymond's internist to implant a venous access port that would allow ongoing therapy with the intravenous medications that were now an integral part of Atkins' life.

Raymond had lived with the knowledge that he had the HIV virus for years. He had remained free of symptoms on oral antiviral medications until a couple of months ago, when a bout of pneumonia proved very difficult to treat, thanks to his compromised immune system.

Brent's mood sagged when he saw Raymond's chart in the rack outside the exam room. His mind flashed back to the incident earlier that day. He looked at the heel of his hand. It was still swollen and discolored around the area where the needle had stuck him.

"Damn!" he mumbled, closing the chart.

"Hello, Raymond," Brent said entering the small examination room. He placed the chart on the table by the door and proceeded to wash his hands, a routine he had adopted years before. "How's the port working out?"

Raymond smiled at him, and Brent noticed his deep-set, hollow eyes. "Just fine, Doc. It sure beats having those nurses digging in my arms looking for a vein every day."

"Good," Brent said, moving toward the examining table. He put on a pair of gloves and removed the small dressing from Raymond's upper chest.

"Hey, this little incision looks good. No signs of infection, and the stitches under the skin will dissolve by themselves," Brent told him. "Dr. Hanneman will keep an eye on it after today. He'll let you know if you need to see me again."

"Thanks, Doc."

"Good luck, Raymond."

Brent left the exam room. *Damn it all! Why didn't Mary move that needle off the instrument tray? Why did I reach for the forceps instead of waiting for them? Why, why, why?*

Brent considered making a trip to the library to look for some specific information about the risk of acquiring an HIV infection as a result of a needle stick. A glance at his watch told him it was too late to do that today. Besides, he could call the librarian in the morning and have her do an online search. That would be the easiest way. And he still had to go to the hospital for evening rounds on his post-ops from that morning.

Pulling himself back to the present, Brent dictated his charts for the afternoon and left the office. Outside, it had begun to rain, and the sky was as heavy and gray as Brent's mood. Rounds took less than an hour.

Fifteen minutes after leaving the hospital, Brent pulled into his garage and locked the car. His home was a two-story, white stucco, French manor that he and Nicole bought when they moved to Houston. At first, they worried about being able to afford the payments, but that was no longer a problem.

Nicole was in the kitchen preparing supper. She stood at an island under a hanging pot rack in the center of the room.

She smiled at him, dark brown eyes twinkling, and tossed a curl of her shoulder-length brunette hair off her forehead.

"Hi, Babe! I'm just about ready to put some chicken in the oven. Can I fix you something to drink?"

Brent walked over, put his arms around her slim waist from behind and gave her a tight squeeze. "Thanks, I'll get something in a minute." He kissed her on the side of the neck and held the squeeze a little longer than usual.

"My, what's that for?" Her arms were locked at her sides, and she held a pepper-shaker in her right hand, a drumstick in her left.

"Just for being here."

She pulled her right arm free and proceeded to dust the glistening chicken with black pepper. "Did you have a rough day?"

"No, it was pretty routine." Brent walked to the refrigerator and took out a bottle of Pinot Gregio. He studied the label for a few seconds, cut the lead cap off the top and extracted the cork then poured each of them half a glass. He put Nicole's near her on the counter top.

She looked over her shoulder at him. "You're kinda quiet tonight. Are you sure there's nothing wrong?"

Brent knew he had to tell her about the needle stick. He just didn't want to alarm her too much when he did.

"I'm just tired after being up most of last night. Had a gunshot wound to come in at one o'clock?" He paused a couple of seconds before continuing, "… and I got stuck with a needle while we were operating on him. Not much damage though, just a little cut."

"I'm sorry. Maybe you can catch up on your sleep tonight. Hungry?"

"A little." Brent picked up the newspaper from the counter top and stared at it. The print blurred, and he blinked, forcing his eyes to focus. A slight throbbing sensation in his hand commanded his attention. The small discomfort made it difficult for him to think about anything else, although he continued to stare at the newspaper. A series of new thoughts now occurred to him. It was possible that he soon could be a carrier for HIV. Unprotected sex was known to be the most common method of spreading the virus. What if he became infected, and Nicole caught it because he neglected to protect her?

Brent put the newspaper aside and looked at the wound in his palm. Nicole walked over and sat beside him.

"Is that where you got stuck?" she asked, looking at the discolored area.

"Yeah, that's the spot."

"Does it hurt?"

"No, it doesn't. It should be all right in a couple of days." He took a sip of wine, swished it in his mouth, swallowed. "I'm a little concerned about it though. I was operating on a patient who is not what you'd call a picture of good health."

"What do you mean?" Nicole said, her smile gone.

"Well, this guy has been using drugs and losing weight. He could have just about anything from syphilis to cancer. I've ordered some blood tests to see if he has anything I need to worry about."

"Oh, no!" Nicole exclaimed, her hand flying to her mouth. "When will you know?"

"The lab results should be back tomorrow morning."

"What are you checking for?"

"Well, I'm most concerned about HIV and hepatitis C. There's not much else I'd be likely to get from a needle stick. And even if he has one of those, I'm not at high risk to catch it."

Nicole kissed him on the forehead. "Oh, Brent, I knew something was wrong." She hesitated, looking into his eyes. "But I'm sure it will turn out all right. Why don't you turn on the news, and I'll watch it with you as soon as I get this chicken in the oven."

The baked chicken with sour cream and mushroom sauce was delicious, but they both left most of their servings uneaten. After supper, Brent excused himself and went upstairs for a shower then straight to bed. In spite of his fatigue, or perhaps because of it, he was unable to sleep. Tossing and turning, his mind wandered back to the time he and Nicole had met.

***

The year was nineteen-eighty-two, almost ten years ago, and Brent had completed half of his last year of surgery residency at Charity Hospital in New Orleans. The demands of his training program were often unrealistic, and the hours and days spent on the large, open wards and in the twelfth floor operating rooms seemed endless at times.

Sometimes, after completing a long stretch on call in the hospital, the young doctors would walk a couple of blocks toward Canal Street to an intimate little place known simply as Joe's Bar. They would have a beer or two and on occasion share a table with some of the off-duty nurses who also frequented Joe's.

In other words, Joe's was a place where singles gathered, and more than a few trips to the altar resulted from romances which began there. With Brent and Nicole, it had been a case of instant attraction.

He had walked alone into the dim room around seven one night and ordered a bottle of Coors. Glancing around, his gaze locked on an attractive brunette who sat with a small group of other young people at one of the tables.

Striking up a conversation had been easy, and he was pleased to learn that Nicole was a nurse and shared an interest in sailing. They soon spent time together on a regular basis.

The couple spent many happy days on Brent's little Daysailer. They explored Lake Ponchartrain and got to know each other in the process. In just a few weeks, they had made plans for a July wedding – not June, because all residency programs ended on the last day of June each year.

Brent looked at several possible places to begin practice, and Houston was first on his list. The city had a reputation for being on the leading edge of medicine. It also was located near Galveston Bay and the Gulf of Mexico, where they could keep a sailboat. And, perhaps most important of all, Brent had received an attractive offer by an older surgeon there to join him in a very busy practice.

They honeymooned for two weeks on a chartered bareboat in the Virgin Islands. It had been the happiest two weeks of Brent's life, sailing among the lush, tropical islands for days on end with Nicole always at his side.

At night, they avoided the more crowded anchorages and sought out smaller, private coves where they could be alone. There, they would sit in the cockpit for long hours late into the night, talking and snuggling in the close confines of the boat, looking up at a clear sky filled with millions of bright, twinkling stars.

Among a host of other things, they talked about the children they wanted to have. He said two or three boys would be about right, and she said the same number of girls would be even better but boys would be okay too. Their future appeared as bright as the brilliant sky.

***

Later that evening, Brent closed his eyes and feigned sleep when Nicole crept into bed. She kissed him on the cheek and soon breathed deeply in peaceful sleep.

Much later, Brent looked toward the darkness of the window by the bed and wondered how much longer it would be until it would be light enough for him to get up and go in for work without alarming his slumbering wife.

In a few short hours, the results of Andy Simmons' HIV test would be known.

Chapter 3

As expected, the following day Brent learned that his ELISA was negative. Also as expected, his patient Andy Simmons tested positive. They both were negative for hepatitis C. It might now take several months of repeated testing to learn if Brent had been infected with the HIV virus.

One of the first things Brent did was to visit a medical library and request a computerized search of the literature on the subject of transmission of the HIV virus by accidental needle puncture. He also asked for a search on the risk of transmission of the virus from an infected surgeon to his patients. He found quite a bit of information and took consolation in the fact that only about one in two hundred accidental sticks with contaminated needles resulted in infection with HIV. In addition, there had been just a few documented cases of transmission of HIV from a surgeon to a patient, and none of those had been in the United States. Brent assumed there would be few instances where infected surgeons would continue to practice.

***

One evening, a couple of weeks after the needle stick, Brent and Nicole lay in bed talking.

"My, you smell good tonight. New perfume?" Brent moved closer to Nicole and put his arm around her. She snuggled closer to him.

"No, just a new shampoo, but I'm pleased you noticed it. Maybe you're coming out of the shell you've been in for the last two weeks." She nestled her head against his chest and tickled the hair on his belly with the soft tips of her fingers. "Got something in mind?"

Brent shifted his position and leaned up on an elbow, causing Nicole to face him and assume the same position.

"Nicole, there's something we need to talk about, Sweetheart." He looked down at the bed and began smoothing the sheet with his free hand.

"Well, what is it?" she asked.

Brent rolled over and opened the drawer in his bedside table then reached in and pulled out a small package. He twisted back to face Nicole and showed her what he held in his hand.

She frowned at the small package, a puzzled look on her face.

"A condom? Brent, a condom? Do I have to remind you that we're trying to have a baby? What in heaven's name are you doing with a condom?"

He lay back on his pillow and took her hand in his then sighed and closed his eyes. "I think we're going to have to put our family plans on hold for awhile, Hon," he whispered, squeezing her hand and pulling it to his lips.

She pulled her hand free and sat up straight. "Brent, why should we? We agreed that we'd have a baby this year. Your practice is going well, and neither one of us is getting any younger!"

He shifted his weight and clasped both hands behind his head. "Well, you know I told you about getting stuck with a needle a couple of weeks ago. Remember?"

"Of course I remember! How could I forget, since the man probably has AIDS?"

"That's what I'm getting at, Nicole. If I should catch the same virus then the very worst thing that could happen would be that I'd cause you to become infected too."

"But you tested negative."

"That just means I didn't have the virus when I got stuck with the dirty needle. It takes time to develop the infection and build up detectable antibodies in the bloodstream. If this happens to me, I won't know about it until the next time I have a blood test."

Nicole lay on her back and looked up at the ceiling in silence for a minute. "We could use the rhythm method, and you can have a monthly test right before I'm due to ovulate. As long as your test is negative, we won't have to use protection. Won't that work?"

Brent shook his head. "It's a good idea, but it could fail."

"How?"

"It takes time – days to weeks – for the blood test to become positive once the virus has multiplied and spread. It's what is referred to as 'the window', and there's no way to tell when you're in the window. Just think, if I did infect you and you got pregnant at the same time, our baby could also become infected. That would be the worst of all possible scenarios."

Nicole sighed and was quiet for a couple of minutes. Still without speaking, she rolled over and kissed him hard on the mouth. Then she reached down and took the small package from his hand and began to open it.

***

Brent's practice was busy. The main reason was that his older partner died about six months after Brent joined him. The older surgeon had built up a large base of referring physicians over the years he had practiced in Houston, and Brent now found himself the recipient of these referrals in what was again a solo practice.

He welcomed the opportunity to work, since work filled his mind and blocked his preoccupation with the date for his next blood test. He put in long hours daily, never postponing anything that could be done before he quit for the evening. As a result, he found himself leaving home before sunup every day and getting home late every night.

The next few weeks dragged by, Christmas came and went, and Brent worked through his daily schedules. The puncture wound on his hand had long since healed, but the wound to his psyche still festered. The incident was seldom out of his mind.

Brent became silent and withdrawn, even in the lounge where the other surgeons sat between cases, trading anecdotes and telling jokes. At home, he tried to occupy himself by reading or watching television. He and Nicole seldom brought up the subject of the accident.

19

After the holidays, the elective case load declined somewhat, but the volume of emergencies more than made up for the slack. One such case was that of a young student Brent was asked to see one evening in mid-January in the emergency room.

The patient was a twenty year old student from one of the local colleges. Her name was Sheila Walters, and Brent paused when he entered the small cubicle in the emergency room.

Sheila's long, silky black hair covered the pillow on which her head rested. Deep-set, dark eyes riveted into Brent's without blinking or turning away. The smooth skin on her face and her dark complexion suggested a Spanish ancestry. She was beautiful enough to be on the cover of a fashion magazine.

"Hello, Sheila, I'm Dr. Dalton," Brent said upon entering the room. "I understand you're having some trouble with a stomach ache." He closed the curtain behind him.

"Yeah, it started early this morning," the young lady replied with a hint of annoyance. "I woke up around three, feeling nauseous. My stomach started hurting right after that."

Brent opened the curtain just enough to signal one of the nurses that he needed her presence for an examination. She entered the cubicle and re-closed the curtain.

"Show me where it hurts," Brent said, pulling the drape sheet down just enough to expose her thin abdominal area.

"Right here," Sheila replied, pointing to the lower part of her abdomen, over to the right side.

"How about over here?" Brent asked, examining the left side first to avoid hurting her.

"Just a little bit," Sheila said. Then, as Brent moved his hands over to the right lower quadrant, both her hands grabbed his and held them off her abdomen.

"Oh, shit! Right there! It really hurts there!"

He removed his hand and stepped back from the table. "I need to do a pelvic exam," he said both to Sheila and to the nurse. "And collect a urine specimen for a pregnancy test, please."

A few minutes later, Brent completed the pelvic exam and looked at the lab reports. The pregnancy test was negative, and Sheila's white blood cell count was elevated. He went back into the examination room, crossed his arms on the front of his chest and looked down at the young woman.

"Well, Sheila, it looks like you may have appendicitis. There's just one good way to treat that, and that's to remove the appendix – an appendectomy."

She appeared crestfallen. "Are you sure it's appendicitis? An operation! Oh, Christ -- shit."

Brent was a little surprised at the girl's reaction but had heard worse on numerous occasions.

"Well, there's no way to be positive that it's appendicitis. A CT scan might confirm the diagnosis, but that's not a hundred percent accurate either. I'd still recommend an appendectomy, regardless of the CT results. You have all the right signs, and your blood tests show an elevated white cell count. There is a risk that it could rupture if we don't go ahead with surgery."

Sheila remained silent for a couple of minutes, rubbing her forehead with eyes closed.

"Then, let's go ahead," she said at last. "My parents are on the way to the hospital. They should be here any minute."

Brent nodded and went to the telephone at the nurses' station. He dialed the number for the surgery scheduling desk. "I've got an appendix down here in the ER," he told the scheduling clerk. "How soon can we get a room?"

"Let's see. Dr. Wilson just started on a ruptured aneurysm in room three, and they're working on a multiple trauma in room five. You can follow whoever gets out first."

"Any estimate on the time?"

"You know how long some of these cases can run. I'd guess it'll be anywhere from one to three hours. The trauma case has been going for awhile, so they might finish first"

Brent glanced at his watch. It was a little after six.

"Okay, I'll either be in the surgery lounge or on my beeper. Let me know when you send for my patient."

The time interval couldn't have been much worse. It was too short to go home and too long to wait in the lounge.

"Would you like for me to call Dr. Morgan to assist?" the clerk asked.

"No, thanks. I shouldn't need any help. It's just an appendix."

Brent decided to watch the evening news in the surgery lounge. There were a few journals there too, and he could read until the OR was ready. He called Nicole to let her know he would be late, again tonight.

"Brent, you've been late every night the last couple of weeks. You're pushing yourself too hard – next thing you know, it'll be you who's in the ER with a coronary."

Brent laughed. "Thanks for being concerned, Hon. I've just been doing this for a couple of years. Besides, I'm not going to wait until I'm fifty years old before I start looking for a partner."

"That's what you need to do, Sweetheart. Why don't you start looking for a partner now. We never have any time for ourselves anymore, and I still want to get started on our family as soon as we know you're okay."

Brent leaned back in his chair and sighed. "Yeah, everything you say makes sense. I'll think about it."

"I'll save your supper in the fridge."

"Okay, Babe. Love you. Bye"

***

Brent drove into his driveway a little after ten that night. Sheila's appendix had been quite infected, but it hadn't ruptured. The appendectomy had proceeded without any problems. She should be home in a couple of days. Nicole was asleep in bed, and he didn't try to awaken her.

In another two weeks, he would have the ELISA repeated.

Chapter 4

In Brent's mind, the next two weeks passed slower than a six-month jail sentence. Gary Morgan spent many long hours working both at Brent's side on rounds and across the operating table from him, and their mutual respect for each other increased by the day. Gary might even have felt he was the only one who knew what had caused the change in Dalton's personality, since he knew the test results on Andy Simmons. Others, however, also became involved.

Jim Shubert, an internist with whom Brent had consulted following his injury, had advised repeating the ELISA in six weeks, although results could change in as little as two. Other than Nicole, Jim was the sole person with whom Brent chose to speak concerning the incident. Now though, he had more questions, and he needed to talk to somebody.

The day before the blood test was to be repeated, Brent called Schubert and asked if he could drop in for a few minutes.

"Of course, Brent. Just slip in the back door. I'm in my office."

Brent took the stairwell down to Schubert's floor and walked over to the small door marked private entrance. He opened the door and went in without knocking, knowing no one was likely to be nearby. Schubert, as he had said, was in his office shuffling through a stack of mail.

The office was small and messy. Bookshelves were filled to overflowing, and stacks of journals rested on every available flat surface. An Audubon print of a snowy egret hung behind Schubert's desk, and the walls were adorned with diplomas and certificates.

"Hello, Brent. Have a seat," Schubert said offering his hand. Brent shook it and sat in the Queen Anne's chair toward which his host pointed. "What's on your mind today?"

"Take a wild guess," Brent said without enthusiasm.

"So you've thought of some questions." Schubert leaned back in his chair and crossed his hands behind his head. "Okay, shoot."

"In just another couple of days, I'll have the second test result back. I'm sure it'll be negative, and we can all relax." Brent crossed his legs and leaned back a little in his chair. "Isn't that what you see happening, Jim?"

"That would be reassuring, of course, but you could still convert to positive at a later time."

Brent stiffened somewhat at this bit of information. He had thought he would know for sure after tomorrow's test result came back. He looked at the internist and shifted in his chair then gazed downward and cleared his throat. "How much later?"

"Perhaps as much as six months, even a year, after the needle stick."

Brent took a deep breath. "That's a long time to have to wait." Crestfallen, he continued to look at the floor while he considered this latest bit of information. Lifting his eyes to look out of the office window, Brent could see bare trees in the distance, bending in the cold, January wind, their branches raised as if in supplication to God above.

"Jim, what happens if I do test positive?" he asked in a low voice.

Shubert leaned forward in his chair and placed his palms together in front of his face, almost as though he were praying. "You know, of course, that the odds for that happening are quite small."

Brent uncrossed his legs and leaned forward, elbows on his knees. "Yes, unless it happens to me. Then it's a hundred percent!"

Jim reached for a mug of coffee sitting on his desk. "How have you been feeling, Brent?" he asked, continuing to avoid Brent's question about what would happen if he were infected.

"Pretty run-down, if you want to know the truth. I may not have been getting enough sleep."

"Anything more specific?" Jim asked.

"Well, I have had some muscle aches and a bit of a runny nose for the last couple of days. Maybe coming down with a cold – hope it's not the flu."

Jim did not respond for a moment. He took another sip of coffee then put the mug back on the desk. "Brent, you may not know this as a surgeon, and I don't want to alarm you, but sometimes a flu-like syndrome can occur after infection with the HIV virus. It's not very specific of course, but it concerns me."

"If I have a fresh cold," Brent asked, "would that interfere with the result of my blood test?"

Shubert scratched his chin. "I doubt it. You'd have to be pretty sick. If your test comes back positive tomorrow then an actual HIV infection will be the most logical explanation."

Brent remained silent for a moment. "Does that mean -- you think I have the virus?" he asked, fearful of the answer.

"Let's wait for the ELISA to be repeated. If it's negative then maybe we'll have some reassurance that you probably don't have the virus."

Brent agreed with Shubert's recommendation and left the office. He knew it would be a long night.

***

Brent did not sleep well that night, and he awoke the following morning feeling achy and tired.

"Brent, your face is flushed, and you feel warm," Nicole said as he pulled on a pair of pants. "Let me take your temperature."

"Oh, that's not necessary. I just didn't sleep well last night," replied, looking away from her.

"Well, at least take some aspirin after you've had breakfast."

"Okay, Sweetheart."

They kissed and then Brent left for the hospital

***

Later that day, exactly six weeks after the incident in the operating room, Brent walked the long corridor to the lab and had another blood sample drawn. He knew the fact that the laboratory technician wore rubber gloves when she took the sample was a routine precaution, but it somehow seemed more personal this time, as though she didn't want to touch him. Her attitude however was cheerful.

"Morning, Doctor Dalton," the tech said. "I see we need just one tube of blood for your test. If you'll have a seat and roll up your left sleeve, we'll have you out of here in a minute."

After having the blood sample taken, Brent took the elevator to the second floor and began making his morning rounds in the Surgical ICU. Most of the time, he would have walked up the stairs, but today he felt drained of energy. It would be twenty-four hours before the results of the ELISA were available. Rounds seemed to take forever.

In the office that afternoon, everyone seemed to be in a chatty mood. Because of the distraction it provided, Brent welcomed a late afternoon consultation regarding a patient with abdominal pain.

The situation was repetitious of the one with Sheila Walters a couple of weeks earlier. Brent scheduled the appendectomy to be done in the first available operating room, but it was after midnight when he drove up the quiet, tree-lined street in West University Place and turned into his driveway.

Nicole waited for him in the den. She lay on the sofa, reading a book. Her hair was gathered in a neat ponytail, and she wore an old, faded blue sweat suit.

"There's some supper in the refrigerator, if you're hungry," she said, sitting up and patting the seat beside her.

"I'm not hungry, thanks. Just exhausted." Brent remained standing.

Nicole remained seated without saying anything for a few seconds, just looking at her husband.

"Brent, you're always exhausted. There's something wrong! You and I both know you're pushing yourself too hard. Why are you doing it? Is it about that needle stick? When are you going to know something?"

Brent knew he had not been open and honest with her for the last six weeks. He had wanted to tell her about the blood test before it was drawn, but when he tried he always failed to follow through. So he had left things with an explanation that he would be tested on a regular basis for a few weeks and implied that it would be up to Jim Schubert to decide when to do it. She had asked that he tell her when it was done, and he said he would.

"I'm sorry, Sweetheart. I know the last few weeks have been – strained," Brent said.

Nicole straightened and looked up into his downcast eyes. He leaned on the door sill and took a long, deep breath then went over to her and sat down.

"I'm sorry, Love. I guess it's been bothering me more than I realized. I had a blood sample taken this morning. It'll take a day or two to get the result back. Maybe then we can relax a little bit." He leaned over and bussed her cheek with his lips. "Right now though, I'm exhausted. I think I'll just go up to bed."

Brent got up from the sofa and made his way up the stairs. Nicole followed later.

***

Brent felt like he had just gone to sleep when the alarm went off at five o'clock. He showered and dressed in a set of scrubs then left for the hospital, trying not to disturb Nicole.

Gary Morgan waited for him in SICU.

Andy Simmons was still in the Unit, having made slow progress after a couple of major complications. First, his kidneys had failed but to his good fortune didn't shut down altogether. Then, his lungs had filled with fluid, making it necessary to put him on a ventilator for a couple of weeks.

Brent's already disturbed sleep pattern had not benefited from the phone calls every night about low urinary output and problems with oxygen saturation, but Andy had improved the last several days. When Brent mentioned Andy's HIV status to him, it became apparent that his patient already knew he was infected with the virus. He just neglected to tell anyone else about it.

"Morning, Brent, how's the cold?" Gary held Andy's chart in one hand while thumbing through it with the other.

"The cold's much better, thanks."

"That's good. It looks like our patient is about ready to leave the unit," Gary said, still flipping pages in the chart.

"Yeah, it's about time," Brent replied. "How about his numbers?"

"Vital signs are stable and normal. Blood work all looks better and has been improving for the last week."

"What about his urinary output?" Brent asked.

"It's averaging thirty to forty cc's per hour," Gary replied.

"Sounds good," Brent said. "Let's take a look at him."

They walked over to Andy's bed at the far side of the large, open room rimmed with cubicles brimming with monitoring equipment. Gary spoke first, an indication of the rapport he had developed with the patient.

"Morning again, Andy. Dr. Dalton wants to take a look at you."

"Sure thing," Andy replied. "He can look all he wants to. Guess he knows more about me than I know myself!"

Gary and Brent exchanged knowing glances without speaking. Brent knew Andy's mood was a reflection of his improved condition, but the attempt at humor failed.

Brent listened to both sides of Andy's chest with a stethoscope then pressed with his right hand on the abdomen, watching for signs of tenderness.

"You've made a lot of progress, Andy. Guess we'll send you upstairs today." He turned then and walked toward the door.

"Want me to talk to the family?" Gary asked.

Brent paused. "Yeah, if you don't mind. I'll finish rounds and meet you in the OR lounge in forty-five minutes." He scribbled a note on the chart and wrote an order to have Andy transferred to the surgical wing then left the ICU.

Later that morning in the OR, the circulating nurse handed Brent a note as he prepared to leave the room after a case. It read: "Call Dr. Martin in the lab when you get a chance."

Brent's heart pounded when he read the simple message. He knew what this call concerned but dreaded making the connection.

He finished the routine duties of writing orders and talking to the patient's family then went into the doctors' lounge.

Inside the room, the other doctors sat around talking and drinking coffee. It was just another day for all of them. Brent wished he could turn the clock back a few weeks and join them without having such dreadful anxiety.

He stared for a minute at a phone sitting on a small desk in the open room then turned and went into one of the private dictation cubicles, closing the door behind himself. He sat down and picked up the phone that was there, noticing that his hand shook as he did so. He dialed the number, and a deep, male voice answered.

"Dr. Martin here."

"Hello, Al. It's Brent. I'm returning your call."

"Brent! Thanks for calling right back. I was waiting for you."

"No problem," Brent replied. "What's up?" he asked, knowing full-well what the call concerned.

"It's the ELISA you had yesterday," Martin said. "Uh --I'm afraid there's some bad news." He paused. "Do you want to come over and talk?" He hesitated for a second or two. "Do you need to call from another phone?"

"No, it's okay." Brent's mouth was dry, and he felt pulses pounding in both sides of his neck. "We can talk now," he said putting his forehead down on the bend of his elbow on the table.

"Well, I'm afraid the ELISA is weakly positive." Martin paused to let this sink in then continued. "It was negative six weeks ago. Brent, uh -- it -- well, it looks like you've converted."

"My God!" Brent gasped. He fought a sudden, almost overwhelming urge to vomit. Although he knew that it was possible for this to happen, he had clung to the hope that everything would be all right. This was the worst thing he could imagine happening to himself, his worst nightmare come true. He had the AIDS virus.

"Brent, are you there? Say something."

Brent took a couple of deep breaths, cleared his throat then lifted his head and spoke again. "Are you sure, Al? Could there have been a mix-up -- or a false positive?"

Al Martin sighed into the phone. "I doubt it, Brent. We'll do some more testing, of course. I know this is devastating news."

"So, what's the next step, Al?"

"We'll get a Western Blot."

"I should know what that is, but why don't you refresh me."

"It's much more specific than the ELISA. So that will be the next step, for confirmation. But given the fact that you were negative six weeks ago, the likelihood of a false positive is slim, at best."

Brent felt drained. All he could think of to say was, "Thanks, Al. Please, whatever you do, don't mention this to anyone."

"Of course not, Brent. Trust me, this is just between the two of us at this point." Martin cleared his throat then added, "You do realize this will go to the Risk Control Committee, don't you?"

Chapter 5

Brent hung up the phone and stared at his feet for several minutes, his head spinning with thoughts.

This can't be happening to me! Not now, at the peak of my career! How can I tell Nicole? What will I tell my patients and colleagues? What will happen to my practice? How will the hospital board and medical staff react? Will the Board of Medical Examiners pull my license?

Brent stood and walked into the open part of the surgery lounge. Inside, several surgeons waited for their next cases to start. They were bent over in laughter from hearing yet another of Jim Wilson's outlandish jokes.

"Hey, Brent, did you hear the one about the tongue-tied peach salesman?" Jim almost shouted at him when he entered the room.

"Yeah, I've heard it," Brent said looking away. He turned and walked back out of the room. He needed fresh air and some solitude to get his head straight. Just get away from this place and these people for awhile, he thought.

True to form, just as Brent contemplated an escape, his beeper went off. He turned the buzzer off and answered the page. It was a message to call the emergency room.

Sheila Walters, the girl on whom Brent had performed an appendectomy two weeks earlier, was in the ER with severe abdominal pain and a high fever. Brent knew before he saw her that she had developed an abscess.

31

Two hours later, Brent pulled off his gloves and left the operating room. He went to the family waiting area to talk to Sheila's parents. They were in a private conference room outside the surgery suite.

Brent shook hands with Mr. Walters. He was a large man, not so much obese as just big. He stood at least four inches taller than Brent's six-foot frame. The grip from his powerful handshake could crush a weaker hand.

"Sheila is on her way to the recovery room," Brent began. "She developed an abscess near the place where her infected appendix was located. I've drained the pus and left a small rubber tube in the abscess cavity. She'll need to stay in the hospital for a few days until we're sure the infection is under control."

"But, she'll be all right?" Mrs. Walters asked, clenching the top of her purse with both hands.

"Yes, she should be fine in a week or so."

Mr. Walters stood in the corner of the room and scowled, both arms folded across his chest. "Doc, why did this happen? Did something go wrong the first time?"

"No, Mr. Walters, nothing went wrong. Her appendix was infected, and some of the infection spread in the area where we operated. This is a common complication after an appendectomy."

"But, shouldn't she have been on antibiotics?" Mrs. Walters asked, fidgeting with her purse. She stared at the wall behind Brent while talking, almost as if she were looking through him.

Brent went over to her and bent at the waist, looking her level in the eyes. "She was given antibiotics for the usual amount of time, Mrs. Walters. When she went home from the hospital, she had a normal white cell count and no fever. There was nothing to suggest persistent infection." He patted her on the shoulder as he rose and stood by the door.

The Walters thanked Brent, but he knew they were unhappy with the course of events. He also knew he had done nothing wrong but sensed they blamed him for their daughter's setback. He hoped that nothing else would go wrong in Sheila Walter's case.

The locker room was empty, and Brent changed into street clothes without having to talk to anyone. Then he went back into the lounge and asked Jim Wilson if he would cover for him through the weekend.

Jim agreed, since he and Brent usually signed out on each other and Brent never took much time off anyway.

Brent gave Jim a list of his hospital patients and told him that Gary Morgan would be available for assistance if needed. As an afterthought, he cautioned Jim about the Walters' attitudes.

Walking out of the surgery lounge, Brent's thoughts turned to Nicole. He felt a sense of despondency when he realized that he had neglected her so much in the past several months. She had been under as much stress as he had, but he hadn't given her the support he should have. Maybe they could spend the weekend on their sailboat. It would be the perfect place for a retreat.

Thirty minutes later, Brent was speeding down Highway 59 toward home in West University Place. He had called his office and told them Jim Wilson would be covering. He also had his appointments for that afternoon and the next day, Friday, rescheduled for the following week. This done, he had nothing scheduled until Monday.

Arriving home, Brent walked through the back door and into the kitchen. Nicole worked every other week with a home health care agency but was off this week. The house was quieter than usual.

"Nicole?" he called. Hearing no response, he walked into the family room.

She was there, sitting on a large, overstuffed sofa in the dim light. She sniffed and dabbed at her eyes with a tissue then turned her head away, not speaking.

"Nicole, what's the matter, Babe?" he whispered. He walked over and sat down by her. He tried to take her hand, but she drew away.

"Nothing." She dabbed at her eyes with a tissue.

"Nothing is wrong." She wiped her nose and sniffed.

"You said last night that something has been on your mind. It's not just that blood test. It's me, isn't it? Is it because we've been unable to have children? That's not my fault you know." She sobbed and buried her head in her lap.

Brent sighed. "No, Sweetheart, it's not you, and it's not because we don't have children." He folded his hands in his lap and hung his head. "I'm afraid I have some bad news, Nicole."

She raised her head and stared at him through red, watery eyes. A tear ran down one cheek and hung on her chin.

33

"Bad news? What is it, Brent?"

"I know I've been acting strange for the last six weeks. It's been a tremendous strain for me to try to act normal while waiting for this repeat HIV test. I know you've been the one to suffer, and I'm sorry. I guess trying to be close to you – intimate – during that time was the hardest thing I had to deal with. I just couldn't do it."

She moved close to him and took his hand. "Brent, you said you had bad news. What is it? Did you get the result from the blood test?"

Brent took her hand in his and lifted it to his lips. He kissed her hand and then closed his eyes as warm tears ran down his cheeks.

"I love you Sweetheart."

Several moments of silence passed before he continued. "My blood test is positive. I found out today."

Nicole's entire body went rigid.

"Positive? Oh, my God! Do you mean you have HIV?" She took her hand from his and stood up.

"Brent, tell me that's not right. You don't have HIV, do you?"

Brent dropped his head, looking at the apparent emptiness of his future on the floor between his feet. "I really didn't believe there was much chance I'd get it, but it's been on my mind every minute of every day. I guess that's why I've found it so difficult to talk to you -- to anyone."

Nicole was silent for a minute, her face a study of grief and shock. Then she erupted in a fresh flood of tears and threw her arms around him. Her body was warm, but she was shivering.

"Oh, Brent, why? Why us? It's not fair! All we've worked for, lost because of a total stranger!" She sobbed harder before looking at him again. "That son-of-a-bitch! I hate him!" Her fists doubled in anger then relaxed as she closed her eyes. "Oh, God, why has this happened to us?"

Brent held her tighter and let her cry. As the sobs subsided, they clung to each other. Neither could know what lay ahead, but Brent had some idea of what might happen.

Chapter 6

The Risk Control Committee for Graham Memorial Hospital met in the Board Room at seven in the morning on the first Friday of each month. Although the committee was small, its role in averting lawsuits was critical, considering the potential for losses. Because the first Friday of the previous month fell on New Year's Day, the committee had not met since December. The agenda was full.

At the head of the table sat the committee's chairman, pathologist Al Martin, a physician with deep-set, dark brown eyes and short, curly black hair. His bronze skin and chiseled features suggested a Mediterranean heritage, perhaps Greek. Dr. Alfred Lewis Martin, at age forty-two, was considered by his peers to be an excellent, if not outstanding, pathologist. He was chairman of his department and also had served for two years as chairman of the Risk Control Committee.

Helen Williams, an administrative secretary who worked for CEO John Kelly, distributed copies of minutes from the last meeting along with additional copies of the meeting agenda and all incident reports from the previous two months. She then took a chair near the head of the table and began recording minutes.

Dr. Martin called the meeting to order. Those in the group who were not yet seated balanced their cups, saucers, and rolls, and drifted to the table.

"If everyone has had a chance to review last month's minutes, and if there are no additions or corrections then we can entertain a motion for approval," Martin announced. The only sounds which could be heard for a minute or two were the shuffling of papers and clinking of coffee cups against saucers.

"So moved," boomed John Kelly, the overweight and graying hospital CEO. "Second," echoed Bill Rudman, one of Kelly's assistant administrators, before Kelly had closed his mouth. Sitting next to the obese CEO, Rudman was a contrast because of his athletic build, dark complexion and black, shiny hair that he combed straight back.

Across the table from Kelly and Rudman sat the two physician members of the committee other than Al Martin. Dr. Tim Richey, director of emergency room services, and Dr. Robin Smith, an internist and one of the youngest staff members. Their heads were together, and they laughed over some private joke.

At the end of the table opposite Dr. Martin sat Louise McArdle, a middle-aged, red-headed woman who scribbled notes while the others talked. She had been employed as a full-time attorney with Graham Memorial for the past five years.

"All in favor, say aye," Martin continued. There were a few grunts around the table. "Any objections?" Hearing none, Martin continued. "The minutes stand approved as read."

After a brief update for the committee by Ms. McArdle concerning the progress of a couple of pending lawsuits, attention turned to new business. Martin called on the Director of Nurses, Nancy Greenblatt, to report new incidents. She was a middle-aged, graying lady who sat stiffly upright in her chair, commensurate with her military background.

"We have six incident reports from the last two months," she reported. "Three concern employees, two concern patients, and one concerns a staff physician."

"The three employee incidents all appear to be of little concern. One involves a fall on a wet floor with no injury. The nurse who fell admitted it was her own fault for not watching where she was walking. The other two employee incidents concern accidental sticks with clean needles. Both of these resulted from attempts to recap the needles after drawing up medication."

John Kelly cleared his throat and interrupted. "Since both these incidents involved sticks with clean needles, there's not likely to be any problem, right?"

"That is correct," Greenblatt answered.

"Haven't all the nurses been in-serviced regarding our policy of never recapping needles for any reason?" asked Robin Smith, now attentive.

"Yes, they have," Greenblatt continued. "Every nurse in the hospital has attended at least one in-service meeting on this topic."

"Then why do we continue to have these needle stick incidents on a regular basis?" interjected Martin. "I, for one, am getting tired of having to deal with this issue on a recurring basis. Next time, the needles may not be clean."

"We have made progress," Greenblatt said. "Last year there were thirty reports of needle sticks, including the two from December, compared to fifty-five similar incidents for the previous year. There were no needle sticks reported for the month of January."

"Well, continue to work on it," Martin said, turning a page. "What about the two patient incidents?"

"One involved a fall out of bed. The guard rails were up. The apparent injuries were a minor abrasion with a contusion over the patient's hip."

"Was anyone else in the room?" Kelly asked.

"No, the patient has close family members living nearby, but they seldom visit and never stay with her overnight. A sitter would have been useful, but the family was concerned about the expense," Greenblatt said.

"Doesn't that absolve us from any liability?" Robin Smith asked, revealing his lack of experience in such matters.

"Not at all," replied McArdle. "We can be held responsible for virtually anything that goes wrong while the patient is at this institution."

"Let's move along," Martin said, shuffling his papers. "What about the other patient incident?"

"That one involved a burn from a hot water bottle that was left on an elderly diabetic patient's foot for an unknown length of time," Greenblatt said.

"Why an unknown length of time?" asked Smith.

"Because the hot water bottle was brought into the patient's room by a relative at the request of the patient. It has been against hospital policy to use hot water bottles in this institution for several years," Greenblatt reported.

"Any injury?" queried McArdle.

Nancy Greenblatt paused and raised her eyebrows before responding. "Yes, the patient developed gangrene and lost her leg."

Groans were audible around the room, and John Kelly covered his eyes with his hand.

"Do you mean we can be liable for this too?" Dr. Smith asked with hands held palm upward, as though unable to comprehend the reality of the situation.

Louise McArdle looked at the young internist with an expression of exasperation. "Of course we will be held at least partially liable, for the same reasons I just explained. We are the ones with deep pockets in this unfortunate situation."

John Kelly sat up straight and looked at his watch then interrupted once more. "Please monitor this incident closely and get reports from all personnel involved. Now, what about this last report concerning one of the staff physicians?"

Although the names of the nurses, patients, and the doctor involved in the incidents were on the reports provided to each of the committee members, they were careful not to mention names out loud. The reason for this practice was that minutes for the meeting were transcribed from a recording, and names were not routinely included in the minutes because of confidentiality concerns.

"I know about that incident," said Tim Richey. "It involves one of our surgeons. He was stuck with a needle while operating on a trauma patient, and the patient turned out to be HIV positive. The surgeon skewered himself in the palm of his hand when he reached for another instrument on the Mayo stand. He cleaned the wound with alcohol, and we had an HIV test drawn to document his status at the time of the incident. It was negative."

"What kind of needle was it?" Dr. Smith asked.

"It was a suture needle," Richey answered. "It had been used to repair a liver injury."

"Most of the documented cases of transmission of the HIV virus from needles have involved being stuck with a hypodermic type needle," Smith informed the committee, now animated. "Suture needles aren't hollow and don't hold much blood or tissue fluid. That decreases the risk of transmitting the virus."

"Did you give him gamma globulin?" Kelly asked.

"No," Richey said. "It's not effective in preventing infection in this situation."

"Too bad," Martin commented then took over the report. "The rest of the story is bad news. The doctor tested negative with the initial ELISA, but converted to positive when he had it repeated last week."

"Has he had a Western Blot?" asked Smith.

"Yes, but the result is still pending. It takes about a week to get it back," Martin said.

"What a nightmare!" Smith shook his head in disbelief. "We all know this sort of thing can happen but never think it will hit this close to home. This surgeon is one of the busiest guys on our staff. He works all the time, days, nights, weekends -- it never seems to make any difference to him."

The room grew silent for a moment then John Kelly spoke. "We'd better get a written statement from the scrub nurse involved. If she was negligent in some fashion, we could be looking at a big liability problem."

"I'll take care of getting a written report," Nancy Greenblatt said.

"What do we do about the surgeon?" Rudman asked, his dark eyes darting around the room. "Do we allow him to continue operating, even though he now has AIDS?"

"Now wait a minute," Dr. Smith interrupted. "He may be infected with HIV, but he doesn't have AIDS!"

"What's the difference?" Rudman asked. "If he is infected with the virus then he's capable of spreading it. You just said he's one of the busiest guys on the staff."

Smith leaned forward on the table. "He can live with the virus for years before he develops AIDS. And the risk of him transmitting the virus to a patient is extremely low, if not nil."

"Does that mean it's okay for him to continue practicing surgery?" Rudman asked, sticking to his point. "I don't want somebody grubbing around in my belly if he's infected with the AIDS virus!"

"I don't think there's anything we need to do or are required to do at this point," Tim Richey ventured. "His attending physician is required to notify the Public Health officials, since HIV is a reportable illness. He also is required to notify the State Board of Medical Examiners. To the best of my knowledge, there is no legal way we can or should attempt to prevent Dr. Dalton -- I mean, the surgeon involved -- from continuing to practice surgery."

"That's absurd!" Rudman blurted out, sliding his chair backwards and sitting bolt upright. "What about our responsibility to the public and to the employees of this institution?" His dark eyes flashed with anger.

"Now wait just a minute!" Smith shouted back. "I may not know much about the law, but I happen to know a bit about AIDS and HIV infection. The risk of a patient acquiring the infection from a surgeon is almost zero."

"Almost?" Rudman asked, raising one eyebrow.

"Yes, and probably IS zero." Smith said.

The room was silent for a few moments while the committee members contemplated this information. Both Rudman and Smith had made their points.

"Are there any applicable laws other than the requirements for reporting?" John Kelly asked.

"I don't think so," McArdle said. "But I'll have to check on it to be sure."

Someone sighed.

"Well, this meeting has run into overtime. If there's no more business to be discussed, we will adjourn until next month," Martin said, gathering the papers in front of him. He rose to leave, and the others followed suit.

***

When the phone rang, Yvonne Walters turned off the vacuum cleaner and hastened across the room on bare feet. She picked up the receiver on the third ring. "Hello?"

"Mrs. Walters?" a male voice asked.

"Yes, this is Mrs. Walters."

"You don't know me, but I'm calling as a friend. I believe your daughter Sheila had surgery performed in the recent past by Doctor Brent Dalton. Am I right?"

"Yes, she did." Yvonne wore an old, faded yellow bathrobe which tied in the front. She stood by a wall phone in her kitchen. Turning, she pulled a chair nearer the phone and sat down. "What about it?"

"You might be interested in the news that Dr. Dalton has the AIDS virus," the voice continued.

Yvonne did not reply right away. Her pulse quickened with the thought of Sheila being operated on by a doctor with the AIDS virus. "Who is this?" she demanded.

"Just a friend with your best interests at heart. Did you know that the AIDS virus can be transmitted by contact with a person's blood?"

"Well, yes. Everyone knows that," Yvonne replied after hesitating a couple of seconds.

"Have you read about the dentist in Florida who infected dozens of his patients with the virus?"

"Dozens! That many?"

"That's right, dozens, maybe more. The newspapers just scratched the surface of the affair. That's why I thought you might like to know about the surgeon, before it's too late. The dentist's patients didn't find out he was infected until after he died. By then, it was too late to do anything about it."

"What can we do about it now?"

"You could at least have Sheila tested for the virus. Then you would know whether or not she got infected when she had her surgery."

"Why should you care whether or not Sheila caught the virus?" Yvonne's nostrils flared and her eyes narrowed. She crossed her legs and bunched her robe up at the neck with her free hand.

"I just want to see justice done where justice is due, that's all. Good-bye, Mrs. Walters." Yvonne heard a click followed by the steady hum of a dial tone.

41

Yvonne replaced the receiver in its cradle but held it in her hand while she sat staring at the floor. After a few minutes, she gathered the robe around her neck and shivered a little before standing up.

Chapter 7

After Nicole had recovered from the initial shock of Brent's devastating revelation concerning his HIV infection, he persuaded her to spend the weekend with him on their sailboat. The change in pace and scenery would provide an opportunity for them to collect their thoughts and perhaps make some decisions about their future.

Little preparation was required. Nicole threw a few clothes and some makeup into a soft bag, and they stopped for food and drinks at a supermarket en route to the marina. They parked near the boat just as the sun touched the western horizon.

Caribe was a well-kept, forty-foot sloop, which Brent and Nicole had purchased a few years ago at a boat show on Clear Lake. For several months, they enjoyed frequent relaxing weekends on the yacht, but during the last year, those times had become rare because of Brent's work schedule. The last time they had been aboard was more than two months ago.

Brent stooped to adjust the lines and brought *Caribe* closer to the dock. He stepped aboard and took the bags of groceries and supplies which Nicole handed him then helped her step aboard. A cool breeze drifted across the open cockpit and rippled the surface of the water behind them.

"It's good to get back to the boat again," Brent said, stretching his arms over his head. He unlocked the entry to the companionway, opened the front of the hatch and latched it in place. Next, he slid back the hatch cover and climbed down the steep steps into the dim, cool interior of the boat, sliding his hands down the smooth, polished wood handrails as he went. The pleasant smell of fiberglass and wood filled the cabin. Brent located the main breaker for the electric power and turned it on then flipped a few light switches. The salon filled with light. Nicole handed down the bags from the cockpit and then joined him below.

Caribe's interior was filled with polished teak and mahogany, and Brent loved the way it looked and smelled. The salon, or living area, occupied the center of the boat. A large seating area built around a dining table took up most of the space in the front of the room.

Behind the dining and sitting area, at the bottom of the companionway steps, was a small galley. Complete with stove, refrigerator, and cabinets for storage, it was quite self-contained. Along the side of the salon opposite the galley and dining area, a long, narrow, built-in sofa stretched along the entire length of the cabin in front of a small navigation station. Private cabins were at the front and rear of the boat, and each had its own bathroom, or head. The cabins could be entered through mahogany doors which separated them from the salon. It was a cozy and functional arrangement.

Although they had never sailed any farther than the outer reaches of Galveston Bay, Brent and Nicole shared pipe-dreams of someday taking *Caribe* south across the Gulf of Mexico to the Yucatan or Belize, or perhaps around the tip of Florida to the Bahamas. Now, it seemed doubtful that those dreams would ever be realized.

Brent knew he had to force himself to stop dwelling on the recent past and all its negative implications. He climbed back up the companionway steps and paused at the top. "If you'll stow our gear, Matey, I'll put some charcoal in the grill."

Nicole smiled up at him. "Okay, Skipper! I'll fix drinks and a salad while you cook the steaks."

An hour later, they sat in the cockpit, talked, and sipped coffee. It had taken just a few minutes to clean the galley after supper, and the marina was almost empty. They enjoyed the privacy.

Gentle breezes pushed waves against the side of the boat and caused just enough movement to let them know they were on the water. Rope halyards clacked against metal masts all through the marina as other sailboats rocked in their slips.

Brent took a sip from his mug and leaned back against the cabin bulkhead. "I love that sound. It's like there are a hundred wind chimes around us."

"Yes, it's very pleasant," Nicole said, looking toward the distant horizon where a few stars twinkled in the east. "I love it too."

They continued with idle conversation for over an hour, avoiding the specter that loomed in both their minds before Nicole broached the subject. "Have you decided what you will do with your practice?"

Brent hesitated for a minute and took another sip from his mug. He sighed and stretched his legs. "No, I haven't. Of course I've thought about it a lot, but there are many things to consider -- and things I don't know."

"What do you mean, 'things you don't know'?"

"I've told you about the Western Blot, so that's still out there. Maybe Somebody up there will decide He likes me, and it'll turn out negative." He swirled the last of the coffee in his mug before tossing it down in one swallow. "Not much chance of that happening though."

After a moment, Brent continued. "And I don't know what the hospital board's reaction to this bit of news will be. To my knowledge, none of the medical staff has ever tested positive for HIV. I don't even know if the State Board of Medical Examiners will allow me to continue practicing surgery. Most important of all, I don't know if patients will continue to see me once news of this leaks out."

Nicole looked surprised. "Leaks out? HIV test results are confidential! No one else should know."

"That's true," Brent replied. "But the reality of today's hospital environment is that medical records are reviewed by every Tom, Dick, and Harry who works for an HMO or an insurance company. It's just a matter of time until word gets out."

Nicole held her warm mug in both hands. "Brent, what if you were to retire? Do we have enough money saved? I can work full-time anytime I want. Could we make ends meet that way?"

"That's crossed my mind," Brent said. "I'm afraid we're not anywhere near having enough money saved for retirement. I couldn't afford to pay my health insurance premiums if I lost my eligibility for group coverage with the medical staff."

Nicole's forehead wrinkled. "I hadn't thought about that. What a potential disaster!"

Neither of them spoke for a few minutes then Nicole broke the silence. "Will you have to start on any treatment or be hospitalized soon?"

"No, I could go for years before developing any symptoms. I'm not sure about treatment, but it's a good thing I've always been healthy up until now. That may give me a little more time before I get sick enough that I'd have to stop working."

They contemplated the future for several minutes, sitting in the cockpit of the sailboat while it rocked in time with the gentle waves. It was a beautiful evening, and the clear, winter sky glowed with stars. They both wore light jackets to ward off the chill of the night air.

"There's our old friend, Orion," Brent said, pointing toward the southern sky. "Over the eons, I guess he's seen lots of bad things happen to us earthlings." He paused for a moment before continuing. "You know, this isn't the worst thing that can happen to a person."

Nicole appeared startled. "What do you mean!? What on earth could be worse?" She sat upright and stared at him.

"Well, at least we have several good years ahead. I deal with people every day who find out they have incurable cancer or some other fatal disease. Many of them can expect just a few weeks or months of a pretty miserable existence before they die. At least, we still have a chance to do some of the things we've always wanted to do."

Nicole leaned back against the cabin and stretched her slender legs out along the seat. She looked up at the sky again. "You mean, like sail to the Virgin Islands?"

After a few moments of thought, Brent said, "Maybe. But for this weekend, Galveston Bay sounds like a reasonable destination."

***

The weekend turned out to be sunny and mild but breezy, creating almost ideal sailing conditions. *Caribe* handled like a dream, and both Brent and Nicole felt their spirits lifting as the time passed.

They discussed their plans for the future several times and decided to take things one step at a time. They would avoid making any hasty decisions. And, perhaps more important, they both resolved not to allow themselves to dwell on the negative aspects of what might happen. Some things were beyond their ability to change, and all they could do was keep their chins up and carry on.

Brent knew the result of the Western Blot would be available the following Thursday.

Chapter 8

Monday morning, Brent left home before seven and drove to the hospital with renewed enthusiasm. The day was bright and sunny, and traffic was light. He parked in the doctor's lot and went into the back of the building through a small, private entry. Everyone he met seemed to share his good spirits.

Gary Morgan waited at the nurses' station on the surgery floor. He had collected the charts they needed for rounds and had stacked them on a small cart.

"Morning," Gary said with a mock salute. "Did you have a nice weekend?" They started down the first hallway together, Gary pushing the cart with the charts.

"Yeah, it was great," Brent replied, taking the first chart off the cart. "We spent the weekend on our boat -- sailed down to Galveston Bay and back again. The weather was perfect." He paused and thumbed through the chart.

Gary glanced over Brent's shoulder and studied the chart while they talked. "I've done a bit of sailing myself. Back when I was in college I used to crew for a friend who did a lot of offshore racing. I'm afraid I'm kind of rusty now."

"That's interesting. It's like riding a bike, you know. You don't forget how." He closed the chart and prepared to go into the patient's room. "Maybe you'd like to go out with us sometime."

"Yes, I would like that. Just let me know when."

Rounds proceeded without incident, and Brent found all of his patients doing well. He and Gary stopped by the dining room before heading to surgery. The room was filled with the robust smells of fried bacon and rich coffee.

Trays filled, the two walked into the crowded dining area and looked for a place to be seated. There were no empty tables, but Brent saw Bill Rudman at a table by himself near the center of the room. They walked over.

"Good morning, Bill," Brent said. "Mind if we join you?"

Rudman looked startled. "Uh -- sure. I mean, okay," he stammered, wiping his mouth with a napkin.

"How are things in Administration?" Brent asked as they seated themselves.

"Oh, fine, I guess," Rudman replied. He put the napkin by his plate, still filled with food, and glanced around him at the other people in the cafeteria.

Brent and Gary sat down and began eating. "Is something wrong?" Brent asked.

"Of course not," Rudman replied. He picked up his fork and stirred his scrambled eggs then looked at his watch. He slid his chair back and took a swallow of orange juice. "I almost forgot. I have a meeting in my office."

Rudman slid his chair back, rose, and walked away from the table, leaving his tray and breakfast.

Brent and Gary looked at each other in surprise. "Wonder what got into him?" Gary puzzled out loud.

"I hope I don't know," Brent said.

"Isn't Rudman the brother of that young woman you've told me about who had AIDS and died last year of post-op complications?"

"Yes, he is. Her name was Carla Brodhurst. She was a sweet and beautiful woman who caught the virus from her husband. He was a drug addict."

"Sad," Gary said, taking a bite of toast. "What happened?"

"She had been ill for several years and then developed a severe gallbladder infection. I was consulted for surgery. We operated as soon as possible and did all we could for her, but she died of sepsis.

Rudman never seemed to accept the fact that we did everything possible."

"I see," Gary replied, finishing his coffee. "How tragic -- in more ways than one."

They finished eating in relative silence then walked to the surgery area to begin the morning's cases.

Brent was concerned about Rudman's peculiar behavior at breakfast. After finishing his last elective case that morning, he decided to drop by the lab and pay Al Martin a visit.

Brent walked through a central receiving area to the histopathology lab where he found Martin peering through a microscope. "Hello, Al. Got a minute?" he asked.

Martin looked up. "Sure, come on in." He pointed to a chair in front of the large table where he sat.

Brent took a seat.

"What's on your mind?" Martin asked.

Brent sighed before he answered. "The ELISA results from last week."

Martin looked back into his microscope. "What do you mean?"

Brent leaned back in his chair and crossed one leg over the other. "Al, is anyone aware of the results other than you and me?"

Martin cleared his throat and looked up from his microscope. "Yes, unfortunately, there are some others. Your incident in the operating room was discussed at last Friday's Risk Control meeting, and the result of your test was mentioned. Don't worry though, it was a closed meeting. Everything discussed there is confidential."

Brent sat bolt upright. For a few seconds, he was speechless. "How in the hell could you let that happen, Al?" he asked, incredulous. "You said this would just be between the two of us!"

Martin got up and walked over to the door and closed it. "Now calm down, Brent. I told you last week the Risk Control Committee would discuss your situation. The information is confidential. The Committee is accustomed to dealing with issues like this. It won't get out."

"How can you be sure?" Brent asked, forcing himself to speak with a steady voice. "Do you have any idea what it will do to me if news of this leaks out?"

"Of course," Martin said. "Have you decided to talk to anyone else about this yourself? After all, someone needs to be managing your case. You can't do it alone."

Brent sat again. "I've talked to Jim Shubert. He knew I was having the ELISA repeated last week."

"Have you told him it was positive?"

"No… I thought we had to wait on the Western Blot results before we knew for sure," Brent reminded him.

Martin sat down again and frowned. "It might be a good idea to have a talk with him. Your case stirred up quite a bit of concern at the Committee meeting, and I think it's advisable that you be under someone else's immediate supervision, just as a precaution."

Brent felt overwhelmed. "We don't even know for sure that I have the virus -- so why was it brought up so soon at the Risk Control Committee?"

Martin looked at his watch before speaking, and when he began speaking, his voice rose in pitch and his words were close together.

"It wasn't brought up before it should have been, Brent. The Committee routinely discusses all incident reports from the previous month. Your incident would have been discussed at the January meeting, but the meeting date fell on New Year's Day, so the meeting was postponed until February.

"It wasn't as if someone was eager to discuss it. We are obliged to deal with all incidents that might have any potential risk for liability to the hospital. And we always gather as much information as possible on each incident before discussing it."

"So this is considered a liability risk for the hospital," Brent said, amazed that his own interests seemed to have been of no concern.

"Of course it is," Martin said, calming down. "Brent, the hospital is responsible for credentialing you to perform surgery. If you should pose any risk to your patients, for any reason whatsoever, the hospital board is at fault and is liable. That's why your case will be of so much interest to the Committee in the future." He paused while his comments sank in.

Brent didn't reply.

"Now, if that's all, Brent, I need to finish reading these slides," Martin concluded, again glancing at his watch.

Brent sat without responding for a minute then rose from his chair. "Thanks, Al. Sorry if I seemed abrupt, but this business has me a little edgy."

"No problem, Brent. I'm always here if you need someone to talk to. And good luck."

Brent left the office. Four days had passed since he had learned his ELISA was positive, and he sensed his world coming apart.

He reminded himself of the decision he and Nicole had made: deal with things as they occurred and keep their chins up. He must avoid slipping into the frame of mind he had been in for the previous six weeks, but he could sense the shadow of depression creeping up on him.

Thursday, he would get the Western Blot result. God, how he hoped it would be negative, and he could get back to a normal life. Thursday seemed years ahead.

***

Sheila Walters appeared to be doing well. Brent saw her in the office on Wednesday for a check-up. Three weeks had passed since her appendectomy, and another week had gone by after Brent had taken her back to surgery to drain her abscess.

She was lying on the exam table when Brent entered the room. Her appearance was about the same as when he first had seen her. Long, black, silky hair flowed over the pillow on the examination table, and dark, deep-set eyes locked on his when he greeted her. A faint smell of good perfume caught his attention. Chanel number something?

Sheila's mother sat in a chair in the corner and nodded without speaking when Brent greeted her. It was easy to see that the daughter had not learned her grooming skills from her mother, who wore no makeup at all.

"How have you been feeling, Sheila?" Brent asked, smiling.

"Like crap," Sheila replied. "The incision still hurts when I move."

"Let's take a look at it," Brent said, pulling the drapes aside to expose her slim waist and lower abdomen. Her drain had been removed, and the incision had closed on its own a short time afterwards. "It looks just fine -- not red at all -- no swelling." He proceeded to palpate her abdomen, when Mrs. Walters interrupted.

"Shouldn't you be wearing gloves to do that?" she asked.

Brent was surprised by the question. "No. The incision has healed, and there are no signs of infection. My hands are clean. Gloves are not necessary."

"Aren't you still touching her?" the mother asked.

Brent was baffled by her attitude. "Mrs. Walters, I'll be glad to wear gloves while touching your daughter, if it pleases you," he said, donning a pair of exam gloves in order to finish Sheila's examination.

Satisfied that there was no infection present, Brent removed his gloves and made a note in the clinic chart while giving Sheila instructions about activity restrictions and driving. When he had finished, she pulled her sweater back down. He helped her off the table then offered his hand to Mrs. Walters as he prepared to leave the room. She ignored the gesture and walked around Brent to get her coat from a hanger near the door.

Puzzled by Mrs. Walters' unusual behavior, Brent left the room. He told Sheila that she needed to see him again in two weeks, unless she had a problem of some sort and needed to come back earlier. Mrs. Walters had remained silent after her questions concerning the gloves.

***

Later that day, in their nice but not very well kept house in Pasadena, Yvonne and Michael Walters talked about the visit to Brent's office. Most of the smell from the nearby refineries was kept outside the house by the air conditioning, and he drank beer while Yvonne prepared supper. He wore a pair of khaki pants and a tee shirt and sat barefoot at the table. She had already told him about the mysterious phone call concerning Dr. Brent Dalton's "AIDS infection".

"I couldn't believe my eyes, Michael. He examined her incision and touched all around it with his fingers without putting on any gloves!"

"Did he seem to be all right?" Michael asked, taking a large swallow of his beer.

"Well, he acted kind of funny. It seemed like he just had to touch us. He wanted to shake my hand before we left, but I pretended not to notice. Do you think he's gay?"

"How would I know if he's gay? Did he act gay?"

Yvonne pondered the question for a minute and took a sip of her beer. "He didn't have limp wrists or anything like that. I don't know. How can you tell?"

Michael stared at the wall and ignored her question. "Yvonne, do you really think Sheila could catch AIDS from him? How would we know if she did?"

Yvonne paused, rubbing her forehead with a thumb and two fingers. "We could take her to Dr. Johnson and have her tested," she said. "She's the one who sent us to that quack in the first place."

"What'll we tell Sheila?"

"Just tell her the truth. Tell her that Dalton has AIDS, and we want to find out if he might have infected her," Mrs. Walters concluded.

Yvonne clapped her hand to her mouth in shock. "Oh, my God! What if he has? She did get an infection from what he did to her. You know, that dentist in Florida infected most of his patients without them even knowing it until after he was dead!"

Chapter 9

Gary Morgan looked up at him, causing Brent to reflect on what had just happened. They were finishing a routine case, a colon resection, and Brent had asked for some three-ought Vicryl when he was ready to close the patient's fascia. It was an obvious error, since the material was much too small for the strong layer of tissue.

It was Thursday, three days after Brent had learned that his test results had been discussed at the Risk Control meeting and a week since he had been told that his ELISA had converted. The result of the Western Blot had not returned when Brent called the lab at seven that morning, and it seemed he couldn't think of anything else.

"Three-O Vicryl? -- for the fascia?" Gary asked, his eyebrows raised in surprise.

"I'm sorry, I guess I'm getting ahead of myself," Brent said in a low voice. "Gary, would you please finish closing -- I need to make a phone call." Turning away from the table, he stripped off his gown and gloves.

"Sure," Gary Morgan replied, but Brent was already out of the room and walking down the hall. He paused at the phone in the lounge then changed his mind and walked toward the laboratory.

Brent found Al Martin in the same chair he had been in when they parted company the previous Monday. "Al?" he said, as he entered the room without knocking.

Martin looked up from his paperwork. "Oh, hello, Brent," he said with a smile. "Have a seat," he said gesturing toward a chair.

"I expected to get the result of the Western Blot back by now," Brent said, ignoring the invitation to be seated. "It's been a week." He paced the floor in front of the desk.

Martin scooted his chair back and got up. "I'll check to see if I can find anything."

Brent followed the pathologist out of the room to a receptionist's desk, where he inquired about serology reports.

The receptionist shuffled a few stacks of paper and shook her head. "They're not here, but we just got some reports back about half an hour ago. They're still in the file room."

Brent continued to trail Martin across the lab. They entered another small room over to one side of the main lab and found a technician sorting a stack of papers.

"Did we get any Western Blot results back from last week?" Martin asked.

"Let's see," the tech said, sifting through the reports. "Yes, -- one," she said, handing a report to the pathologist. "It's coded. Do you want me to print it out?"

Brent's heart began beating faster, and again he could feel his pulse throbbing in his neck. He was glad his name was not written on the report for everyone to see.

"That's all right," Martin replied, looking at the slip of paper. "I can de-code it in my office."

They walked back to Martin's office, and Brent looked over Al's shoulder while he typed in some information on his computer. Within seconds, the machine blipped a few times, and a printed message appeared on the screen. First was Brent's name, followed by a string of numbers and the date of the test then the date of the report. Then, after skipping a couple of lines, the word "INDETERMINATE" appeared in the column for results.

"Indeterminate!" Brent slammed his fist down on top of the table. "How can that be? I thought the Western Blot was the final answer!" He was shaking with frustration.

"This happens sometimes," Martin said. "Sorry, but I don't know anything else to say. I know how important this is to you, but we'll just have to wait awhile and repeat it."

"Wait! How long this time?" Brent couldn't believe this was happening to him.

"Another six weeks," Martin replied. "Even then, the results could still be indeterminate. Then we would have to wait another six weeks."

"How long can this go on?"

Martin shrugged and wrinkled his brow. "Most of the time, not longer than three months, but we'll test you for a year unless you test positive before that time."

"Isn't there some other test available?"

Martin shook his head. "Not at this time. This doesn't look good, you know. An indeterminate test result is actually a weak positive. But the lab won't report it as positive until the result is unequivocal."

"What about the Risk Control Committee? What will happen there?"

"Well, of course they will have to be kept informed of developments." Martin leaned back in his chair and looked at his watch, a habit that Brent was beginning to find annoying.

"What about my rights to privacy? How can this be discussed without my permission?" He put his hands on his hips, not yet ready to end the conversation.

"It's a bit late to think about that. After all, you were the one who filed an incident report about the needle stick. That's tantamount to a written request for the case to be discussed by the Risk Control Committee." Martin looked at his watch again and folded his arms across his chest. "Sorry, Brent, but I have work to do. Do you want me to send a copy of the report to anybody else?"

Brent studied the man for a few seconds. He knew the pathologist was his friend, but he didn't appear that way now.

"You can send a copy to Jim Shubert," he said, turning to leave the room.

"All right, Brent, but you need to understand what is going on here," Martin said. "Nobody wants anything bad to happen to you, but there are others who are concerned too."

"Sure there are," Brent said, slamming the door behind him. Now, he had to go home and tell Nicole about this new development.

Chapter 10

As usual, Nicole stood at the island in the center of their kitchen when Brent got home that evening. She held a bottle of skim milk in one hand and a bunch of carrots in the other, and several bags of groceries rested on the counter top. "Hi, Sweetheart," she said when Brent walked in. "I just got back from the grocery store."

"Hi, Babe," Brent replied. He opened the refrigerator door for Nicole and gave her a squeeze around the waist when she reached to put the milk away. He walked around the island and sat on a stool across from her. A bouquet of fresh flowers decorated the countertop in front of him.

"Is anything wrong?" Nicole asked, pausing in front of the refrigerator. "You're not saying much. Anything going on that you want to talk about?"

"Well, sort of, I guess. It's something I should have mentioned to you earlier," Brent cleared his throat before continuing. "The HIV test I had done last week; it was just a screening test. It's not specific."

Nicole froze in her tracks, mouth agape. "Brent, what are you trying to tell me?"

"I had a confirmatory test; it's called a Western Blot. I just got the result back this morning."

Nicole remained frozen to the spot in which she stood. "What are you trying to tell me, Brent?" she repeated. "Is there a chance you don't have an HIV infection?" Her face brightened at this prospect.

Brent shook his head. "I—I'm not sure. At least I don't think that's the way it will turn out. My test came back indeterminate."

"Brent, that means it's not a sure thing that you are infected! That's great news! Aren't you glad?"

Brent hung his head. "I guess I'm too afraid to be glad. Al Martin explained that an indeterminate result is just a weak positive. They just won't call it positive until it's more definite."

"But there's still some chance the next test could come back negative! Brent, that's good news! I can't believe you're not excited." Nicole ran around the island and threw her arms around him. He hugged her back, and when she closed her eyes, tears ran down both cheeks.

***

That night, Brent tried to help in the kitchen, more just to be with Nicole now than for anything else. He was grateful to have her for a confidant and needed her support, but the need for support was new to him. He had become accustomed to being the support figure for countless others over the years, but now the tables were turned. The isolation he had felt for the last seven weeks had been miserable. He didn't want to repeat the experience.

Brent busied himself de-boning a boiled chicken. Nicole rolled dough out on the countertop to make dumplings. Chicken and dumplings was one of Brent's favorite dishes.

"Do we have to wait another full six weeks?" Nicole asked. "I'll go crazy not knowing what's going to happen. Isn't there some other test we could have done now?"

"No. I asked that same question. There are some things we don't have any choice about," Brent said. "This is just one of them. Al Martin said he expects the next result to be confirmatory."

"Tell me again, if it's a weak positive, why do they call it indeterminate?" Nicole asked.

"It boils down to a liability problem for the lab. If they ever made a mistake and called a test positive, and it turned out negative later on, you can imagine the consequences."

"I guess there is a tiny fraction of a chance that the next test will be negative," Brent admitted. "But I'm too much a realist to hope for that happening." He walked over to the stove and added the deboned chicken back to the broth from which he had removed it earlier.

"What do you think Jim Shubert will have to say?" Nicole asked. "Will he have to report the test result?"

"He won't have much to say. He'd have to report a positive test, but I doubt if he will report an indeterminate one. That means it will be a few weeks before the State Board gets wind of this."

"Do you think you will be able to continue practicing surgery?" Nicole asked, raising the issue that bothered Brent so much.

"That's the big question. I need to get some information from somewhere, but I'm not quite sure where to start."

Nicole began dropping the dumpling strips into the pot of chicken broth. "I guess it's like we said last weekend. We'll just have to take things one -- at a -- time," she said, her words timed with the dropping of the dumplings.

***

The weekend passed without incident. Brent covered for Jim Wilson and made the usual rounds at the hospital. He also fielded a few phone calls, but there were no emergencies.

Monday morning, Brent and Gary Morgan met for rounds on the surgery wing at six-thirty, as was their custom. "Morning," Gary said, smiling.

"Morning," Brent said back to him, reflecting on the young man's perpetual good mood. "Did you enjoy the weekend off?"

"Sort of," Gary replied, pulling charts out of a rack and putting them on a cart. "I spent most of it on a quick trip to Austin. There's a surgeon in solo practice there who's looking for a partner. It looks pretty attractive."

"How large is the hospital?"

"The one where he does most of his work is about two hundred beds, but there are several others in town, just like here."

"Did you agree to go in with him?" Brent asked as they pushed the cart in front of them down the first hall.

"Not yet. To tell the truth, I wanted to talk to you before I made any final decisions." He pulled a chart out of the rack and began turning pages.

"I'm flattered," Brent said, pleased with the compliment. "Maybe we can talk in my office later today, after surgery."

The cases for that Monday consisted of a couple of hernias and a gallbladder, and they were finished by eleven thirty. After changing clothes, they walked together to Brent's office, which was in an office complex adjoining the hospital.

Entering the back door to the office, Brent read his phone messages and answered a few questions that Susan, his office nurse, had about some calls. He asked Susan to order a couple of sandwiches then he and Gary went into Brent's private office and closed the door. They took seats on opposite sides of Brent's large desk.

"Did you have anything specific you wanted to ask me," Brent asked, leaning back in his swivel chair, "or did you just want to talk in general about the possibility of going to Austin?"

Gary smiled. "To get to the heart of the matter, I was wondering if you might be looking for a partner anytime soon."

Brent was surprised. He hadn't thought this was what Gary wanted to discuss, and the possibility of taking in a partner was the last thing on his mind today, in view of recent developments.

"It's obvious that you are pretty busy, and I know you don't take much time off," Gary continued. "I thought you might be getting to a point where you need another man. You could spend more time on your sailboat and enjoy life a little."

Brent scratched his head and smiled back. "In all honesty, I haven't given it a thought. But the possibility sounds interesting." He propped his lanky legs up on the corner of the desk. "When do you officially finish your residency?"

"I finished my stint as chief resident at County Hospital at the end of last October. When I finish my rotation with you at the end of June, I'll be through."

"Well, that's not far away, Pilgrim," Brent replied in a poor imitation of John Wayne. It had been weeks, he reflected, since he had done any of the corny imitations he once did so often -- when his spirits were high. He felt good.

Gary laughed out loud. "It would be a pretty smooth transition, since I already live here in Houston, and I'm not married. We both know we work well together."

"That's true," Brent said. "You know, operating with another surgeon is a lot like finding a good dancing partner. There's a certain rhythm –- an anticipation of the next move. Some have it, some don't."

"Does that mean you'll give it some thought?"

"Without a doubt!" Brent said, rising from his chair to answer a knock at the door. It was Susan with their sandwiches.

Gary began to ramble on about where he might live in Houston, the call schedule, and other such matters, but Brent became pensive. He paused from eating his sandwich for a moment and leaned forward in his chair.

"Gary, I'm flattered that you've come to me with this -- proposition. I think it's something that could work out well if we decide to go through with it." He looked down at his sandwich. "There is something you don't know about that may have a significant impact on your decision."

He took a sip of the tea Susan had brought, swished it in his mouth and swallowed before continuing. "Do you remember the night we operated on Andy Simmons, and I was stuck with a needle?"

"Sure -- yes, of course I do," Gary said.

"Well, I filled out an incident report on the accident and had some blood drawn that morning for an ELISA."

"I knew that."

Brent continued, "The initial ELISA was negative. I had it repeated six weeks later, and it had converted."

Gary's mouth hung open. "You converted! You mean you tested positive?"

"I'm afraid so. I had a Western Blot drawn last week, and it came back on Thursday. It was indeterminate."

"I can't believe what I'm hearing," Gary almost shouted. "This is terrible!" He got up and began to pace the floor then stopped.

"An indeterminate Western Blot? How can that be? I thought the Western Blot was the final answer."

"Believe me when I tell you I was even more frustrated than you are," Brent said. "It will be another six weeks before we repeat the Western Blot, and I'll know for sure. But there's a small chance the results could still be indeterminate at that time."

"It could also turn out negative, couldn't it?"

"Yes, of course. If you believe in miracles."

They looked at each other in silence for a moment, before Gary spoke again. "This does shed a different light on things, Brent. Will you be able to continue practicing surgery?"

"I think so," Brent replied. "In a worst case scenario, I should still have a few years of good health ahead of me. With a little luck, I could have ten years or so before the disease gets a grip on me. By then, they may have a cure."

Gary smiled at the attempt at optimism. "But what about public perception? Will people let you operate on them if they know you have -- the virus?"

Brent frowned. "That's the big question," he replied, looking down. "I doubt they will."

"Will you have to put up some kind of sign in the office advising patients you have HIV, or can this be kept confidential?"

"That's something I don't know. And there are a lot of other things I don't know either. I'll have more answers soon, I hope."

They dropped the subject for the time being and finished their sandwiches in relative silence, chatting about routine cases between bites. Gary appeared to get over his initial shock, and his usual good mood returned. "It looks to me like you are going to need a partner now more than ever," he said, tossing his napkin in a wastebasket by Brent's desk.

"Looks that way, Pilgrim," Brent agreed with a wink. "Think about it."

"I will," Gary said.

Chapter 11

A few days later, William Rudman sat at his desk reviewing files. Deep inside, he fumed about Brent Dalton continuing to practice as though nothing were wrong. He felt it was sweet irony that Dalton now had the same virus his late sister had, since Dalton had let his sister die following complications of gallbladder surgery.

Rudman pushed an intercom button on his desk and asked his secretary to get Louise McArdle on the phone. Minutes later, his intercom buzzed. "Ms. McArdle is on line one," the secretary said.

Rudman picked up the receiver and turned his back to the door of his office. "Louise, this is Bill Rudman. I want to talk to you about the surgeon we discussed at the Risk Control Meeting. -- that's right, Dalton. Can we get together later today to discuss that incident? -- yes, three o'clock would be fine. My office or yours? -- okay then, I'll expect you at three. Thank you, Louise."

Rudman hung up the phone and buzzed his secretary again. "Anita, mark off half an hour at three o'clock for a meeting with Louise McArdle here in my office. And bring me the folder on Dr. Dalton from the Risk Control file."

"Yes, sir," Anita said, rising from her chair.

***

Just before three, McArdle arrived and was shown into Rudman's office. Anita closed the door behind her as she left the room.

"Thank you for coming," Rudman said, gesturing toward a chair in front of his desk. "Have a seat." He ran his fingers through his long, dark hair and leaned back. "I was reviewing the minutes for the last Risk Control meeting and noticed that you were going to look into the guidelines for healthcare workers infected with HIV. Have you learned anything?"

"Yes, a little bit," McArdle replied, taking a seat. "For starters, the CDC eased its guidelines a few months ago."

Rudman raised his eyebrows. "Eased its guidelines? Why would they do that?"

"It was in response to evidence that transmission of HIV from a healthcare worker to a patient is rare. The CDC now recommends supervision of such professionals by individual states."

"What's being done here in Texas?"

"Texas is in compliance with these relaxed guidelines and doesn't place any restrictions on allowing an infected physician to practice."

Rudman drummed his desktop with the eraser of a pencil while he thought about McArdle's comments. He was disappointed. "Do you mean we will be forced to allow Dalton to continue practicing surgery in this facility?"

"If the Board of Medical Examiners feels he is not a significant risk to the public then we may not have a choice."

Rudman leaned back in his chair and frowned at the attorney. "There may be more than one way to solve this problem," he said. "Thank you for coming, Louise."

"You're welcome, Bill," McArdle replied, rising from her chair.

* * *

Another week passed, and everything seemed to be as normal as ever. Brent continued to do cases, make rounds and see new patients. His practice had blossomed over the last few years to the point he had difficulty getting all his work scheduled. He had been pleased with this course of events until last week.

He reflected on his conversation with Gary, and the more he thought about it, the better the prospect of taking in a partner sounded. He also had discussed Gary's offer with Nicole, and she had been excited about the possibility of him getting some relief from the demands of his practice. The thought of having every other weekend off seemed too good to be true.

Jim Wilson had agreed to cover for Brent that weekend, and the Daltons had invited Gary to go sailing. Brent's dark blue Suburban was loaded and ready to leave by two o'clock Friday afternoon.

"Did you put the steaks in the ice chest?" Nicole asked as they left the driveway.

"Yep, sure did," Brent replied.

"How about the lettuce?"

"Yes -- and the drinks, and the sandwich meat, and the mayonnaise, and the breakfast rolls, and the... "

"Enough, already!" Nicole laughed. "I guess we haven't forgotten anything."

"It looks to me like we've got enough food to feed an army," Gary said from the back seat. "When do we start eating all this?"

"Anytime you get hungry," Brent said, taking the exit to Red Bluff Road. Friday afternoon traffic was always heavy, but it was still early enough that they were able to make good time. They headed southeast toward Kemah, near Clear Lake on Galveston Bay. In less than an hour, the Suburban pulled up at the marina. Minutes later, they had the boat loaded and ready to sail.

Brent started the diesel engine, and the threesome backed *Caribe* out of her slip with Brent at the helm. Gary helped Nicole on deck by taking off sail covers and preparing to raise the mainsail.

Nicole uncleated the main halyard and took a couple of turns with it around a winch. "Gary, if you'll crank, I'll tail the line for you," she said to the second mate.

"Aye, Matey!" Gary said with a snappy salute. He took the winch handle and began to turn it then remembered to uncleat the mainsheet to prevent the sail from catching wind while he was in the process of raising it. "Point her into the wind," he shouted to Brent.

Brent smiled. "You see, Pilgrim, it's just like riding a bike. You don't forget how."

"I think you're right!" Gary shouted back. "I feel like I was on deck yesterday doing the same thing I'm doing right now,"

"Deja vu all over again!" Brent quipped. Gary and Nicole laughed.

It was a clear, sunny day. The wind blew at a steady fifteen knots out of the southeast, and *Caribe* sliced through the waves like a scalpel. High, scattered cumulous clouds drifted overhead. They tacked several times, and Gary took a turn at the wheel to see if he remembered how to steer.

"You handle the boat well," Brent said after they completed another tack and Gary eased off the wind.

The younger man looked up and studied the shape of the sails. "Thanks. I had forgotten how much fun this is."

The sun was low on the western horizon when *Caribe* nosed back into her slip at the dock. After the deck lines were cleated, they soon were lounging in the salon with cocktails. Nicole breezed around tidying things up and getting a few dishes out for supper.

"I love your boat," Gary said. "What's her displacement?"

"About twenty tons," Brent replied. "She has a full keel, which can be a disadvantage in these inland waters, but she's capable of sailing around the world if we wanted her to do it. The navigation equipment is state of the art."

"How much water and fuel does she hold?"

"About four hundred and fifty gallons of water and a hundred and fifty gallons of diesel fuel," Brent said. "Loaded, she draws about six feet of water."

"I would have to agree, she's a world cruiser," Gary said, taking a sip of his Bloody Mary.

"The only thing she lacks is a galley slave," Nicole said. "If we are going to have steaks for supper, someone needs to get the charcoal out and start a fire in the grill."

The two men laughed and rose from their seats. Brent followed Gary up onto the deck and pulled a bag of charcoal from one of the lockers. He poured some of it into a grill which was attached to the railing then saturated it with liquid starter. Soon, the charcoal blazed with a warm glow, and they sat in the cockpit.

The men talked about sailing and boats for awhile. Then, as it almost always did, the conversation turned to medical topics. The climate of private practice changed as fast as cars switching lanes on the Interstate. With the encroachment of managed care, solo practitioners like Brent were becoming dinosaurs, part of a dying breed.

Brent sipped his drink and gazed toward the horizon. He cleared his throat.

"Gary, have you thought any more about the possibility of us working together?"

Gary watched the flames in the cooker for a minute before he replied.

"Yes, I have. A lot. It's been on my mind almost all the time. I wish I could say that I have made a definite decision, but I can't. I'm sure it would work -- if that, uh -- problem we discussed doesn't become a nightmare."

Brent looked down into his half empty glass and swirled its contents. A couple of moments passed before Gary spoke again.

"Sorry, Brent. I didn't want to bring that subject up."

"It's okay. I understand." Brent put his glass down and stretched. "We'll just have to wait and see about that, I guess. On a brighter note, we haven't talked yet about salary and benefits," he said. "I can promise you they'll be generous, probably better than you'll find anywhere else -- under the present circumstances."

"I'm not concerned about salary," Gary said. "I just don't know what to do about this joker that's been dealt. What if the practice dries up?"

"I appreciate your frankness," Brent said after a minute. "I've thought about that too, and all I can say is, I would be willing to step out of the practice if it appeared that was happening."

"You mean retire?" Gary asked.

"I'm not sure I could do that. I would like to do whatever I could to continue working. That might mean doing something without patient contact."

Gary shook his head. "What a loss. A talented surgeon shuffling papers for a living." He studied the reflection of the moon across the water. "Do you think that's what could happen?"

"Anything can happen," Brent replied. "I don't expect anything drastic to take place overnight, and that's one of the reasons I need a partner. By bringing you into the practice while I can still work, we can shift things toward you over a couple of years, and I can fade out. Within two years you could find yourself in one of the busiest surgical practices in Houston, and I could salvage something in the process. That's a lot better than just closing the doors and watching it all go down the drain."

"I hadn't thought about it that way," Gary said. "You make it sound attractive." Pausing a minute, he added, "I should be able to give you a definite answer by the end of the week."

"Excellent, Pilgrim," Brent said with a smile. "Now I'd better get those steaks on the grill, or we'll be eating them raw."

***

Saturday and Sunday were sunny and warm for late February, and Brent, Gary, and Nicole sailed down into Galveston Bay both days. They took turns at the helm and put *Caribe*'s colorful spinnaker out when running before the wind on the return trips to Kemah. The large, parachute-like sail looked like a hot air balloon in front of their boat, and they found themselves back at the marina in record time Sunday afternoon.

The boat tugged at its lines like a playful puppy while the threesome transferred gear to the Suburban. They then proceeded to wash down the topsides to get rid of dried salt spray that had accumulated over the weekend. Brent and Gary talked about sailboats and surgical cases all the way home, but the subject of their possible partnership was not brought up again.

Brent felt tired but relaxed and happy when he and Nicole went to bed that night. Ten weeks had passed since he had been stuck with the needle, but his life had changed less than he would have predicted at this point. He and Nicole made love on a regular basis, but they did take precautions so she was protected.

Chapter 12

Sheila Walters' parents had not allowed her to return to Brent's office in spite of the surgeon's instructions to see him again two weeks after her last visit. Instead, they chose to see Dr. Catherine Johnson, a pleasant, middle-aged family practitioner. It had been a month since Sheila's appendectomy.

Dr. Johnson whisked into the examination room with Sheila's chart in her hand. Her auburn hair was done up in a French twist, and she wore a white lab coat over her knee-length, brown dress.

"Hello, Sheila." Dr. Johnson said, smiling. She turned to the parents and nodded then flipped through the chart. "I see the last contact I had with you was when I referred you to Dr. Dalton with possible appendicitis." She continued turning pages. "Let's see -- here's a letter from Dr. Dalton -- looks like we were right, the appendix was hot. How have you been doing?"

Sheila's mother answered for her. "Not very well," she said. "Sheila still has pain in her incision, and she's lost five pounds of weight since her surgery."

"What does Dr. Dalton think about that?" Dr. Johnson asked.

"We've been back once. He had to operate on her again because he botched the first operation, and she got infected. She just got off antibiotics last week." Yvonne paused, glaring at the physician. "Why did you send us to that quack?"

Dr. Johnson was surprised at the response. "What do you mean, 'quack'? Dr. Dalton is one of the most respected surgeons in Houston, and he has one of the busiest practices in town. His patients all love him!"

"I'll just bet they do," Yvonne replied. "Maybe that's why he has AIDS!"

"AIDS! Brent Dalton? Why, I've never heard such a ridiculous thing in my life. I send patients to him all the time. He's a married man and looks healthier than a college athlete!" She paused and took a deep breath. "Where did you hear that he had AIDS?"

"Never mind where we heard it," Yvonne said. "It was from somebody who is in a position to know, and we don't have any reason to doubt that it's true. We want Sheila tested."

"Tested for what? For HIV? That's absurd!" Johnson said.

"Absurd or not, we want her tested," Michael Walters interjected, speaking up at last. "Sheila got infected after Dalton operated on her, and if that sombitch gave her AIDS, he'll pay for it!" Michael Walters' clenched fists emphasized his meaning even more than his rippling jaw muscles.

Dr. Johnson could tell that it was useless to try to talk them out of their request. And she saw no harm in doing as they wanted, since she had no doubts about Brent Dalton. She completed a cursory examination, found nothing out of the ordinary, and ordered an ELISA to be drawn.

"I should have the result by Friday," Dr. Johnson told them. "I'll call you when it comes in." Pausing in mid-stride as a new thought occurred to her, she faced the Walters again. "You do understand, don't you, that even if Sheila's test is positive, it doesn't mean she caught HIV from Dr. Dalton." Then without another word, she turned toward the door and left the room, white coat flying behind her.

***

March came in like the proverbial lion, and a blustery, cold wind blew across southeast Texas. It was the first Friday of the month, and Graham Memorial's Risk Control Committee convened in the conference room. Al Martin called the meeting to order, and after approving the minutes of the previous meeting, they moved to a discussion of old business.

John Kelly, true to his position as CEO and always quick to forge ahead, opened the discussion. "Has anything happened as a result of the patient who had the leg amputation because of the incident with the hot water bottle?"

"Yes," Louise McArdle replied. "We have already been served papers, and we are now in the process of scheduling depositions with the appropriate individuals." The attorney shuffled some papers lying in front of her and cleared her throat before proceeding. "It will be a few weeks, perhaps months, before some of the smoke clears and negotiations begin. If they push hard enough, we'll be prepared to settle."

"And the patient who climbed out of bed and suffered a hip contusion?" Al Martin asked.

"Nothing has come of that, and I would be surprised if anything did," McArdle answered. "There was no significant injury involved, and the patient went back to a nursing home."

"Well, that brings us back to the surgeon who was stuck with a needle in the operating room and appears to have contracted HIV," Martin said. "I've been monitoring that situation myself, and I'm sorry to report that his Western Blot came back indeterminate."

"What does that mean?" Bill Rudman asked, brushing his hair back with his fingers. "Does he have the virus or not?"

"He probably does have it, considering the situation." Martin said.

"What do you mean 'the situation'?" Rudman asked.

"The situation is this: a negative ELISA at the time of a nasty puncture with an HIV infected needle, followed by conversion to a positive ELISA six weeks later, and now a weakly positive -- correction, indeterminate -- Western Blot. It looks pretty bad for poor Dr. Dalton. Excuse me, the surgeon involved."

"What's the next step, Louise?" John Kelly asked, directing his gaze toward McArdle.

"I don't think we need to do anything at this time," McArdle replied. "When the test results are reported to the State Board, they will be the ones to take action if anything needs to be done."

"And in the meantime, Dr. Dalton continues to practice surgery in our hospital and could infect any number of innocent people with the AIDS virus," Rudman added.

"What would you have us do?" Dr. Robin Smith asked, interrupting with a scowl on his face. "Take away the man's hospital privileges at this stage of the game?"

Rudman's face grew red, and his nostrils flared. "Yes! And I would remind you that this is not a game, Doctor," he replied to the young internist. "We stand to lose millions of dollars in liability suits if we allow Dalton to continue practicing and a single patient becomes infected as a result of it."

"Now, just a minute," John Kelly said. "This may be a first for us, but it can't be the first time a surgeon has tested positive for HIV. And I'm sure it won't be the last. Guidelines must be available, and the State Board will be acting on this matter in due course. Let's keep our sanity. If we act too fast by suspending the doctor's privileges now then we also stand to lose a lot of money if he should sue us." The CEO glared at the faces around the table. "I agree with Louise. We do nothing at this time."

Kelly turned to Al Martin. "What do you think, Dr. Martin? You've been pretty quiet about the issue of whether the surgeon poses any risk to anyone else."

Martin leaned back in his chair and rubbed his brow. "I want all of you to know, although the surgeon involved is an old friend, I'm inclined to agree with Mr. Rudman. That may surprise some of you, but we're dealing with an infectious disease here. If a patient gets infected as a result of this surgeon's work, there'll be hell to pay. It's potentially a huge liability."

Dr. Robin Smith threw his pen down on the tabletop. "I can't believe this! You two act like we don't know anything at all about HIV. It may be infectious, but you'd have to work at it to infect a patient. After all, it's the surgeon who is in contact with the patient's blood, not vice-versa. If you want to prevent the spread of the virus then test the patients, not the doctors." He paused, and no one spoke. "After all, that's how the surgeon got infected in the first place -- from an infected patient."

The Committee members pondered Smith's comments for a minute.

"When is the Western Blot supposed to be repeated?" Dr. Richey asked.

"Six weeks after the last one," Martin said. "That would be in about two more weeks."

"Will the result be definite at that time?" Kelly asked.

"I certainly hope so," Martin said. "But there's a slight chance the Western Blot could still be indeterminate."

"Is Dr. Dalton seeing another physician?" Smith asked.

"Yes, Martin said. "He's seeing Jim Shubert."

"To change the perspective," John Kelly interrupted, looking at Louise McArdle, "what about the potential liability of the hospital for the surgeon's accidental infection?"

McArdle shuffled some papers in front of her before replying. "It appears that the accident was the surgeon's fault." She cleared her throat again and adjusted her half-frame glasses, warming up to the subject. "The hospital has the obligation to provide a scrub nurse for surgical cases, and it's the nurse's responsibility to pass instruments. The surgeon is supposed to ask for whatever he wants, and the scrub nurse hands it to him. In this case, he violated the usual procedure by reaching across the scrub nurse for an instrument. He injured himself, and it wasn't anybody else's fault."

Kelly and Rudman smiled at McArdle. At first, no one commented on the attorney's opinion until John Kelly broke the silence.

"Of course, that's just an opinion. Is there any indication that the doctor will try to sue us?"

Blank stares answered the question when Kelly looked around the table.

Martin wrote a note on a legal pad then proceeded with the meeting. "Is there any new business to be discussed?"

"Yes, two more nurses were stuck with needles," Nancy Greenblatt reported, her gaze directed downward. A short discussion followed, and the Committee adjourned.

***

Al Martin tapped Bill Rudman on the shoulder as they walked down the corridor outside the meeting room. Rudman stopped and turned to face the doctor.

"I just wanted to tell you I agree with you about not allowing the surgeon to continue practicing in this hospital," Martin said. He looked over his shoulder before continuing. "I don't think there is much available in the way of guidelines for this circumstance, but you are right on target concerning the liability issues."

Rudman nodded and pushed his hair back again. "I know. But it seems that everybody else is afraid to step on any toes -- afraid the surgeon will sue them, I guess. Myself, I think a lot less of him than the others on the committee do, but that's a personal matter."

Martin gazed at Rudman for a minute, puzzled by the comment then looked around again to be sure no one was listening. "Listen, Rudman, I don't need to tell you how confidential all this is, do I? If word about Dalton being infected leaks out then he'll be ruined, career-wise."

Rudman grinned at the pathologist. "Right. And we wouldn't have to worry about taking away his privileges if that were to happen. Patients wouldn't come to see him anyway."

Martin nodded his head then patted Rudman on the shoulder. "You take care, now. I'll see you later." They both wandered off down the hall toward their respective work spaces.

***

Later that morning, Yvonne Walters busied herself at home and debated with herself whether or not to call Dr. Johnson for Sheila's test result. Sheila had returned to her part time job at one of the large department stores, where she worked in the cosmetic section. She said she planned to move back to her own apartment soon.

When Sheila stayed with her parents, which had not been often until her appendectomy, she would return from classes or from work in late afternoon. On Fridays, she liked to take a long nap before going out in the evening. It was not uncommon for the Walters to see little of her on weekends, due to her habit of staying out until the wee hours then sleeping all the next day.

Yvonne looked at the telephone for the hundredth time that morning but recoiled when it rang. "Hello?" she said, her voice quivering.

"Yvonne? This is Dr. Johnson. I have Sheila's test result and would like to talk to you both here in the office, if possible. Can you come in?"

"No, I can't," Yvonne said. "I'm here alone. Michael and Sheila are both at work. Why can't you give me the results over the phone?"

"I can, if you want me to, but I'd rather not," Dr. Johnson said. "Yvonne, I would prefer that you come in so that we can discuss the test -- and its interpretation."

"What do you mean, 'discuss its interpretation'?" Yvonne asked, becoming alarmed. "Does my daughter have HIV?"

There was no immediate reply.

Dr. Johnson cleared her throat then said in a hushed voice, "I'm afraid the initial test result is positive, but we will need to do another, more sensitive test for confirmation when Sheila can come in."

Yvonne Walters stared at the cabinet door in front of her face for a moment and closed her eyes. "We'll be in this afternoon, when Sheila gets back from work," she said in a low voice. "Good-bye, Dr. Johnson."

***

Sheila and her mother had returned home from Dr. Johnson's office by the time Michael came in from work. The women sat unspeaking in the living room when the back door slammed.

"Yvonne?" Michael called from the kitchen.

"We're *--sniff--* in the living room," Yvonne replied in a tone so low it could barely be heard.

Entering the room, Michael sensed that something was wrong. The two women sat opposite each other in the semi-darkened room, a box of tissues resting on the coffee table between them. Mounds of used tissues rested by their chairs. Their crying had dried to the point of mere sniffles, and their eyes were red and swollen.

Sheila got up and faced her father when he entered the room. "Oh Daddy, it's terrible! She said I have the AIDS virus!" she blurted out in a new flood of tears. She ran across the room to her father, throwing her arms around him.

"What?" Michael said, pushing her back at arm's length. Confused, he looked first at his daughter then at his wife then back to Sheila again. "AIDS? Sheila, what are you talking about? Did you talk to Dr. Johnson?

Mrs. Walters explained what had happened. When she had finished, Michael looked at his daughter in silence for a moment. "It was that goddamned surgeon, wasn't it, Sheila? You couldn'a got this nowhere else could you?"

"No, Daddy -- of course not! What do you think I am?" Sheila collapsed back into her chair and resumed sobbing, her face in her hands. Her long, black hair hung down over her hands in moist tangles like black ropes.

Michael felt distressed over the news of his daughter's infection, but they had never shared a close relationship. Sheila had distanced herself from both her parents while she was still in high school. Things had gotten worse when she started college then found part time work and moved into her own apartment.

Her father had never been tolerant of grief or crying. He paced the room awhile then stopped by the window and looked out. The two women sobbed in the background.

Michael pounded his fist into the other hand and said, "I'll talk to a lawyer. We'll sue that sombitch blind. Take every penny he's got."

"What good will that do?" Yvonne said, looking at her pathetic daughter. "Sheila will still have the virus. Suing the doctor won't change that."

"No, by God, but it'll give her the money she'll need to take care of herself -- and then some," Michael replied, grimacing. "I'll make that bastard think twice before he infects somebody else."

***

The Daltons had invited Gary Morgan over for supper that same, eventful Friday evening. It had been a week since he and Brent talked in the cockpit of the boat, and Brent hoped for an answer to the partnership proposition. He answered the doorbell when it rang promptly at seven.

"Come in, Gary! Let me take your coat." The visitor smiled and stuck out his arm with a bottle of wine. "Thought you might enjoy this sometime."

"Ah, Napa Valley Cabernet! One of our favorites. Thanks."

Brent hung the coat in a closet by the foyer then lead the way into the living room. "Have a seat, Gary," he said, gesturing toward an overstuffed chair. The spacious room was furnished with large, leather-covered sofas and chairs, carpeted floor, and several contemporary oil paintings by regional artists. A wood fire burned in a fireplace on the back wall, next to a large window that looked out over two huge, moss-draped live oak trees. It was dark outside, and floodlights illuminated the low, sprawling limbs of the massive oaks.

"What a beautiful view!" Gary got up from the chair and walked to the window. "If I had a view like this, I'd spend most of my time standing by the window staring at those trees."

Brent laughed. "You get used to it. I once thought the same thing, but it seems you grow accustomed to your surroundings. There's always some place a little nicer just around the corner."

"I never thought about it quite like that, but I'm sure you're right." Gary said, moving to the fireplace. He held his hands out toward the warm blaze and rubbed them together. "Where's Nicole?"

"She's in the kitchen putting some last minute touches on supper. Can I get you something to drink?"

"Sure. How about a scotch and water, light on the scotch."

"Coming right up." Brent walked over to a small wet bar near the corner of the room and pulled out a couple of glasses.

"Well, this has been a busy week," he said, filling two cocktail glasses with ice. He poured a generous splash of a twelve year old single malt into each. "I would've had a difficult time doing all those cases without your help." He added water to the glasses, wrapped a small napkin around them then handed Gary's to him.

"Thanks," Gary said. "I'm enjoying working with you." He swirled his drink in the glass and stared at the fire.

"The surgeon I talked to in Austin is older than you, but he's not near as busy. Makes me wonder why. Maybe because he doesn't have much bedside manner, or he's a clutz with his hands." He paused. "I think it would be hard to work with him for very long."

A smile flashed across Brent's face. "Does that mean you've made a decision?"

"Yes, I have," Gary replied. "Your offer is very attractive, and I know we work well together."

The fire popped and shot up a bright flame.

Gary smiled and looked over at Brent. "I've decided to stay here in Houston -- and work with you."

"Terrific!" Brent exclaimed, raising his glass for a toast. "Here's to a successful partnership."

They drank to the future and then shook hands.

Nicole walked into the room as the men celebrated their association. She wiped her hands on an apron. "Hello, Gary!" she said, smiling. "This looks promising. Do you have some good news for us?"

"He sure has," Brent answered. "Gary has decided to join me in practice. We just drank a toast to our success. Care to join us?"

Nicole clapped her hands and beamed a bright smile. "Yes, I'm thrilled! Oh, Gary, this will mean so much to us. I'm so glad you decided to stay here." Nicole stood frozen for a couple of beats before her brow furrowed and her lower lip quivered just a little. Turning her head, she wiped a tear from her eye. "I'll -- just be a minute. I need to check the roast." She went into the kitchen.

"I'll have someone start the necessary paperwork Monday," Brent said, avoiding the temptation to plunge into sentimentalism. "When do you want to start?"

"My residency ends on the last day of June," Gary replied. "A week or two to visit home should be ample enough time off before starting to work. Is there enough room for me in the office?"

"We have enough square footage, but I think we'll need to knock out a wall between two empty exam rooms to make an office for you. Where is home, by the way?"

"Marshall, up in the East Texas piney woods." Gary sipped his drink. "It's about a three hour drive from here."

"I've heard of it. Nice country, good people." Brent looked out the window at the huge oak trees. "There won't be too much else to take care of, since you already have an apartment. Do you think you'll want to move to a new place right away?"

"No, my apartment should be just fine for awhile. I don't need much space."

"Good. Apart from the office modifications then, there isn't much else to do except for the paperwork. You'll need applications for joining the medical staffs of the various hospitals and for malpractice insurance and membership in the county medical society," Brent recited, thinking out loud. "I'll have Elizabeth start getting those together for us Monday morning."

Nicole came back into the room and sat by her husband. "I just thought of something." She had a serious look on her face. "After Gary joins us in practice, we won't all be able to go sailing together. One of you will always be on call!"

The men laughed. "Oh, I'm sure Jim Wilson won't mind covering for us occasionally," Brent said, a smile on his face.

***

The next week passed almost without notice. Elizabeth had requested applications from various institutions, and some of them already had arrived. Brent hired a contractor to plan for an additional office, and construction was scheduled to begin later in the month, to be completed in two or three weeks.

Pushed into the background, but nowhere near forgotten, was the repeat Western Blot which Brent was to have drawn in mid-March. Both he and Nicole had resigned themselves to the fact that the likelihood of the next test being negative was almost nil. Facing reality was something they both had learned to do a long time ago.

Brent sat at his office desk late Tuesday afternoon, two days before the date for the repeat test, when Elizabeth's voice came to him over the phone intercom. "Dr. Dalton, there's a Mr. Atkins at the front desk, and he says he has something to deliver to you. You'll have to sign for it. Should I bring him back?"

Brent felt the hair rise on the back of his neck, since Registered Mail and other deliveries which had to be signed for rarely contained good news. "Show him back, Elizabeth," he said into the intercom.

Atkins was thin, wore a western-style shirt with snaps for buttons, and his cowboy boots looked like lizard skin. "Dr. Brent Dalton?" he said, entering the room.

83

"Yes, I'm Dr. Dalton," Brent answered, rising from his chair and extending his right hand.

Atkins reached as though to shake hands, but instead placed a thick envelope in Brent's palm. "Sorry to be the bearer of bad tidings, but I need you to sign for this."

Brent looked at the envelope, which was addressed to him and had an official Harris County return address in the upper left hand corner. "What is this?" he asked.

"It's a lawsuit, sir, and you've just been officially served," Atkins replied. "If you don't mind, just sign right here. I've got a couple more of these to deliver today."

Brent signed in the appropriate place, and Atkins, backing toward the door, touched his forehead as though tipping his non-existent hat. "Thanks, Doc," he said then left the room. The entire process had taken only a couple of minutes.

Shocked and instantly demoralized from the news of being sued, Brent sat again at his desk and opened the envelope with sweaty hands. He unfolded the long, thick stack of papers and began to read.

Twenty minutes later, Brent sank down into his chair and stared at the wall. He felt devastated, drained, empty. He was being sued by Sheila Walters and her parents for causing Sheila to become infected with HIV through some unspecified act of negligence. They wanted twenty million dollars for future medical costs, pain and suffering, and several other things.

In addition, Brent read that the Board of Directors at Graham Memorial Hospital was named in the suit for allowing him to practice surgery there. His mind raced. How had the Walters learned of his infection? What would Gary think about joining him in practice now that this had happened?

He knew that the first thing he needed to do was notify his attorney and arrange a meeting with him so they could file a response to the suit. He looked up the number for Todd Ward, a Houston attorney with an excellent reputation for medical malpractice defense and dialed it. Ward was not in the office, but Brent made an appointment to meet with him the next afternoon.

***

William Rudman was in the process of ending an impromptu meeting with John Kelly in the CEO's office when the secretary buzzed. She announced that a Mr. Atkins was waiting with something that required the CEO's personal signature.

In short order, the procedure which had taken place in Brent's office had been repeated, and Kelly examined the lawsuit while Rudman stood by the window, combing his long hair with his fingers and trying to appear disinterested.

"Well, I'll be damned!" Kelly exclaimed after a minute. "One of Dalton's patients is suing us -- and him -- for infecting her with HIV." He rubbed his chin. "I didn't expect anything like this so soon."

Hiding a smile with his hand, Rudman walked over to the back of Kelly's chair so he could look over the CEO's shoulder. "Not such a big surprise," he said. "It was bound to happen sooner or later. I guess McArdle's work is cut out for her now."

Rudman could hardly contain himself when he left Kelly's office. He tried to appear casual while walking the short distance back to his own office. Once there, he closed the door and looked up the number for a local tabloid.

Whisper enjoyed wide circulation in the Houston area and had a reputation for sensational news backed up by less than accurate facts. Rudman was delighted. He had thought of a way to deal with Dalton that would halt his practice within days, if Rudman knew anything about human nature.

The receptionist at *Whisper* connected him with a reporter who had special expertise in legal matters. Speaking anonymously, Rudman asked, "Can you print allegations from a lawsuit before it goes to trial?"

"Yes, of course. If it's anything of interest to the public, we're glad to print allegations."

"What about libel and things like 'right to privacy'?"

"As long as we report the allegations as such and don't claim that they are facts then we're safe. Lawsuits are in the public domain. There's no 'right to privacy' involved."

Rudman smiled to himself and combed his hair back with his free hand. "If you will go down to the courthouse and look up a suit filed last week for Michael and Yvonne Walters and their daughter versus Dr. Brent Dalton, I think you'll find the allegations worth printing. They involve a Houston surgeon with the AIDS virus who is still practicing surgery."

"Well now, that should make interesting news all right. I'll do that, first thing tomorrow morning. Thanks for the tip."

"Don't mention it," Rudman said, hanging up the phone. He rubbed his hands together with glee, still smiling in the privacy of his office. *Now we'll see how much surgery Dr. Dalton will do,* he thought.

Chapter 13

Brent drove into the garage just after dark and entered the kitchen through the back door. Nicole stood at the sink, washing lettuce for a salad. She looked up at him when he walked over to her, put his arms around her and gave her a tight hug.

"What's wrong?" she asked with her uncanny intuition.

"Why do you think something is wrong?"

"I could tell something was wrong the minute you walked through the back door. And you always give me an extra tight squeeze when something's wrong." She pulled away from him and resumed washing the lettuce. "Now, tell me what it is."

"Nikki, you amaze me." He took a seat at the table and looked down at the empty tabletop, clasping his hands in front of him. He took a deep breath. "I was served with a lawsuit today."

Nicole exhaled as though she had been punched in the stomach. "Oh, no!" She dropped the lettuce into the sink and stood there, staring at him. "As if we didn't have enough to worry about already! Is this one of those frivolous suits?"

"Not this time. This case definitely isn't frivolous." Brent picked up a salt shaker from the table and examined it as though it could shed some insight into his dilemma. "It involves a patient who discovered she was HIV positive a few weeks after I did an appendectomy on her. She's blamed me for the HIV infection, and she's suing for twenty million dollars. I know I didn't infect her, but convincing a jury of that may be difficult."

Nicole went to his side, pulled up a chair and sat by him. She kissed him on the cheek and put her hands on his. "Oh, Brent, I'm so sorry. This shouldn't be happening. You haven't done anything to deserve it."

He smiled at her and shook his head. "Maybe worse, a case like this will cause a lot of talk around the hospital and the medical community. Even if I win the lawsuit, I could lose my reputation."

Nicole patted his hand. "Remember what we decided that weekend on the sailboat. We'll deal with matters as they come up and won't dwell on the negative."

Brent sighed and squeezed her hand. "That's my girl. You make me feel better every time we talk. A lawsuit may be depressing, but it's just part of practicing medicine today. Life still goes on. Right?"

"Right. Now, can I get you a glass of wine before a scrumptious supper?"

***

The next afternoon, Brent arrived at Todd Ward's office at the appointed time. A plump, middle-aged receptionist with hair rolled into a tight, no-nonsense bun showed him into the office. Ward was sitting at his desk when Brent and the receptionist walked in, and he rose when they entered the room.

The attorney appeared to be a little older than Brent, and he was even taller, standing at least two inches over six feet. He was thin, with gray eyes and matching hair and wore round, wire-rimmed glasses.

"Dr. Dalton," the attorney said, offering his hand. "I'm Todd Ward. Just call me Todd."

"Glad to meet you," Brent said, shaking hands. "And most people just call me Brent."

"Please have a seat," Todd said, resuming his place behind a massive desk which was cluttered with stacks of paper and books.

After they both were seated, Todd asked Brent to show him a copy of the lawsuit, which he reviewed. He then asked the receptionist to make a copy for their file.

"It appears that the plaintiff in this case has the HIV virus and is accusing you of infecting her with it," Todd said. "She further states that you have been practicing surgery with the knowledge that you are infected with the virus. Any truth to that?"

"No, to both allegations."

"Why don't you tell me how all this happened, Doctor, in as few words as possible. And you can start with an explanation of how you came to be infected -- if you are infected -- with HIV."

Brent took a deep breath and sighed. "Back in mid-December, I operated on a patient with HIV and got stuck with a bloody needle. On the day of that incident, I tested negative for the virus. Six weeks later, when retested with an HIV screening test, I tested positive, but the confirmatory test was indeterminate. I'm to have a repeat test drawn tomorrow."

Todd looked at him for a minute without replying. "That's some story, but it's still not quite clear to me." He cleared his throat. "Do you have the virus or not?"

"I may have the virus," Brent replied. "We won't know for sure until the Western Blot, that's the confirmatory test I mentioned, is either positive or negative, not in-between."

"And will you know that tomorrow?"

"No, I'll have blood drawn for the test tomorrow, but the results won't be available for about a week. Of course, I'm hoping the test won't be indeterminate again."

"Well, I can guess that you won't be sleeping very well for the next week," Todd said, "but let's get on with your story. Where does the Walters girl enter the picture? If you are infected with the virus, is there any way you could have infected her?"

"Absolutely not," Brent said, slamming his fist on the edge of the attorney's desk with a sound like a hammer hitting a board. "My blood would've had to come in contact with her incision. There's no way that happened."

"What kind of surgery did you do on her?"

"An appendectomy."

"Did she have any problems after the surgery?"

"Yes, she developed an abscess, but that's not uncommon after an appendectomy. I had to take her back to surgery to drain the abscess."

"Did you know that you might have the HIV virus at the time you did her surgery?"

"Not at the time of her original surgery, the appendectomy. I had just found out that my ELISA, the screening test, was positive on the day I drained her abscess."

Todd's brow wrinkled. "That could be a problem -- knowing that your test was positive at the time you did her second surgery. He made a note on a yellow legal pad. Did you have any cuts or other type of injury on your hands when you did her surgery?"

"No, I didn't. Furthermore, I didn't cut or stick myself with anything during the case."

"Did you have an assistant who can validate that?"

"No, I didn't have an assistant on her particular case, but I did several other cases earlier that day and also the following day with a surgery resident who can testify that I had no visible wounds on my hands."

"Would there be any written record or other verification of that?"

"The scrub nurse should remember whether or not I injured myself during the case. Any break in technique would have been recorded in the circulating nurse's notes, and I would have mentioned it in my operative dictation as well."

"What about the girl?" Todd asked. "I mean, what's she like?"

"She doesn't have any risk factors as far as I know, other than being sexually active. I recall that she was on birth control pills at the time of her surgery. We didn't talk about whether or not she used protection, or how many partners she has had."

"Do you know if she uses drugs?" Todd asked.

"No, I don't. I didn't ask her about that when I took her history, but I guess I should have." He paused a beat. "Anyway, I doubt she would have admitted to using drugs. Most of the time, users deny it."

"No needle tracks on her arms?"

"Not that I can recall."

Todd made more notes on the legal pad while they talked. He sometimes paused in order to finish writing before continuing his questions. "How did the Walters girl learn about your HIV status?"

"Now that's a very good question." Brent pulled on his earlobe and thought for a minute. "I'd like to know the answer to that myself. Results of those tests are supposed to be confidential. I don't know how she found out."

"Well, who else knows about the test results?" Todd asked, turning a page on the yellow pad.

"Well, there's Nicole my wife, and Dr. Gary Morgan, the surgery resident I mentioned, and Dr. Jim Shubert, my internist. There's also Dr. Al Martin, the head of the pathology department and chairman of the Risk Control Committee. My God! The Risk Control Committee! There must be seven or eight people on that committee." He rubbed both of his cheeks with his fingers. "That might be where the news leaked out. I don't guess there's any way we'll ever know for sure."

"It may not even be all that important -- unless you do test negative for the virus and decide to sue someone yourself, of course."

"If I test negative for the virus, suing someone will be the last thing on my mind." Brent mumbled in a tone so low it was barely heard by the attorney.

Todd Ward smiled at the comment then turned another page and began writing again. "I'll need a few other things from you, like schools attended, residency training, honors received, and so forth. Do you have a current CV?"

"Yes, I think so."

"Good. I'll also need certified copies of all the records, of course. Can you take care of that or would you rather I subpoena them from the hospital?"

"Sure, I'll take care of it. I can have copies of my office records sent over today. I should be able to get a copy of the hospital records to you tomorrow. Will that be satisfactory?"

"Yes," Todd said. "I'll file a response to the suit and notify your insurance carrier tomorrow. I've taken cases for them in the past, so there probably won't be any problem with my representing you. Why don't we meet again after you get the results of the next blood test? And in the meantime, any additional information you can get on the

Walters girl could be valuable as far as your defense is concerned. It sounds to me like she picked up her infection by some means other than your surgery, but we may have to convince a jury of that."

"Let's hope not. But I'll see what else I can find out."

"All right, Brent. I guess that about wraps it up for now," Todd said, putting his pen down on the desk. "We'll get things started as soon as possible." He rubbed his chin before picking up his pencil again. "By the way, do you know the names of any other doctors that the Walters girl has seen in the past?"

"She was referred to me by Dr. Catherine Johnson. Cathy practices here in Houston and is on the staff at Graham."

"Good," Todd said, picking up the pen and writing again. "I'll subpoena her records, just so it's official. That will take a little time, so I'd appreciate it if you would provide me with copies on your own. Just be sure to have them certified as true copies. Maybe we can find something of value there."

"No problem, Todd."

They shook hands again, and Brent left. He had a few more patients to see in his office before going home, and he wished for a little slack time so he could mull over the conversation he and Todd just had.

***

That night, Brent was restless again, and Nicole gave him a couple of aspirin and a glass of warm milk around midnight. He felt like he had been up for a week by the time he left home the next morning.

Instead of going straight to the hospital to meet Gary Morgan for rounds, Brent went by his office to review the file on Sheila Walters. He had requested that a copy of the record be sent over to Todd Ward right after their meeting the previous day but hadn't found time to look at it himself.

While reviewing his history and physical exam notes from the night of Sheila's surgery, Brent could remember the girl vividly. Her dark beauty was striking but contrasted with her personality. And she had quite a vocabulary too, he recalled, judging from the expletives she used.

He turned another page and found a startling entry under her past medical history: Sheila had had an abortion performed a few months before her appendectomy. It was possible she might have had a test for HIV at that time, but that information might be hard to locate without her help.

Brent knew he needed more hard evidence than the record contained to convince a jury Sheila had contracted her infection from some source other than himself. The obvious question was, where would he get it? Acting on impulse, he jotted Sheila's address on a note pad and put it in his pocket. He wasn't quite sure at this point what he would do with the note but felt it might come in handy later.

Between cases that morning, Brent went to the lab and had a blood sample drawn for the repeat Western Blot. He didn't have much doubt about what the result would be, but there was always a slim chance it would turn out negative; and he would be vindicated. *God, he thought, what would it be like for that to happen and get my life back like it used to be?*

Brent and Gary finished the last case of the day around noon, and Gary headed for an afternoon clinic. Brent went by the Medical Records Department to complete some old chart work and asked that two certified copies of Sheila's records be sent to his office. When they arrived, he would send one copy to Todd Ward and keep the other for his own reference.

***

That evening after supper, Brent and Nicole sat on their back patio talking and drinking coffee. The night was warm, the temperature that afternoon had climbed into the low eighties. Locusts sang from live oaks all around, and countless crickets contributed a syncopated harmony. It seemed as though the trees themselves orchestrated the performance. Nicole put her cup on a side table and rested her head on Brent's shoulder.

"Do you think the Walters' lawsuit will go to trial?" she asked.

"I don't know what would prevent it, because I have no intention of settling out-of-court. What we need is some evidence that Sheila was infected before I did her surgery."

Nicole tugged at a strand of her hair and twirled it around a finger. "What kind of evidence would that have to be?"

"Well, I'm not real sure," Brent said. "The perfect piece of evidence would be a positive blood test for HIV taken prior to the appendectomy, but I doubt that exists. In lieu, it would take some pretty convincing circumstantial evidence to persuade a jury she didn't get the infection from me." He stared into his coffee cup and swirled the dark liquid.

"Do you mean evidence of IV drug use, or something like that?"

"Yes, something like that. I'm convinced she couldn't have gotten the infection from me, so there has to be some other explanation for how she did get it."

Nicole retrieved her cup from the table at the side of her chair and took a sip of the cold coffee. "How can we find out, hire a private detective?"

Brent shook his head. "Not just yet. First, I want to look into this a bit myself. Some of what needs to be done will be easier for me than it would be for a private investigator."

"Like what, for instance?" Nicole asked, pouring herself another cup of decaf.

"Like tracking down results of a previous blood test. HIV results are pretty confidential, and I may have trouble getting them myself. Something else that might be of help would be a frozen sample of Sheila's blood that was drawn before the surgery. We could have it tested now and it might prove she already was infected at the time of the appendectomy."

"Why would a blood sample be frozen for such a long period of time?"

"If Sheila donated or sold blood to a blood bank, a sample might have been saved," Brent said. "On second thought, if it had been saved under those circumstances then it would already have been tested for HIV. If it tested positive, she would have been told, and the blood wouldn't have been saved."

"Do you think Sheila knew she was infected?"

"I don't know. If she did, I don't think she told anyone about it. That's just something I suspect from the brief contact I had with her." He rose to get himself another cup of coffee.

"How do you go about trying to find an old blood sample?" Nicole asked.

"I know Sheila had an abortion a few months before her appendectomy. I need to find out where that was performed then I can see about getting the records."

"Can you do that?"

"If it relates to my defense, we have every right to access old records. Todd Ward will know how to go about doing it legally, so we can use anything we find."

"What about the possibility of drug use? How will you get information about that?"

"That could be more difficult. I might need to do a little detective work myself," Brent said, grinning at his wife.

"Something tells me we had better find a good private detective. I can't picture you in a trench coat, sneaking down dark alleys late at night!" She rose and began to gather their cups and utensils.

"We'll see," Brent said, his eyes sparkling.

Chapter 14

Friday morning, William Rudman drove like a heavy-footed teenager on his way to check the newsstand. He parked his car in the lot of a supermarket near the hospital and went directly to the checkout stall with the shortest line. The usual array of tabloids and magazines was there, and it took him just a few seconds to locate and pay for a copy of *Whisper.*

Walking almost at a trot, Rudman went back to his car, climbed in, and scanned the front page of the paper. There it was, in the lower, right-hand corner: "Houston Surgeon Accused Of Infecting Patient With AIDS Virus!"

The article went on to itemize the accusations in the lawsuit, mentioning Brent's name in every paragraph. It also reported his office and home addresses and listed all the hospitals where he had medical staff privileges. There was even a comparison of the situation to the one involving the well-publicized case of a Florida dentist back in the eightys, who had died before the discovery of his secret.

Rudman sped to his office where he made multiple copies of the defaming story. These he distributed by hand throughout the hospital, taking particular care to leave several copies in the surgery lounge. Feeling quite smug then, he went back to his office and waited for things to start happening.

***

Brent and Gary completed rounds as usual that morning and went to the cafeteria for breakfast before starting their cases. Just as they were seated, Brent's pager went off. He answered from a wall phone near the table.

The answering service gave Brent a message to call a number in the hospital. When he called, John Kelly answered.

"Dr. Dalton," the CEO said. "Could you please come to my office right away? I'm afraid something important has developed."

Brent's heart sank. He knew Kelly had to be referring to the lawsuit.

"Something important?" Brent said. "What?"

"I'd rather not discuss it over the phone," Kelly replied. "I'll be in my office."

Brent replaced the receiver and walked back to the table. "I just had a request to come to John Kelly's office. He said something important has happened, and he needs to talk to me. Why don't you finish breakfast and I'll meet you in the surgery lounge in a few minutes."

"Sure," Gary said, looking puzzled. "I hope it's nothing bad."

Brent reflected on the fact that he had not yet told Gary about the lawsuit, and he suspected this urgent summons to the office of the chief administrator had something to do with the suit.

Brent drank his orange juice in three large gulps and left the remainder of his breakfast on the table. He then walked from the cafeteria to the administrative area of the hospital. John Kelly's secretary was expecting him and ushered him into the private office, where Brent found the CEO with Dr. Jerry Sherman, the Chief of Staff. They kept their seats when the surgeon entered.

"Please have a seat," Kelly said, frowning. "Dr. Dalton, are you aware that the hospital has been sued along with you by one of your patients and her family?"

"Yes, I'm sorry about that," Brent said. "I have no idea how news of any of this got to them."

"Do you read *Whisper*?" Kelly asked.

"No. Isn't it just one of those cheap tabloids that prints anything sensational?" Brent asked.

"Yes, it is," Kelly agreed. "Unfortunately, it enjoys wide local distribution." He handed Brent a copy of the article Rudman had left on his desk. "You'll find this interesting, I think. It's from today's edition."

Scanning the article, Brent felt his face grow warm then hot. "I was afraid something like this might happen," he said after a minute. "Another nightmare come true."

"Brent, are you familiar with the Medical Staff Bylaws?" Jerry Sherman asked, entering the conversation like an attorney in a cross-examination.

"Well, sure. To a certain extent, I guess. Why?" Brent asked, puzzled.

"Do you know what a summary suspension is?" Sherman continued in his abrupt fashion.

Beginning to understand what was happening, Brent replied, cautious as a cat approaching a sleeping dog. "I think so, but I get the feeling you're about to enlighten me, right Jerry?"

Handing Brent a copy of the Bylaws, which had been opened to the section dealing with disciplinary action, Sherman read aloud: "A summary suspension of a medical staff member's hospital privileges can be declared by the Chief of Staff, in concurrence with the hospital CEO, when they have reason to believe that the staff member poses a threat to any of his patients or to any hospital personnel, for whatever reason."

"Are you implying that I am a threat to my patients?" Brent asked, astounded.

"Yes, I am," Sherman replied. "In light of this article, I'm afraid we have no choice. I'm sorry, Brent."

"Why, that's absurd! I have patients in the hospital that are not well enough to be discharged. I even have several surgical cases posted for today," Brent said. "What about them?"

"I'll take care of getting someone to take over your inpatients, and I've already called the scheduling desk and canceled all your cases for surgery," Sherman said. "You'll want to talk to your patients yourself, I'm sure. What you tell them is your own business. Be aware, however, that you are not to leave any orders, written or verbal, on any of the patients. You no longer have any privileges whatsoever in this institution." The Chief of Staff paused before adding, "I'm sorry to have to do this to you, Brent."

Inside, Brent seethed with anger. He suppressed a sudden impulse to grab both men by their necks and instead sat in silence, contemplating what Sherman had just said. He rose from his chair with deliberateness and looked at the other physician. "Okay, Jerry. If that's the way it's going to be, I'll get on with it. I expect there will be a hearing in a few days... so I can present my side of this?"

"Yes, it's all spelled out in the Bylaws. There must be a hearing with the Executive Committee of the medical staff within three days. That would be Monday -- why don't we say eight o'clock? You have a right to have an attorney present, you know," Sherman said.

Brent squared his shoulders and stood glaring at the other two men for a moment then turned to the door and walked out. "You can be sure I'll have an attorney present," he said over his shoulder.

***

Outside Kelly's office, Brent paused to allow his anger to settle. He thought about what had just happened. *What am I going to say to my patients? How do you explain that you have lost your privileges because you may have HIV? It's so damned unfair!*

Brent went first to the pre-operative holding area and talked one at a time to his patients there. He explained that an emergency situation had arisen, and he would have to postpone their surgery or refer them to another surgeon. He thought about telling them he could schedule their surgery to be done at one of the other hospitals where he was on staff, but he realized that an immediate summary suspension of his privileges at the other institutions would occur as an automatic reaction to what had just happened at Graham Memorial. His patients expressed regret over losing him as their surgeon, but they all were willing to be referred to another surgeon.

Next, Brent retraced his steps from earlier that day and revisited his inpatients. Most of them were post-ops. He gave them each a similar explanation for having to transfer their care to another surgeon. Some seemed puzzled, but none of them pushed the question about why that would be necessary.

At last, Brent walked to his office and called the surgery lounge. Gary Morgan answered.

"Gary, this is Brent. Listen, something unexpected has developed, and I'd appreciate it if you'd come to my office so we can talk. The cases for this morning have all been canceled. Can you come right now? Great -- I'll see you in a few minutes."

While Brent waited for Gary to arrive, Jim Wilson called and explained with obvious embarrassment that Jerry Sherman had asked him to take over care of the patients Brent had in the hospital. He had seen the copy of the newspaper article in the surgery lounge and expressed his surprise and sympathy. He offered to cover Brent's practice for a couple of weeks or so until things got sorted out, and Brent expressed his gratitude. His mind spun like a slow-moving dust storm by the time he hung up.

Gary Morgan arrived just after Brent replaced the phone on its cradle. It was obvious from the expression on the young surgeon's face that he had seen the tabloid article. He sat in a chair in front of Brent's desk and folded his hands in his lap, looking almost on the verge of tears.

"Gary," Brent began, "I'm sorry I didn't tell you about this before you read it in a newspaper. I was served with a lawsuit just three days ago, and wham! Just like that, it's all over the front page," he said, striking his fist against his desktop for emphasis.

"I can't say I was totally taken off guard," Gary said, still looking down. There has been a little talk in the lounge. You know, just speculation -- about the needle stick that night. I haven't said anything to a single person," he hastened to add.

"I know, Gary," Brent said. "I just regret not telling you sooner about this suit, especially in light of the fact that we've been planning on becoming partners. In all truthfulness, I intended to tell you about the whole thing this weekend, when we would have had more time to talk in private."

"What are you going to do?" Gary asked. "Can you continue to practice?"

"Yes, and no, to the last question," Brent answered. "I can continue my office practice, but that's not much good, as a surgeon. If I can't do any surgery then there's not much use in seeing surgical patients in the office. That is, providing that there are any patients out there who would be willing to see me in the first place."

"A real catch-22."

"Yes, it is. And as to what I will do…" he continued, "well, I'm not sure at this point. There'll be a hearing with the executive committee on Monday. At least, I'll have a chance to be heard."

"What if they don't restore your surgical privileges?"

"If that happens, I'm not sure what I'll do." Brent frowned and sighed. "Maybe I'll take an extended cruise on *Caribe*." He paused a few beats before continuing. "And I need to give my office people a little warning about what to expect. They'll want to start looking for other jobs."

"I wish there was something I could do to help," Gary said. "In just another three and a half months, I could take over the practice. But now, who'll see your patients?"

"Jim Wilson has agreed to cover for me for awhile, but I'm not sure if he will do it for three months, if it comes to that," Brent said. "You might want to see if that opportunity is still open in Austin."

"Brent, if there's any possible way to see this through with you, I'm going to stick it out," Gary said. "I don't think it's time to abandon ship."

"I appreciate that, Gary," Brent said. "But things look pretty bad at this point. I wouldn't blame you if you want to look elsewhere."

"Not right now," Gary said. "We'll see what happens in the next few weeks." He rose from his chair and walked over to Brent then extended his hand to shake in solemn support of his colleague.

Chapter 15

Brent spoke by phone with Todd Ward who assured him he would be with him Monday morning. He also left instructions with his office personnel regarding the referral of patients to Jim Wilson and then headed home. By the time he arrived there, Nicole had taken the telephone off the hook and was waiting for him in the den. She had received the first call about the tabloid article right after Brent had left for rounds, and had grown weary of explaining that this whole affair was probably just a big mistake.

Nicole ran to meet him as Brent entered the room, and they clung to each other in silence for a few minutes. The situation was too grave, far too serious, for tears.

Facing Nicole with both his hands on her shoulders, Brent spoke in a soft voice. "I know you've heard about the newspaper article, but that's only part of the bad news. Right after rounds this morning, I was paged and asked to go to John Kelly's office. Kelly and Jerry Sherman were there and told me they were declaring a summary suspension of my privileges because of the article."

"A summary suspension? What's that?" Nicole asked, pulling away enough that she could see his face.

"It's a means of immediately taking away a doctor's hospital privileges. And it's used only in dire circumstances," Brent replied. "It's also done to protect patients from a dangerous or an incompetent doctor." He shook his head and looked down at the floor. "This is the most humiliating thing that's ever happened to me."

103

Nicole moved nearer and put her head on his chest. "Oh, Brent, this is terrible." Suddenly she pulled her head up. "Incompetent! My God! Surely they don't think you are incompetent just because you may be infected with HIV!"

"I'm sure they didn't do this because they feel I'm incompetent," Brent said. "But it does appear they think I'm dangerous."

"Why would they think that?"

"Because they feel that allowing me to continue my practice would place them at risk for more lawsuits from patients who could claim they contracted the virus from me."

"But you told me there hasn't been a single case where that's happened. Don't they understand?"

"Maybe not. I wasn't aware of it myself until all this business started, and I did some reading about it."

Nicole walked over to the sofa and sat down. "Who will take care of your patients?"

"Jim Wilson has agreed to cover for me. I hope some of the smoke clears in the next week or so, and we can make some more permanent arrangement. Gary Morgan says he is still interested in coming into practice with me, but I suspect when he becomes more aware of the gravity of this situation, he'll change his mind."

Nicole looked surprised. "I hope not. He's such a sincere person. Do you have any recourse as far as getting your privileges back?"

"There's to be a hearing on Monday morning at eight o'clock. The entire executive committee will be there, and I've asked Todd Ward to appear with me. Maybe there are a couple of committee members who are informed well enough to make a rational decision about this."

"Yes, but it appears that even if you get your privileges back, you might not have any patients." Nicole pointed out. "What if your practice dries up?"

"I suppose I could try finding a job with an insurance company, reviewing claims or something like that." Brent hung his head and clasped his hands together. "or we could consider running away to some other place where there hasn't been so much publicity."

Nicole looked startled. "Something tells me that would be the worst choice we could make -- trying to run away. Please don't consider that. But what if you gave up surgery and practiced as a general practitioner?"

"That might work. I hope it doesn't come to that."

She put her arm around him, and they sat for awhile and talked about how this series of events would change their lives. Brent reflected on Nicole's inner strength and felt warm inside from knowing she was his ally. Their lives had been turned upside down, and their aspirations for the future were dubious, at best.

Now, talking about their dreams, they both realized that most of the things they always thought mattered now meant nothing at all. What mattered now was that they were together.

***

Later that evening, while preparing to change clothes, Brent pulled the piece of paper with Sheila's address from his pocket. Looking at it, he wondered if he might be able to do something himself to learn more about this mysterious girl who was now his enemy. The more he pondered the question, the more the idea intrigued him. He decided to try it.

Brent pulled on a pair of faded jeans and an old, blue and green flannel shirt then put on a pair of sneakers. He selected a crumpled baseball cap with "Astros" across the front and put it on then went back into the living room where Nicole sat staring at the opposite wall.

"Well, do I look like Sam Spade?" he asked, walking into the room.

Nicole turned, her eyes open wide in surprise. "Brent Dalton, you never cease to amaze me. What do you think you are getting ready to do?"

"Just a little gumshoe work. I thought I would see if Miss Walters is out on the town tonight."

"And how do you propose to go about finding her in a city this size?"

"I've been thinking about that," Brent said. "Young, single people don't leave home to go out until pretty late. I can park near her house and watch for her to leave then just follow her."

"You make it sound so simple. What if she sees you?"

"It's a free country," Brent said. "There isn't anything wrong with my being out on the street. Besides, I doubt that she will recognize me, dressed like this."

"What you need is a wig and a beard," Nicole snickered, seeming to warm up to the idea. "What time are you planning to leave?"

"Around dark, I guess."

"I've got an idea!" Nicole said, her eyes lighting up. "Why don't I call the Walters house and pretend to be someone Sheila knows from school? Maybe I can learn something about where she's going or when she's leaving."

"Do you think that would work?" Brent smiled at her excitement.

"Why not? It's worth a try, and what have we got to lose?"

Nicole went to the telephone near the corner of the room and retrieved a thick directory from a drawer in the table underneath. Turning to "W", she found a long list of Walters. "What are Sheila's parents' first names?"

"Michael and Yvonne," Brent replied. "Here's their address." He showed Nicole the piece of paper with Sheila's address written on it.

"Here it is," Nicole said, scanning down the column. She jotted the number on the piece of paper with the address for future reference then picked up the receiver and dialed the Walters' home.

A man's voice answered. "Yeah?" he said into the mouthpiece.

"Mister Walters?" Nicole said in a high-pitched voice.

"Yeah, who's this?" Michael said.

"This is, uh -- Sandra Matthews," Nicole replied with a deliberate slow, southern drawl. "I'm a friend of Sheila's -- from school. Is she there?"

"No, but she should be at her apartment. She lives a couple of blocks from here, on Oak Street."

"Could you please give me her number?"

Nicole jotted the number on the pad and thanked him then hung up and dialed Sheila's apartment.

A thin voice with a distinctive nasal twang answered. "Hello."

Nicole winked at Brent and gave him an "okay" sign with her thumb and index finger in the shape of a circle. "Hi, Sheila? This is

Sandra Matthews. You probably don't remember me, but we met at school a few weeks ago. I'm from Alabama and just started classes this semester -- remember? We were talking about places to hang out, and I was wondering if you were going out tonight."

Sheila didn't answer right away. "Where did I meet you? Oh, yeah, aren't you in my music appreciation class?"

Nicole rolled her eyes upward as a sign of relief. "Yes, that's it," she replied. "I'm bored to tears, just sitting around in my little apartment. Where do people go around here for a little fun?"

"Well, I like to go down to the Montrose Street area, myself," Sheila said. "It's not far from the Rice campus, and there's lots of neat little sidewalk cafes and singles bars. You can have a great time and not spend much money, if you meet the right people."

"Oh, good!" Nicole said. "What time do things start happening down there?"

"I usually leave home around ten o'clock," Sheila said. "I live in Pasadena, so it takes me about half an hour to get there."

"What's your favorite place?" Nicole asked.

"I always start in Attaboy's, on France Street. That's about two blocks off Montrose up at the north end. Most nights, there's a good crowd there."

"Super!" Nicole said. "I'll probably see you there! Thanks a million for the help."

Nicole hung up the receiver and turned to Brent, beaming. "Got it!" she said.

Chapter 16

S tanding by the phone, Sheila wondered just who Sandra Matthews was. She remembered talking to someone a few days ago about places to hang, but she couldn't picture the face that went with the conversation. She didn't waste much time thinking about it, however, since she assumed the girl was someone she had met at school and just couldn't quite place. Like Sandra said, they had talked.

Getting ready to go out on Saturday night was a big production for Sheila. The process began with a shower and shampoo, followed by a long session with a hair dryer and curling iron. Another long session in front of a make-up mirror then a little touch-up on her fingernail polish finished the tedious part. Next, she slipped into her sweater and tight skirt, sans bra and underwear. Then, a little perfume to strategic places, a few final strokes with a hairbrush, and voila! She was ready.

Driving her red Mustang, Sheila left Pasadena via Edgewood Drive then took the Gulf Freeway into downtown Houston. In a little less than a half hour, she found a parking place just off Montrose and walked down France Street past a couple of bars and diners. A few doors before the entrance to Attaboy's, she walked into a small pub and nodded to a figure standing at the bar.

The room was dim, and the air was thick with smoke, but the figure nodded back. He moved to a table in the back corner of the room and pulled out a chair. Sheila sat down opposite him, and they spoke for a minute before she laid her hand on the table. The man reached out and covered her hand with his for a few seconds then pulled his hand back and put it in his pants pocket.

They talked a couple more minutes then he put his hand out on the table and the procedure was reversed, except for Sheila reaching inside her purse instead of into a pocket when she withdrew her hand. It all proceeded with such smoothness that their movements appeared to be nothing unusual.

Sheila rose and walked into the ladies room, and the man went back to his place at the bar. A few minutes later, she left through the front door and walked the remaining half block to Attaboy's.

***

Brent had arrived at the nightclub about nine-thirty. He took a seat near the back of the room where he tried to appear inconspicuous. Loud, country music boomed from a jukebox at the side of the room, and a few couples danced. The room itself was long and quite wide. A large, rectangular bar occupied the center space. Forty or fifty people sat or milled around circular tables, and Brent noticed a few same-sex couples who held hands or talked at their tables.

Brent ordered a bottle of Lonestar and pulled his Astros cap down low on his forehead, almost covering his eyes. Slouched in his chair and nursing the beer, he blended with the crowd but felt he stood out because of being alone. Nicole had tried to talk him into letting her come along, but he had refused. He now wondered if that might not have been a good idea, since there weren't many unattached people in the room.

"Mind if I join you?" a low voice said over the music. Looking up, Brent saw a thin young man wearing a cowboy hat, alligator skin boots, and tight jeans. He was smiling and holding a bottle of Heineken in his right hand.

Seizing the opportunity, Brent pushed a chair out from under the table with his foot and gestured toward it with his hand.

"Nice crowd," the young man said, sitting down. He took a pull on his bottle of Heineken. "Come here often?"

"No. First time," Brent replied. "How about you?"

"Just about every weekend, on Saturday night," the stranger replied. "There's always a good group of people here. Some of the other places can get pretty rough. By the way, the name's Randy," he said, extending his hand.

"Uh, mine's Sam. Glad to meet you, Randy," Brent replied, shaking the limp hand. "You need a beer or something?"

"Yeah, I could use another one," Randy said.

Beckoning to one of the waitresses, Brent pointed to their bottles and held up two fingers. She nodded then went to the corner of the bar.

Brent sat facing the front of the room. If Sheila came in, he wanted to see her right away. He didn't have to wait long.

She strolled into the room about ten forty-five and went over to the bar. Several pairs of male eyes followed her across the floor. She took a seat and ordered something then lit a cigarette. Before her drink arrived, a middle-aged, plumpish little man wearing western clothes approached her and spoke. They were too far away for Brent to hear what they said, but the little man took a stool beside Sheila and they appeared engrossed in their conversation. Brent noticed that the man paid for her drink.

"That's a nice-looking young lady over there at the bar," Brent said, nodding toward Sheila. "Know who she is?"

Randy turned a little in his chair then looked over his shoulder toward the bar. "You talking about the dark-headed girl talking to the fat guy?" he asked, turning back to Brent.

"Yeah, that's the one."

"That's Sheila," Randy said. "She's down here just about every Saturday night. Hangs out with an older guy most of the time. But she'll hang with anybody'll buy her drinks if he's not here. Might even be a hooker, but I'm not sure. Interested in setting something up?"

"No, not at all," Brent replied, looking away. "I was just curious."

"Good. Then maybe you and I should get a little better acquainted." Randy said, grinning at Brent.

Brent ignored the comment and took another swallow of his beer. Then he put some bills on the table and pushed his chair back.

"Hey, you're not leaving already, are you?" Randy asked. "The crowd's just getting here."

"Yeah, I need to hit the road," Brent said. He felt like he had gotten what he had come for, so there wasn't any need to hang around any longer.

"Why don't you come over to my place? We can have some drinks, listen to a little music -- might even smoke a couple 'a joints, if you want to," Randy pleaded.

"No, I don't think so," Brent said, rising.

"Are you coming back here next week?" Randy seemed desperate.

"I don't think so," Brent said, walking away.

"Well, shit then."

Brent pulled his cap even lower over his eyes when he passed behind Sheila, still engaged in conversation with the same man. He breathed a sigh of relief when he left Attaboy's and walked up the semi-dark street toward his car.

The street grew darker as Brent left the vicinity of the nightclub, and there were few people on the sidewalk.

"Hey, you," someone said from a dark doorway as Brent passed.

Brent turned and could see the dim outline of a shabby, bearded man wearing an overcoat and a cap similar to his own. "Got a couple of bucks for a hungry vet'ran?" the figure asked.

"No, I don't," Brent said, turning to leave.

"Hold it, asshole! Gimme your wallet and your watch," the figure said. Brent saw a metallic object in the man's hand and knew instantly it was a gun. He put his hands in the air, and the robber reached up and detached Brent's watch with a flip of his wrist.

"Where's your wallet?" the man asked.

"It's in my left back pocket," Brent answered.

"Put one hand down and give it to me. Slow, now!"

Brent reached into his back pocket and retrieved the wallet. He gave it to the man.

"Step over here and turn around," the man said. Sensing that he was about to be hurt, Brent hesitated, wondering if he should run for the street.

"Move!" the man said.

Suspecting he would be shot if he resisted, Brent had just stepped over to the shadowy doorway and turned around when a blinding, white light filled his eyes and a sharp pain shot into the back of his head. He slumped to the ground, ears ringing with a sound like a million crickets singing. In the distance, he heard footsteps running down the sidewalk.

Everything was quiet. Brent found himself on all fours at the entrance to the dark door. Rolling over to a sitting position, he felt the back of his head, where a large lump had formed. He felt something wet and knew it was blood, but there didn't seem to be much of it.

Shaking all over, Brent got to his feet and took a few deep breaths. Assessing himself, he recalled the events of the evening, beginning with Nicole's phone call to Sheila. He asked himself the date and location, and was relieved to discover that his memory was still intact. He decided he had not suffered a concussion and should be all right.

He made his way back to the Suburban and unlocked the door. At least he still had his keys. He thought about turning on the dome light to inspect his injury but yielded to the impulse to get away as fast as possible. He started the engine and pulled into the street then turned south on Montrose. It was just a short drive to Main Street and the Medical Center, where Brent turned west onto University and followed it home.

Amazing, he thought when he pulled into his driveway, *Here I am, no more than a couple of miles from home and my office, and I've been mugged!*

***

Meanwhile, back at the bar in Attaboy's, a slim, dark-haired, middle-aged man walked over to the couple engaged in a conversation over their drinks. Sheila looked up at the man and broke into a smile with white teeth gleaming through a crescent of ruby-red lips, like a double row of pearls surrounded by ripe, plump strawberries.

"Hello, handsome. You're late," she said, reaching to brush his hair off his forehead with her fingers.

He smiled back at her, ignoring the man who sat beside her. "Sorry, got tied up at work." He cast a quick glance at the other man then looked back at her. "Let's find a table."

Sheila finished the remainder of her drink in one swallow and rose. "Thanks for the drink," she said to the man beside her. She and the second man went to an empty table in a corner of the room. The short, fat guy sat with a puzzled expression on his face, sipping his drink and staring at the couple who had just left him.

***

Nicole was waiting for Brent when he got home. He walked into the living room, and her hand flew to her mouth to suppress a startled scream. "Brent, what happened?" she asked as she leaped from her chair.

Brent looked a lot worse than he felt. He had lost his cap, and his hair was tangled and matted with dried blood. Blood had also run down the back of his neck and stained his shirt. The knees of his pants were torn and dirty, and his shoes were scuffed on the toes. Nicole helped him to the nearest chair, where he collapsed.

"I'm all right," he said. "Just got mugged and hit on the head. It looks worse than it is." He felt the back of his head and located the large knot. Grimacing a bit, he rose from the chair and made his way down the hall to the bathroom.

"Please sit down," Nicole said with concern. "I'll clean you up. Are you dizzy?"

"No, I'm okay." He reached into a bottom drawer, took out a pair of rubber gloves and gave them to her.

"Wear these, Nikki. Blood can be dangerous."

She hesitated for a brief minute and then put them on.

"Just help me get washed up so I can take a look at this damn cut."

He leaned over the sink while Nicole cleaned his hair with gentle fingers and exposed the cut. "It looks like the bleeding has stopped," she said. She located a hand mirror so he could inspect the back of his head.

"It doesn't look too bad," he said, turning his head from side to side while looking at the mirror. "It could use a couple of stitches though."

"Do you want me to take you to the emergency room?" Nicole asked.

Brent thought a minute then pulled on a fresh shirt. "No, I'll just call Gary Morgan. He won't mind meeting me at the office. He can sew me up without all the hoopla that'd be involved with a trip to the emergency room."

Brent looked much better after getting cleaned up and changing into some fresh clothes. He called Gary, and within a few minutes, they were all in Brent's office.

Gary inspected the wound.

"Gary, please be careful," Brent said. "I can't imagine anything worse than being responsible for giving this virus to someone else -- especially you or Nicole."

"I know," Gary said, pulling on a pair of rubber gloves. "I'll be careful."

"Are you sure you didn't lose consciousness?" Gary asked while he prepped the cut with some Betadine. "This is a pretty nasty gash."

"Ouch, that hurts!" Brent replied, grimacing. "No, I didn't lose consciousness. He just knocked me down and ran off with my billfold and watch."

Gary parted the hair around the gash. "I could shave this a little, but under the circumstances, I think the less conspicuous the wound, the better."

"You're right," Brent agreed.

"Have you notified the police?" Gary asked, injecting a local anesthetic.

"No," Brent said through clinched teeth and with eyes closed down to slits. "I started to call them, but I'll never get my stuff back. I just don't want the publicity that would go along with a police report."

Gary began to sew the edges of the cut together. "Brent," he said after a couple of minutes had passed, "I don't want to seem nosey, but what in the world were you doing up on Montrose Street at this hour of the night?"

"Playing detective," Nicole interjected. "He was following Sheila Walters so he could learn more about her lifestyle."

"Gosh, Brent," Gary said. "I thought you knew better than to go up there alone late at night. The north end of Montrose can be a pretty seedy area." He tied another stitch while he talked. "So, did you find out what you wanted to know?"

"I think so," Brent said. "I saw Sheila hanging out at one of the bars. She appeared to be waiting for someone. A fellow I met in the bar told me she's a regular and might be a hooker. But she usually keeps company with one particular, older man."

Gary appeared puzzled. "So, how is that going to be useful to you?"

"Well, if the lawsuit against me goes to court, it could be helpful to prove Sheila is a prostitute. I don't think any reasonable jury would believe that she got her HIV infection from me under those circumstances."

"How can you prove she's a prostitute?" Gary asked, putting in the last stitch.

Brent rearranged an arm under the drapes and rubbed his chin for a minute. "Good question. I'd need something more than just a suspicion."

"I'm single," Gary said. "Maybe I could try to line something up with her. I wouldn't mind testifying for you in court. In fact, it would be a pleasure."

"That goes beyond the expectations of friendship," Brent said. "She is HIV positive, you know."

"Oh," Gary said, shocked. "Believe me, I don't plan to do anything. I'll just confirm the fact that she's willing to sell her body."

"If you had listened to me in the first place," Nicole said, "this all could have been avoided. We need a private eye -- a real detective. They do this kind of thing all the time." She looked hard at Brent who still lay on his stomach on the treatment table with a sterile drape over his head. "And they never get hurt."

Brent groaned. "Yeah, right. Okay, that's something I can take care of Monday. Gary, I do appreciate your offer, but that's too much.

We'll hire a private eye. I'll take care of it right after the executive committee hearing." His voice sounded muffled, coming out from under the drape.

Gary removed the drape and helped Brent sit up. "I can take the stitches out anytime next week. Just let me know when the time is convenient."

"Thanks, Gary. We've kept you up most of the night," Brent said. "I appreciate your help, my friend."

"The offer to do a little detective work is still open," Gary said, taking off his gloves.

"Thanks, again. I'll let you know if I change my mind," Brent said.

They went out through the back door, and the three walked together to their cars. In a short time, they were all headed home.

Exhausted, but unable to doze more than a few minutes at a time, Brent dreamed. In his dream, he saw Sheila Walters, her face contorted and smeared with lipstick, with John Kelly and Bill Rudman -- even Al Martin was there -- and they all were laughing and pointing fingers at him. He stood outside an operating room wearing a surgical cap and mask, and from his neck to his toes he was stark naked .

Chapter 17

In response to Nicole's diligent use of ice packs, the swelling around Brent's cut had diminished in size by Monday morning. In fact, his scalp injury had been so well repaired that close scrutiny was required to determine that he had even been injured.

Todd Ward was at Brent's office a little before seven that morning. He wanted to review what had happened and formulate some sort of plan.

Todd asked for a copy of the medical staff bylaws and read the section regarding summary suspension of a staff member's hospital privileges.

"It appears that Dr. Sherman and Mr. Kelly followed the correct procedure for the summary suspension. Now, it's up to us to convince Graham's executive committee that you represent no threat to the patients of their institution," Todd said in his rather formal style. "Is that the way you interpret the situation?"

"Yes, it is," Brent replied, reflecting on the attorney's use of the term 'their institution' before continuing. "And I've collected some articles from the medical literature to support my position, too."

"Tell me something else, Brent," Todd said. "How is it that things have gotten so far at this stage of the game? I mean, you haven't even been proven to be infected with HIV, have you?"

"No, I haven't," Brent said, casting his eyes downward. "But I'm afraid that it's just a matter of a few days until it will be definite. I had a repeat Western Blot drawn a few days ago, and the result should be back later this week. The possibility of it being negative is small."

"Don't you think it would be a good move to insist on delaying action regarding your staff privileges until the result is back?" Todd asked.

"Maybe so," Brent said, pleased that the attorney had thought of some tactics. "But the main thing we have to do is convince the executive committee that I don't pose a threat to my patients. The fact that my latest test result is pending could be used to our advantage."

"Do you have any information about similar cases?" Todd asked.

"There hasn't been much published about specific cases, in particular, none involving surgeons. I've reviewed the literature up through ninety-one, which is pretty current, and I do have articles stating that there has never been a documented case of transmission of the virus from surgeon to patient," Brent said, reaching for a stack of papers on the corner of his desk.

"Very well then," Todd said. "And we know that the State Board of Medical Examiners doesn't prohibit infected physicians from continuing to practice. It appears that their decision is based on facts, not just 'doctors protecting their own' -- if you'll pardon the expression."

Brent smiled and began to relax somewhat. "Yes, I would agree with that, and no offense taken."

"Then I suggest we gather our material and walk over to the hospital," Todd said. "And remember, stand tall and look 'em in the eye. You've done nothing to be ashamed of."

"Thanks, Todd. It's good to know there's someone out there who understands that," Brent said, sensing butterflies in his stomach in spite of the reassurance.

***

The hospital board room began to fill a few minutes before eight o'clock. The Executive Committee consisted of ten medical staff members, all elected by their peers, and the hospital CEO John Kelly, who was an ex-officio member and therefore could not vote. Louise

McArdle arrived to represent the hospital, and a staff secretary took a place near the corner of the room, where she could take notes and record the meeting for later transcription. They were seated around a long, rectangular table, and a smaller table with a coffee pot and a tray of donuts stood off to one side of the room.

Brent and Todd Ward entered the room promptly at eight. They took seats at the end of the table, and Brent placed the papers he had brought on the table in front of him. A few of the medical staff members nodded at him when their eyes met, but none attempted to speak. He felt isolated, naked and alone in the midst of these people whom he had known and worked with for years. A flashback of his dream went through his mind, and he forced it away.

Conversation around the table began with strained smiles and low voices. All eyes flicked toward Brent but looked away when he returned the gaze. Jerry Sherman called the meeting to order at five minutes after eight by tapping on an empty glass with a spoon and as much authority as he could muster. "Let the meeting come to order!" he said in a loud voice.

After the inevitable shuffling of papers and scraping of chairs, the room silenced.

"I assume we all know why this special hearing has been called," Sherman continued. "We are here to discuss the recent summary suspension of Dr. Brent Dalton's hospital staff privileges." He reached for some papers lying on the table in front of him.

"If you will distribute these documents among yourselves, you will see that the action taken on Friday by Mr. Kelly and myself was not capricious. It was well investigated and took place in order to prevent any further risk of lawsuits and bad publicity which might occur if further allegations against Dr. Dalton arise." He proceeded to pass out copies of the lawsuit against Brent and the hospital and copies of the article from *Whisper.*

"Dr. Dalton," Sherman continued, "do you have anything to say to the committee?"

Brent felt his heart hammering in his chest. He rose to his feet and looked into the eyes of the committee members seated around the table.

121

"Yes, I do," he said in a clear, strong voice. "To begin with, everything you have in front of you, provided as evidence by the Chief of Staff, consists of unsubstantiated allegations. There is no way in the world that the Walters girl contracted HIV from me, and I think all of you know that to be the case. Furthermore, I have not tested definitely positive for the virus myself, although the plaintiff in this case has. My Western Blot test is still pending, and the results should be available by the end of this week. I feel that a suspension of my privileges is unjustified and would also be unjustified even if my Western Blot were known to be positive."

"Thank you, Brent," Sherman said. "The result of your test will be of major interest to this committee and to the hospital board. Do you have anything else to say?"

"Yes," Brent added, "I do. I have some copies of recent medical literature here which indicate there has never been a documented case of transmission of HIV from surgeon to patient." He proceeded to distribute copies of the articles to the committee members.

"Evidence such as this has been the basis for the absence of recommendations from the CDC or State Medical Societies and Examining Boards for the withdrawal of medical licenses from infected practitioners," Brent told the committee. "And I will say it again, even if my Western Blot should return positive, there is no basis for termination of my staff privileges."

"Thank you, again," Sherman said, shuffling his papers and avoiding Brent's eyes. "If that is all you have to say then you are excused. The committee will discuss this matter in private, and you will be informed in writing by Registered Mail of its decision within five days. In the meantime, the suspension is still in effect."

Brent and Todd left the room and walked back toward Brent's office. The mood was somber. "I had hoped the committee would make a favorable decision this morning, while we were still there," Brent said.

"I didn't expect that to happen," Todd said. "When a matter like this gets to this point, all the t's have to be crossed, and all the i's have to be dotted."

"What do we do now?" Brent asked.

Todd scratched his head. "How's the research on the Walters girl's background coming along?"

"Interesting that you should ask," Brent said, lifting a portion of the hair on the back of his head to expose the recent wound. "See this?"

"Wow, that looks painful! How did it happen?" Todd said.

"Come into my office, and I'll tell you all about it," Brent said, opening the back door with a key. They stepped in and went into Brent's office. He buzzed the front desk to let the receptionist know he was in then closed the door for privacy. Within a few minutes, Brent had related the events of the weekend to the attorney.

"My God, man," Todd said after Brent had finished his story. "Don't you know better than to go down to an area like north Montrose late at night, by yourself and on foot?"

Brent felt foolish. "I didn't realize the area was as rough as it is. At least I got a little information."

"A little is right," Todd replied. "But what we need is something we can use in court." He paused for a minute and scratched his chin. "Have you considered hiring a private investigator?"

"Yes, Nicole and I've talked about it. Do you think it would help?"

"Yes, I do," Todd said. "Those guys can dig up stuff you wouldn't believe. They know how to collect evidence that will stand up in court, too."

"How do I go about finding one?" Brent asked. "Should I just look in the Yellow Pages under detectives, or what?"

Todd put his briefcase down across his lap and thought for a minute. "There's a guy I've worked with several times in the past that I could recommend, if you like. Would you like for me to set up a meeting?"

"Yes, and as soon as possible too," Brent said. "I'm anxious to get things moving."

"I'm pretty sure I can arrange something for tomorrow, providing he's in town," Todd said, rising from his chair. "I'll call him from my office and let you know as soon as possible."

"I'll be waiting for your call," Brent said, extending his hand. "Thanks for all your help."

"And, Brent …"

"Yes?"

"Don't forget to cancel your credit cards and apply for a new driver's license."

"I called about the credit cards yesterday and will go down to the Driver's License office today. Thanks for reminding me."

They shook hands and Todd departed, leaving Brent alone in the room to ponder the situation further. An hour later, Todd called to say he had arranged a meeting with the PI.

Chapter 18

Next afternoon, Brent met Todd in the attorney's office at two. A few minutes later, he shook hands with Mitchell Jackson, private eye. "Just call me Mitch," the young man said, taking a seat.

Mitch was dressed in a neat sport shirt and slacks and appeared to be in his early thirties. He had gray hair streaked into brown which was distributed in a ring around the sides and back of his head. The top of his head was bald and shiny as a fried egg, giving him somewhat of a gnomish appearance. He was medium height, a little stocky, and spoke with a southern drawl that suggested to Brent he might be from Mississippi or Georgia. And he wore small, almost undetectable hearing aids in both ears.

"Todd tells me that ya'll need a little background infa'mation about a young woman who's suin' you," Mitch said, coming right to the point. "How 'bout tellin' me a little about huh and the suc'umstainces."

Brent leaned forward and looked into the younger man's deep-set, brown eyes. "The young woman is a former patient of mine who has HIV. She claims she caught it from me when I did an appendectomy on her in December."

"Did she?" Mitch asked without mirth.

"No, of course not," Brent replied without blinking. "There's no way that could have happened."

"Why'd she think she caught it from you?" Mitch asked.

"I'm not sure she does think she caught it from me. But she's claiming she did," Brent said. "I think she sees that as a way to get money from me, or maybe she just doesn't want her family to know how she really got the virus."

"And how'd that be?" Mitch asked.

"We don't know for sure, but the most common ways are by having sex with someone who is infected or by sharing needles while using drugs," Brent said. "That's what I need you for -- to find out how she got the infection. We may not be able to pinpoint the exact person she caught it from, or when she got it, but if she is sleeping with everybody she meets or is mainlining drugs, we should be able to build a decent defense against her."

"That don't sound like too much to find out," Mitch said. "What so't o' time frame ah we lookin' at?"

"No trial date has been set for the case," Todd said. "But the sooner this can be resolved, the better."

"One thing botha's me, Docta Dalton," Mitch said, his accent a little less pronounced. "How can this woman claim to've caught the virus from you? Do you have the AIDS virus too?"

Brent dropped his head and looked at the floor for a few seconds before looking back at Mitch. "I might have it," he answered. "The test has not been conclusive for several weeks, but I might have the virus."

"Would 'ja mind if I asked how ya' caught it?" Mitch asked.

"No, not at all," Brent replied. "I caught it from a needle stick while operating on a patient who had HIV."

Mitch looked relieved. "Just curious. Didn't mean to pry."

"That's all right," Brent said. "I didn't mind your asking."

"If ya' would, please jot the lady's name and address down for me," Mitch said, handing Brent a small notebook. "And if ya know anything else about her that might be helpful, tell me about it."

"Weekends, she likes to go to a place called Attaboy's just off Montrose Street. She hangs out there with an older man, according to what someone told me the other day," Brent said. "There's a possibility that she might even be a hooker. I don't know whether or not she is using drugs."

"Well, that's someplace to start," Mitch said with just a trace of an accent. "You wouldn't have a picture of her, would you?"

"No, afraid not," Brent said. "What happened to your accent?"

Mitch burst out laughing. "I have to practice that Southern drawl sometimes, since I grew up in Wisconsin. The accent helps me in certain situations, if you know what I mean."

Brent laughed a little. He wasn't sure if he wanted an actor for a detective.

Todd reassured Brent that Mitch was genuine. After discussing the detective's fee arrangements, they asked that he report back to them as soon as he had any news. Mitch agreed then left, still chuckling to himself.

"Are you sure this guy's for real?" Brent asked when Mitch had left. "He even wears hearing aids in both ears. How's he going to do any snooping?"

Todd laughed out loud. "Yes, he's for real, and he's at least pretty good, even if not the best. The advantage with Mitch is that he enjoys his work and is like a bulldog when he gets on to something. And he's a lot cheaper than the big agencies. His hearing is no problem, as long as he has batteries in his hearing aids and keeps them turned on."

"Well, okay -- if you say so," Brent agreed.

"To get back to the subject of concern, have you heard anything from the hospital?" Todd asked.

"No, but I sort of expect they will wait until the results of the Western Blot are back," Brent replied.

"That doesn't surprise me," Todd said. "What are you going to do in the meantime?"

"Nicole and I thought we would spend a couple of days on our boat while we're waiting. I can let the girls at the office know how to reach me if anything happens before we get back." Brent rose from his chair, walked over to the window and looked out.

"Todd, what do you think we should do if I don't get my privileges back? I mean, if I'm positive for HIV, will it be worth while to fight the hospital?"

"That's a question only you can answer," Todd said, twirling a pencil in front of his face, leaning on his elbows. "It all depends on what you want to do in that situation. Would you want to continue practicing surgery in the face of all the negative publicity that will accompany such a challenge? Will patients be willing to see you?"

Brent sighed, still looking out the window. "I'm afraid there's no easy answer," he said, turning back to face the attorney. "I've asked myself those same questions a million times. Right now, even though I fear I know what the outcome will be, I feel I can't make any more decisions until my test result is back."

"Speaking of the test result," Todd said, "do you think there's any problem with letting your entire future hang on the thin thread of one test result from a single laboratory? In particular a lab that is part of the hospital you may end up fighting in court?"

"That thought has occurred to me too," Brent said. "What you say makes sense, but I can't imagine any reason for the results not to be accurate. After all, if I test negative then everything else is moot."

"I'm sure you're right," Todd said, putting the pencil down on the desk and sitting up straight. "If the current test turns out negative then there's nothing to worry about. But if it's positive -- at least think about it."

"I will," Brent said.

***

Later that same day, Brent and Nicole strolled along the dock near *Caribe*. The sun had sunk to the horizon, and the western sky glowed with brilliant orange-red florescence streaked with purple clouds. Seagulls circled and mewed, darting between dozens of sailboats whose tall masts jabbed at the sky.

"Tell me more about Mitch," Nicole said.

Brent stopped to watch a gull fly by before answering. "He's a bit strange, but he struck me as competent," he replied, smiling at the thought of the gnomish little man with a southern drawl. "...even if he does seem to have a humorous side. His job doesn't seem all that difficult." He glanced at Nicole to test her reaction to that comment and was pleased she didn't remind him of the mugging. " ... for a person in his line of work, that is."

"Has Todd worked with him before?"

"Yes, Todd recommended him and arranged the meeting."

"Is he from around here?"

"He's from Wisconsin but has a background in the Houston police department -- as a detective, I think. He's been on his own as a PI for the last five years. That's all Todd told me about him."

Darkness had begun to close around them, and they decided to walk over to the Brass Parrot for supper. They went aboard *Caribe* to freshen up, and a few minutes later Nicole stepped over the toerail and back onto the dock.

"Are you taking your cell phone with you?" she asked, waiting on the dock.

Brent finished closing the companionway. "No, I don't think so. No one will call us before Friday, when the result of the Western Blot is ready." He stepped onto the dock beside her, and they walked over to the restaurant at the edge of the parking lot. Within a few minutes they sat at a table on the covered, back deck studying the menus, sipping draft beer. In front of them lay the channel connecting the harbor to Galveston Bay.

A full moon began a slow climb over the Bay and its yellow light beamed across the harbor straight toward their open air table. Brent covered Nicole's hand with his and squeezed it, They looked at each other in silence for a few moments then nibbled like overfed wedding guests when seafood platters brimming with hushpuppies, fried shrimp, fish and oysters arrived at the table.

***

In the moonlight, *Caribe* frolicked on her lines, but there was no one aboard to answer the cellular phone when it rang in the empty salon.

Chapter 19

Next morning, Brent and Nicole climbed out of their bunk in the captain's stateroom. They dressed in light clothes in anticipation of a warm day sailing in the Bay. Nicole poured them each a cup of coffee and had just taken her first sip when the phone rang, startling her so much she spilled some of her coffee onto the tabletop.

Brent reached for the phone.

"Dalton here."

"Brent, this is Todd Ward. Where have you been? I tried to call you several times last night."

"Sorry, Todd. We went out to eat," Brent replied. "Got back to the boat pretty late. What's happened?"

"I received a call from Dr. Sherman last night. Said he had tried to call you at home and wanted me to track you down. Seems that the Executive Committee met again yesterday afternoon late and voted to restore your privileges, pending the result of the Western Blot test."

"You mean I can operate again?"

"Yes, at least until Friday. He made it clear that your surgical privileges would be suspended again if the test result is positive. He also said they would allow you to remain on the staff and practice non-invasive medicine if you test positive."

Brent stood gazing out of a porthole at the surface of the water as he let Todd's words sink in.

"Brent, are you still there?" Todd asked.

"Yes, sorry. I didn't expect anything to happen before Friday. I guess I'm a little overwhelmed."

Nicole waved her hands in the air and did a little dance in front of Brent. "What is happening?" she hissed in a stage whisper.

Brent covered the receiver with his hand. "I've got my surgical privileges back again! Start packing our clothes."

***

Thursday morning, Brent left home later than usual. He had no hospital patients left to see on rounds, and his elective cases had all requested referral to other surgeons. Even Gary Morgan had been assigned to work with somebody else.

Brent had spent Wednesday in his office catching up on the paperwork that piled up on a regular basis. There were a few phone calls from post-op patients who needed prescriptions refilled or had questions about their dressings or wound care. The receptionist had managed to reschedule a few post-op visits so they could be seen Thursday, just to keep things moving. There were no new referrals and no requests for consultations.

So Thursday morning, Brent decided to have breakfast in the cafeteria before going to the office. He thought he might bump into some of the other doctors there and get a sense of what they were thinking. More than that, he wanted his colleagues to see him looking alive and well.

Passing down the buffet breakfast line, Brent piled his plate high with bacon and scrambled eggs. He ladled on grits then added biscuits with butter and jelly on the side. This was the way he had eaten years ago, before he had realized that he too was susceptible to the same laws of biochemistry and physiology that governed everyone else. Today, for some reason, that didn't seem to matter.

Seeing no other doctors in the cafeteria, Brent took a seat alone near the side of the room and attacked his breakfast with gusto. He could almost make himself believe the time was fifteen years earlier. He and Nicole hadn't met at that time, and he was working his tail off as a junior resident at Charity Hospital in New orleans, the "Big Free" as it was called.

The residents on the surgery service almost never had time to eat breakfast in the doctors' dining room. They met on the large, open wards to begin their morning rounds at five AM. Rounds always took at least two hours with the first year house officers and a queue of medical students in tow. One by one, they visited the patients, checked charts to look at temperatures, vital signs, and laboratory data then changed dressings and examined their patients.

Brent had loved what he was doing. He enjoyed teaching medical students the rudiments of surgery on rounds: when to get patients out of bed, how to remove dressings and put on new ones, how to write orders for IV fluids and how to select and use antibiotics and narcotics. These were basics.

More complicated subjects, such as examination of patients with abdominal pain and making decisions about necessity for surgery took more time and individual tutoring. What had become obvious to Brent back then as a resident and even today as a practitioner was the difference in aptitudes among those who trained with him.

They all were bright and had above average IQ's, or they wouldn't have gotten as far as they had. The obvious difference was that a few were gifted with common sense and an ability to use their hands. Those with both talents were potential surgeons of high caliber.

"Hey, Brent!" Gary Morgan stood at the side of the table with a big grin on his face. "Mind if I join you?"

"Hey, yourself! Sit down! I was just thinking about you," Brent lied. "Don't you have any cases to assist with this morning?"

"We have a late start today. I'm helping Dr. Wilson with a couple of laparoscopic cases starting at ten thirty, and we've finished with rounds." Gary paused while taking a seat and began buttering a biscuit.

"It's good to see you back in the hospital again. I heard about the decision of the executive committee. It's been a hot topic for conversation in the surgery lounge."

"Oh?" Brent said, studying his near-empty plate. "What are they saying?"

"Well, nothing bad about you," Gary said in the process of making a bacon sandwich out of his biscuit. "Everyone agrees that you're an innocent victim in this whole mess. Opinions vary as to what should be done."

"Mind giving me some examples?" Brent asked.

Gary placed his biscuit-sandwich on the edge of his plate after taking a large bite. He chewed while looking at a wall above Brent's head then washed the food down with a swallow of coffee. "Dr. Wilson has been one of your biggest supporters. He says there's no law against practicing surgery with an HIV infection because there's no evidence of risk to the patient."

"That's right," Brent added. "I know that from the reading I've done. What else are they saying?"

"There's someone from administration who has dropped into the lounge a couple of times this week. He's the same dark-haired fellow who took off from the breakfast table that morning when we tried to join him a few weeks ago, remember?"

"Rudman? What has he got to say about this?"

"Nothing good, I'm afraid," Gary said. "He says the hospital is liable for anything that goes wrong, and he doesn't think you should be allowed to practice at all. He thinks the risk is too great."

"Where's he coming from?" Brent asked. I wonder why he feels that way? I know he has hard feelings about his sister dying, but I don't understand why he has this paranoia about people with HIV."

Gary looked around him to see if anyone was within earshot. "The word in the surgery lounge is that he has a son who is gay and is infected. I don't have any way of knowing for sure, but that's what they're saying."

"Wow, first his sister, now his son. I guess something like that could make a person see things through a different colored glass all right," Brent said. "But you'd think those circumstances would make him more empathetic to those infected, wouldn't you? He sits on the Risk Control Committee too. That could be the source of some of the trouble I've had."

"I wouldn't know about that," Gary said. "The vast majority of what I hear is supportive of you, like I said. All the technicians and scrub nurses, the nurses in the ICU and on the floor, they all have been asking about you."

"That's good to know," Brent said. "They're all good people."

Gary finished his biscuit in one big bite and washed it down with the remaining coffee from his cup. "Guess I'd better get moving. Don't want to be late for my assists."

"Thanks for the information," Brent said. "And don't be a stranger. I'm in the office quite a bit now, so drop by when you have a few minutes to spare."

"I will." Gary gathered his breakfast items on the tray and left.

Brent sat at the table alone again, staring out the large set of windows at the end of the room. While he watched, an attractive young woman with long, dark hair walked by and took a seat at a table nearby. She reminded him of someone he had known a long time ago.

Outside, flowers bloomed, and fresh, green foliage covered shrubs and trees. The scene was reminiscent of a rural landscape in spite of its downtown location. He watched a mockingbird hop from shrub to shrub in search of food and realized that the first day of spring had just passed without him even being aware of it.

He daydreamed, and the year was nineteen sixty seven. He was finishing his senior year in high school, and the world was his. He had just fallen in love for the first time.

Her name was Juanita, and she had long, black hair and sparkling, dark eyes that constantly shined. She loved the outdoors. Weekends, they hiked trails and canoed inland lakes. They were in love not just with each other but with the great outdoors. Looking back now, it seemed like another lifetime.

They spent every possible minute together. It was a happy, carefree time. They birdwatched while they hiked and canoed, and they collected rocks and fossils. Brent felt then that whatever he did for a career would have to involve the natural world, the outdoors. How different things were now. It seemed until a few days ago he could never find time to get away from his work.

College derailed their plans. They both enrolled at the University of Texas in Austin and majored in biology. But during the first year, their interests changed. Juanita enjoyed chemistry, and Brent's grades were so good that his advisor had talked him into changing his major to pre-med.

They saw less and less of each other over the next year, and she had started dating other guys. Brent hadn't minded, since by then he had other interests himself.

Through four years of college, followed by four more years of medical school and five years of surgical residency, his only true mistress was medicine. As time passed, he drifted little by little away from his former love, the great outdoors.

Now, sitting in the cafeteria and looking out on a beautiful spring day, he wondered what he would be doing and what his life would be like if he had not gone into medicine. What if he had majored in forestry or wildlife management, like he had started out to do?

Deep down inside, he knew he had no regrets about his career choice. He had loved medicine from the start and still did. His career and his life were presently threatened by the bizarre circumstances in which he found himself, and now he yearned for what he had left behind, the great outdoors. He regretted the years he had let slide by without spending more time in the woods and streams that abounded around him.

He smiled at himself, recognizing what was happening. He was looking for an escape, a refuge from what threatened him. He knew he wouldn't find a solution to his problems by dwelling on the past or by daydreaming, so he gathered his empty dishes on the tray and carried them toward the conveyor belt at the back of the room.

Crossing the room, Brent recognized the husband of one of his patients sitting alone at a table. The man was Freddie Sanders, and his wife had required a mastectomy a couple of weeks ago because of breast cancer. She was thirty-seven years old, and her cancer did not appear to have spread outside the confines of the breast. They were hopeful that she was cured. He walked over to the table.

"Hello, Freddie. Is Julie back in the hospital?"

"Oh, hello, Doc!" the man said. He appeared pleased to see Brent. Rising from his chair, he reached to shake hands. Brent rested his tray on the back of a chair so they could talk.

"Yes, I'm afraid Julie's having some problems. She started having pain in the calf of her leg a few days ago. We called your office, and the nurse told us Dr. Wilson was covering. He said Julie has blood clots. Wanted to keep her in the hospital for a few days on blood thinners."

"I'm sorry to hear that. How are the kids?" Brent asked.

"They're doing as well as can be expected, under the circumstances. They're both old enough to know what's going on, and they're a big help at home."

"I'm sorry Julie is having trouble," Brent said. "I'll run by her room and say hello later today."

"That's nice of you," Freddie said, "but you'll have to make it pretty quick. She's supposed to be discharged this morning. I'm going to check on her after I've had a bite of breakfast."

"I'll go right now," Brent said. "Good luck."

"Bye, Doc. Thanks for stopping."

Brent caught the elevator to the fifth floor and moved down the corridor to the surgical wing. It was a familiar area.

When he entered the nurses' station to look up Julie's room number, Brent noticed that something appeared to be happening in one of the rooms down the corridor. Three nurses stood talking outside the room, and several other hospital personnel passed in and out of the room.

"What's going on?" Brent asked a young ward clerk who was seated behind a computer screen at a long desk.

The clerk glanced up from the screen. "Oh, hello, Doctor Dalton. Just had a Code Blue in five-sixty-two. It wasn't successful, I'm afraid."

"Too bad. Let me know if I can help," Brent said. He turned to the patient list on a blackboard on the back wall and scanned it for 'Sanders'. The name appeared about half-way down the second column. To the left of the name was the room number: five-sixty-two. A wave of nausea swept across him when he saw the name and room number.

"I hope this is wrong," Brent said, pointing his finger at the name.

The clerk looked up again. "What's the matter?" she asked.

"Didn't you say that the patient in room five-sixty-two just expired?" Brent asked.

"Yes, that's right."

"This list has Julie Sanders in that room. There must be a mistake," Brent said.

The clerk scanned another list she had at the desk. "No, I'm afraid not," she replied. "Her name was Julie Sanders. Age thirty-seven. She was admitted to Dr. Wilson. Do you want to talk to Mrs. Dinkins?"

"Yes, is she in charge?" he asked, choking back a surge of bitter bile, his heart sinking. It was hard for him to believe this was happening. Julie was such a bright, cheerful person. She had everything to live for. And two young children at home.

"Yes, Sir. She's down by the room."

Brent walked down the hall to the group of nurses. He recognized Charlotte Dinkins standing by the door.

"Charlotte, I've just been told that Julie Sanders expired. Can you tell me what happened? She was a patient of mine."

"Hello, Dr. Dalton," the charge nurse said. "I'm sorry. We didn't realize she was also your patient, or we would have called you."

"Just tell me what happened," Brent repeated.

"She was admitted earlier this week with DVT in both legs. She's been on heparin and Coumadin and was hoping to go home today."

"I think I know the rest," Brent said grimmacing. "She got up to go to the bathroom and collapsed. Right?"

"Something like that. We found her on the floor with no vital signs. We called a full code but she never regained a heartbeat."

"Dr. Wilson just saw her on rounds about an hour ago and ordered some clotting studies to be done this morning," the charge nurse continued. "They hadn't even been done."

"Was CPR started right away?" Brent asked.

"Yes, one of the anesthesiologists happened to be on the wing at the time the code was called, and he started CPR as soon as he got to the room. Her EKG showed a flat line when we connected her to the monitor."

"What did you do?"

"We gave epi and atropine a couple of times and continued CPR, but the monitor still showed a straight line. Her pupils were dilated and fixed. We just got there too late."

Brent shook his head and grimaced. "What a shame. She has two beautiful, young kids at home. I just talked to her husband in the cafeteria. He thought she would be going home today."

"I'm sorry," the nurse said. "Would you like for me to go down and bring him up to the conference room?"

"Thanks, Charlotte. I'd appreciate that. I'll go there in a few minutes and talk to him." Brent wondered what he would say. In spite of having gone through this sort of thing before -- the unexpected death thing -- it never got any easier. There just wasn't any easy way to tell people that their wife, or husband, or child was dead. Especially when it was an unexpected death.

Nurse Dinkins disappeared down the hall, and Brent went back to the nurses' station. Jim Wilson was there, looking at Julie Sanders' chart.

"What a terrible thing," Wilson said, looking up. "I just saw her a little while ago on rounds. If her clotting studies looked all right, I was going to discharge her on Coumadin."

"Hadn't she just been in for two or three days?"

"Yes, but her INR was in the therapeutic range, and her HMO was pushing me to get her out of the hospital." Wilson shook his head and looked back at the chart. "This could have happened there, right in front of the kids."

Charlotte Dinkins entered the station from the doorway. "Hello, Doctor Wilson. I'm sorry about your patient. Mr. Sanders is waiting for the two of you in the conference room. He has no idea why you need to talk to him."

Brent led the way down the corridor. In spite of the fact that Julie had been under Jim Wilson's care, he felt she was his patient. He needed to be the one who told her husband what had happened.

Freddie Sanders stood against the back wall of the small conference room when they walked in. He looked a little pale. "Doctor Dalton, Doctor Wilson -- is anything wrong? Is Julie OK?"

"I'm afraid we have some very bad news, Freddie," Brent began. "Something unexpected... has happened."

"What is it?" Freddie asked, the remainder of color now drained from his face.

Brent pulled a chair out from the small table in the center of the room. "Have a seat, Freddie."

Freddie stumbled as he walked around the side of the chair. He fell into the chair and put his face into his trembling hands. "Is Julie OK?"

"No, I'm afraid not, Freddie." Brent felt his throat tighten as he spoke. "She had a cardiac arrest a few minutes ago. Her heart stopped. We weren't able to get her back." He put a hand gently on the man's shoulder.

"Oh, God, no! She's not dead!" Freddie's lower lip trembled as he looked up through wide eyes filling with tears.

"I'm sorry, Freddie," Brent said. "It was totally unexpected. One of the clots which had formed in Julie's leg broke loose and went to her heart when she got out of bed a little while ago. It was very quick and painless."

Large tears ran down Freddie's cheeks. He sat without speaking for a minute, staring at the door. His mouth hung open.

"Stay here as long as you like, Freddie," Brent said, patting him on the shoulder and edging toward the door.

"Why did this happen?" Freddie asked with a cracked voice. He stood up and looked at the two doctors. "She did everything you told her to. She wanted to live. Why did you let this happen?"

Brent glanced at Jim Wilson, who hung his head and frowned. "We're sorry, Freddie," Wilson said. "It's nobody's fault. These things happen sometimes. We can't tell you why."

Freddie sat down again and buried his head in his folded arms on the table. His body shook as he began to sob out loud. "Please, just leave me alone," he said with a muffled voice.

Charlotte Dinkins had tiptoed into the room while they were talking. She nodded at the doctors. "I'll stay here," she said. "The Chaplain is on his way up."

They left the small room with Freddie and the nurse still inside. At the nurses' station, Jim looked at Brent. "That was pretty rough. It's always hard when you lose a patient, but it makes matters a lot worse when the family blames you for it."

"You're right about that, Jim. Thanks for your help."

Brent left the wing and walked back to his office with a pace slower than that of a tortoise and a mood darker than the clouds that had begun to gather in the western sky. This was not turning out to be a good day.

Chapter 20

A short time after leaving Freddie Sanders in the conference room, Brent walked into his office through an entrance in the back. He needn't have taken the back door, since the waiting room was empty. The office nurse sat behind a sliding glass window adjacent to the reception room. She stared at a computer screen in front of her, hands folded in her lap.

"Morning, Elizabeth. Any messages?"

"Oh, good morning, Doctor Dalton. I didn't hear you come in. I put a couple of notes on your desk -- nothing urgent." She got up and began filing some charts. "You're here a little early. Appointments don't start until one."

"I know. It makes the morning kind of long when there's not any surgery scheduled. Any consults?"

"No, I'm afraid not. There were a couple of new patients on the schedule from last week, but they both called and canceled."

"Has that happened often?"

"Yes and no," Elizabeth said. "There haven't been many new referrals to begin with for the last week. Ever since that horrible story came out in *Whisper*. And the ones we had all called and canceled."

"What about the post-ops?" Brent asked. "Have any of them canceled?"

"A few have. Most of those were several weeks post-op and were due their final check-up."

"Why don't you give me the charts on those who don't come in," Brent requested. "I may need to be sure some of them get checked by someone else if they don't want to see me."

"I'll get some for you now," Elizabeth said. She picked up the appointment schedule and began pulling charts from the files.

Brent walked into his office and sat down. On his desk lay a few phone messages about requests for prescription renewals, but nothing of much importance. He swiveled in his chair and gazed out at the tall buildings around the office.

A few pigeons flew by the upper story window, and a shadow fell across the scene when a large cloud drifted across the sun. The sudden dimness matched his mood. He sighed and leaned back in the chair.

Brent wondered if he was a failure. He had just lost a young patient whose husband blamed him for her death. Maybe it really was his fault. He wasn't getting any new patient referrals, and his colleagues had deserted him in the midst of this crisis. For the first time in his life, he regretted his decision to practice medicine.

***

Early the next morning, which was Friday, Brent climbed out of bed after a long, fitful night. He had dreamed about storms encountered while sailing on a clear day then of being trapped in a quagmire, unable to proceed in any direction.

Today was the big day. Today, he would get the result of the Western Blot. He had asked Al Martin to call the result to him as soon as it became available, so now he had to find something to do to help the time pass.

He went into the kitchen and put on a pot of coffee then walked out to the end of the driveway and retrieved the morning paper. He managed to drink three cups of coffee by the time Nicole came downstairs and joined him in the kitchen.

"Morning, Sweetheart," Brent said to the person he had come to realize meant more to him than life itself. After Julie Sanders' sudden death the day before, he had reflected for a long time on what it must be like to lose a wife. And to lose her unexpectedly when things appeared to be going well, as had happened to Julie, would be more than he thought he could bear.

"Good morning," Nicole said. She stood behind his chair and slipped one of her small hands under the front of Brent's bathrobe then leaned over and kissed the top of his head.

"Did you get any sleep at all last night?" Nicole asked.

"Oh, yeah," he fibbed. "I slept like a log. How about you?"

"I didn't get much sleep," Nicole confessed. "You tossed and turned all night, talking in your sleep. What in the world were you dreaming about?"

Brent smiled. He had learned long ago that he could never get away with trying to lie to Nicole, no matter how good his intentions or innocent the fib.

"I had crazy dreams, about sailing and getting caught in storms and getting stuck in mud -- things like that. What did I say?"

Nicole poured herself a cup of coffee and sat beside him. "You mumbled a lot... things I couldn't understand... and you even shouted out loud a couple of times. Something like, 'Look out!' and 'Get away! Get away!'"

Brent blushed a little and smiled at her. "Sounds like I was worried about something. I didn't expect it to be that obvious."

Nicole refilled Brent's cup. "I think it's obvious what you are worried about." She sat beside him and stirred her coffee. "Today's the big day. Maybe today, we'll finally get a definite answer and be able to move ahead with the rest of our lives."

Brent didn't reply immediately. "Yeah, I certainly hope so," he said at last, but without much enthusiasm. He recognized that while he was eager to get the test result back, he also dreaded learning what he feared was the unalterable truth.

"Did you ask Al Martin to call you at the office?" Nicole asked.

"I didn't specify where to call me. He knows how to track me down when he's got the report."

"Do you think there's much of a chance the test will turn out negative this time?" Nicole asked.

Brent got up and began pacing the kitchen floor. "There's not much chance of that," he replied. "I've asked Jim Schubert about the possibility of the previous results all being false. He said it's not likely. But he also said that an acute viral illness can cause a false positive, and I did have an episode resembling flu this past winter. It was at the same time I found out that my ELISA had converted to positive."

"Could an acute HIV infection cause a similar picture?" Nicole asked.

It appeared she had done some reading, Brent reflected.

"Yes, I'm afraid so," he admitted.

"At least you have your hospital privileges back," Nicole pointed out. "You can continue working, no matter what the result of the test."

"Maybe so and maybe not," Brent said. "The executive committee's decision was that I could practice non-invasive medicine if the Western Blot returns positive. That's not much good for a surgeon. Most of my office appointments have been canceled, and I haven't had a single new patient referral or a consult in the last week. Everything seemed to come to a stop when the article came out in that tabloid."

Nicole got up and tossed the remains of her coffee down the drain. "We'll do whatever we have to in order to keep going. Like you have told me before, if you do have the virus, it might be years before you really get sick. You'll find something to do."

Brent moved over and put his arm around her. "Thanks for sticking with me, Babe. I don't think I could have kept my sanity without you."

Nicole looked at him. "No matter what happens, Brent, we'll be together and be there for each other. I've never been surer of anything. I love you, and nothing will change that."

They embraced in the kitchen. Brent brushed Nicole's hair back from her face with the back of his hand and kissed her on the cheek. "I love you too, Nikki. And nothing will ever change that."

***

Brent had decided to go to the office and wait for Al's phone call there, rather than pace the floor at home. He had no patients left in the hospital, so there still were no rounds to make. He also had decided not to go to the cafeteria because he didn't want to talk to anyone on this particular morning.

One by one, Brent reviewed a stack of recent laboratory test results that had returned during the last couple of days. When the stack was gone, he turned to a pile of mail. It had already been separated into two sub-piles, one for first-class mail and the other for the rest.

While Brent read his mail, the phone rang several times. Each ring caused him to pause, hoping to hear a voice on the intercom telling him that Al Martin was on the line and wanted to speak with him. But the intercom remained silent.

A little before noon, the phone rang again. Brent's heart rate increased when he heard his phone intercom hiss as it turned on.

"Dr. Dalton," Elizabeth said. "Mrs. Dalton is on line one."

"Thanks, Elizabeth," Brent said, picking up the handpiece. "Hi, Honey. What's happening?" Although he knew why Nicole was calling, he couldn't stop himself from trying to appear casual.

"Brent, have you heard anything yet?"

"No, nothing yet. I don't know what's causing the delay. Maybe I'll walk over to the lab and check on things."

"Why don't you do that? This suspense is driving me crazy," Nicole said.

"I'll let you know as soon as I hear anything."

"Thanks, Honey. I love you."

"Love you too. Bye."

Brent went to the front desk and told Elizabeth that he would be in the hospital for a little while but had his beeper in case he was needed. A few minutes later, he walked into the laboratory and looked around for Al Martin.

He found the pathologist sitting near some microscopes inside the back office with his back toward the door. Brent walked through the door without saying anything and waited for him to turn around. Al appeared to be engrossed in a phone conversation.

"Okay, Jerry. I knew you would want to be the first to know. I'll talk with you later... 'bye." Al hung up the phone and swiveled around to face the front of the room.

"Good morning, Al," Brent said.

"Oh, Brent! You startled me." Al blushed and began to shuffle some papers on top of his desk. He looked flustered. "When did you come in?"

By Al's reaction, Brent knew that the phone conversation he had just overheard in part pertained to him.

"I just got here," Brent said. "I've been waiting to get a call from you all morning. Have the test results come back yet?"

Al hesitated a moment. "Have a seat, Brent. I was just getting ready to call you."

Brent grabbed the nearest chair, dragged it over in front of the desk and sat down.

"The report just came in," Al said, still shuffling papers.

"Well, what is it? Good God, man, spit it out! It's not indeterminate again, is it?"

"No, it's not indeterminate this time," Al said, looking down. "It's positive."

For the second time in the last twenty four hours, Brent felt a wave of intense nausea sweep over him, felt his skin crawling as though covered with worms. He had known this could happen, but somewhere in the back of his mind he had held onto the hope that he would test negative. Now, his career was over. He had just heard his death sentence. He closed his eyes and sat without responding for what seemed like an eternity then stood and looked at Al. The pathologist sat expressionless, staring at his desktop.

"Then I guess that's it. There's nothing else to do at this point, is there? Do we need to do some other confirmatory test or anything?"

"No, nothing else needs to be done now." Martin looked downward, avoiding Brent's eyes.

"Thank you, Al," Brent said in a low voice then left the office.

Brent felt strange, as though he were walking in a dream. He shook his head a time or two to remind himself that he was awake. The office seemed the logical place to go for the time being, since he knew he didn't want to talk to anyone right now.

Faceless figures mumbling incoherent words walked past him while he worked his way through the lunch crowd clogging the hospital corridors. Some of them spoke to him, but he neither heard nor saw them.

He thought about the years he had worked, the sleepless nights in residency, sometimes working until he felt like a zombie. Then followed the years of struggling to build a practice after the death of his first partner. It had all been for nothing.

Brent thought about Nicole as she had been when they first met. Sweet, unassuming, and smart. Most of all, beautiful and loving. He had thought she was the most beautiful girl he had ever seen in his entire life. He still thought so.

He walked into his office and closed the door then collapsed into his chair. He leaned forward, placing his forehead on the back of his clasped hands. He closed his eyes.

If he had been a religious man, Brent might have prayed. But he wasn't, so he didn't. Formal religion had too many rules as far as he was concerned, too many threats. Just change the name of their deities, and they were all about the same anyway. He had always felt that if he treated others with fairness and compassion, that was about all that could be expected of him. Jumping through hoops to the rhythm of some authority figure standing in a pulpit wouldn't seem to add much.

He thought about his future. He knew now he would not be able to continue practicing surgery. If Gary Morgan could join him right now, Brent might be able to salvage something from the practice he had worked so hard to build over the years. But Gary still had three months left in his last year of residency.

Money would be a problem. Nicole could continue to work, and that would help. There were some savings in his retirement fund, but the government would take most of that in taxes and penalties if he tried to use it before retirement age. And to his dismay, most of the investments he had tried outside his retirement fund had not worked out, so there wasn't much money to be obtained from that source.

The equity money in their home and in *Caribe* was the only remaining source for money that he could think of. There would only be enough for them to live on for two or three years. He would have to find something to do.

The intercom on Brent's credenza came to life behind him. "Dr. Sherman is on line one for you, Dr. Dalton."

Brent raised his head and rubbed his eyes, turned, and picked up the phone. "Dalton here," he said in a low voice.

"Brent, Jerry Sherman. I spoke with Al Martin a little while ago. He told me about your Western Blot result. I'm sorry, but you know what this means."

"Yes, Jerry, I know what it means. It means a good deal more than you'll ever know, but I know why you're calling, if that makes your job any easier."

"I just called the operating room supervisor and told her that you no longer have any surgical privileges, Brent. It was a difficult thing to do. If you don't mind my asking, what are you going to do?"

"I'm damned if I know, Jerry. If Jim Wilson will cover for me, I'll probably take a leave of absence while Nicole and I try to sort things out."

"That sounds like a good idea. Good luck, Brent. Please keep me posted on whatever happens."

"Sure, Jerry. That'll be right at the top of my list." The sarcasm in his voice was not well-hidden.

"Good-bye, Brent."

Brent hung up and prepared to leave the office. He knew Nicole waited at home for his call, but the telephone wasn't the way to tell her.

Chapter 21

Before leaving the office, Brent called Jim Wilson and asked if he would be willing to cover for an indefinite period. After hearing the developments, Jim agreed without hesitation and expressed his regrets over the way things had turned out.

When Brent buzzed the front desk to tell them he was leaving, Elizabeth answered and asked if she could speak with him for a few minutes before he left.

She entered the office with her head downcast, taking slow steps. He knew what she was going to say before she opened her mouth.

"Dr. Dalton, I know this is a bad time for you, and I'm sorry. This is difficult. I've worked for you for seven years, and I've loved it." She hesitated before continuing. "It looks like things are getting slow here at the office. You don't have a single appointment for next week, and there's no surgery scheduled. I'm a person who likes to stay busy, so I looked around some this week. I've found a position in another office, and they would like for me to start as soon as possible."

Brent wasn't surprised. He had wondered when something like this would happen. He had just three employees. Elizabeth was the office manager as well as his nurse. He also had a receptionist and an insurance clerk who worked for him. In a way, Elizabeth's leaving was a relief, since he knew he would be forced to cut back on staffing in the immediate future.

"I understand, Elizabeth. It appears things are going to get slower here, perhaps even come to a halt. I've just signed out on Dr. Wilson for an indefinite period. We won't be seeing any patients here in the office for awhile."

Brent walked over to Elizabeth and put his hands on her shoulders. "I wish you well, Liz. You'll succeed and be happy, wherever you go. You're a good person and a hard worker, and that's what counts."

Elizabeth leaned into Brent's chest and burst into tears. "Oh, Dr. Dalton, I'm so sorry that all this is taking place. You're a wonderful surgeon, and this is such a tragedy. I just don't feel like I have any choice." She sobbed and wiped her eyes with her hand as she backed away from him.

Brent reached for a box of tissues on the credenza and handed her one. "Elizabeth, things happen that we can't control. Somehow, life goes on. You did what you had to do, and I don't have any hard feelings."

"Is it all right with you then, if I start my new job on Monday?"

"Yes, that's all right with me. I'll mail your check on payday."

"Thank you, Dr. Dalton. I've learned a lot, working with you. And I hope things get better for you." She held out her hand. "Good-bye."

***

Brent left the office and drove home. Nicole met him at the garage door. Words were unnecessary.

The couple embraced in silence for a few minutes before Brent finally spoke. "This time, the test was positive. There's no doubt. I've got the virus."

Nicole didn't cry. She held him close and rocked back and forth a little, as though comforting the child they were never able to have. Finally, she stood back and looked at him.

"What are we going to do, Brent?"

He took her hand. They walked into the kitchen and sat at the table. He placed both of his hands on top of hers, and they looked at each other for several minutes before breaking the silence that hung in the room like a dense fog.

"I'm closing the office." Once the words started, they flowed like water released from a dam. "It's obvious I'm not going to be able to continue practicing surgery. Even if patients were willing to see me, which they're not, I don't have any surgical privileges. I might get them back if I took this to court, but it's not worth the fight."

"Are you going to try something else?"

"I'll have to. We don't have enough money saved to retire. To tell the truth, Nicole, I don't even want to continue practicing medicine. I just don't know of anything else I can do without going back to school." He hung his head and looked down at the floor.

"Should we stay here in Houston?"

Brent ran his fingers through his hair and thought about it for a few seconds. "No, I don't think so. It's too unpleasant here. I'd rather go somewhere else for a fresh start. I know we talked about not running away from this earlier, but there's no good reason to stay here now."

Nicole got up from her chair and began to take slow, measured steps around the kitchen. "When do you want to leave?"

"I'm not sure. I know there's a rural area out there somewhere that needs a doctor. Maybe we can be relocated by the first of July. That would give us three months to sell the house and get moved."

"Then let's get started." Nicole took the yellow page directory out of a drawer and turned to Real Estate. In less than ten minutes, she had spoken with a realtor who would come to the house the next morning and list it for sale.

"There. We've started," she said with a note of finality to her voice.

"Brent, I hope this isn't running away."

***

Mitch Jackson hadn't wasted any time after being hired by Brent the previous Tuesday. After getting Sheila's address, he had staked out her apartment and identified her from Brent's description when she arrived home that afternoon.

Following Sheila from her apartment to school and then home again began to bore the detective. The only change in her routine was related to her part-time work in the cosmetic section of a large department store. This was located in one of the malls near Pasadena, and she worked there for a few hours three days a week.

Friday night, Mitch sat outside Sheila's apartment in his eighty-three Pontiac listening to country music from somewhere in Kansas. He spotted her when she walked from her apartment to the red Mustang and stared from his cramped and slouched position, unwilling to take his eyes from her curvaceous figure.

Sheila's long, black hair hung past her shoulders, and she wore a dark skirt that had a split up the side, exposing a lot of leg. She climbed behind the steering wheel of the Mustang and backed out of the driveway.

Mitch started his car and pulled into the street a short distance behind her. He followed her out of Pasadena into downtown Houston. They drove up Main Street past the Medical Center then turned left onto Montrose Street.

Sheila pulled into a parking spot several blocks up Montrose, forcing Mitch to pull into a private parking lot which was unattended. He climbed out of his car and followed her down a side street.

Montrose Street was lit by a few overhead and club lights, but the side street was dim and forced Mitch to stay closer to the girl than he would have preferred. Sheila displayed no signs of suspicion that she was being followed.

She followed her usual routine, as Mitch would later discover. First, she stopped in a small bar for a few minutes and spoke with someone at a corner table. They exchanged something while trying to hide their transaction. Next, she went into the ladies' room for a few minutes before leaving the bar and walking a little further up the street to Attaboy's.

Mitch lit a cigarette and smoked outside for a few minutes then ground it out on the sidewalk and walked into the nightclub. Sheila sat at the bar with her back to the front door. She was seated next to two men who were on her right, and the stool on her left was unoccupied.

Not wanting to appear too conspicuous, Mitch took a seat at a table near the bar but out of Sheila's direct line of vision. "Lonestar, longneck," he told the waitress who came to his table a short time later.

Before Mitch's beer was half empty, a trim, dark haired man who appeared to be in his mid-to-late thirties walked into the bar and over to Sheila. He leaned over and kissed her on the cheek then took the seat next to her.

Sheila smiled at the man and kissed him back. They talked in low tones for a few minutes then got up and walked over to a table near the back of the room.

Mitch now found himself at a disadvantage. He wanted to be able to hear what the two talked about, but he didn't dare try to get any closer for fear of attracting the couple's attention.

Instead of moving closer, Mitch put his hand across his forehead, as if to shield his eyes from the overhead lights, and watched Sheila's lips. As a result of his hearing impairment, he had long ago learned to read lips, a valuable skill in his profession.

Sheila's friend sat with his back to Mitch, so he could read just the girl's lips. As luck would have it, she did most of the talking.

"Another longneck, Sir?" The waitress interrupted Mitch's concentration just when he was beginning to get the gist of the couple's conversation.

He looked up at the waitress and smiled. "Why not?"

Sheila had been saying something about taking a trip, and it appeared her friend planned to go with her. Mitch found it difficult to interpret every word, but he could make out enough of the conversation to follow it.

Now, they appeared to have changed the subject. "How did ... (something)... the news?" Sheila asked the man.

The man shrugged, as if to say that he didn't know.

Mitch couldn't understand what Sheila said next. Something to do with settling. He wondered if they were planning to settle somewhere they had talked about during the conversation about traveling or if she was referring to her lawsuit against Brent.

The bar grew more crowded, and Mitch had increasing difficulty interpreting the couple's conversation. People walked between them so much that Sheila was hidden from his view most of the time.

Mitch spotted a seat at the bar that would put him a little closer to the couple's table. He prepared to move, but just as he got up, Sheila and her friend also rose. The man laid a few bills on the table, and they walked toward the door.

Mitch grabbed his wallet as fast as he could and put a ten dollar bill on the table. He took the last swallow of beer from his longneck then followed the couple out onto the street. They walked back toward Montrose Street.

Mitch had no difficulty staying out of sight on the dim side street. The couple walked as though time had no meaning, pausing a few times to talk or kiss. The man placed his arm around Sheila's shoulders while they walked, and she rested her head on his shoulder. *A couple of regular lovebirds*, Mitch thought.

At Montrose, they walked south, in the direction of the two vehicles left earlier by Mitch and Sheila. When they reached her car, they continued walking another half block and stopped beside a black Lexus. The man opened the doors with a remote device then helped her into the passenger side and walked around the vehicle, climbed in, and started the engine.

This is no low quality bum she's with, Mitch thought. *Opens the doors for her and everything.*

Mitch crossed the street and jogged back to his car. He breathed a sigh of relief when he found it undisturbed where he had left it.

The black Lexus pulled into the street then stopped and turned around. Tires squealing, it sped down Montrose toward Main Street.

Mitch had no trouble following the couple. They turned right onto Main then drove just a few blocks before turning into the parking area for one of the large hotels near the Medical Center.

Leaving his vehicle parked on the street, Mitch walked into the front lobby, which was empty except for a single bellman standing next to Sheila and her friend at the registration desk. They appeared to be signing in.

Taking a seat near the elevators, Mitch picked up a discarded newspaper and hid himself behind its pages. His eyes followed the pair across the lobby to the elevators. The man carried a small bag, and they stepped into one of the elevators.

When the elevator doors closed, Mitch got up and went over to the front desk. He laid a twenty dollar bill on the counter. "Pa'don me, but I was wond'rin if you might be of some assistance," he said to the night clerk in his best southern drawl.

"That's a definite possibility," the clerk replied, eyeing the bill. "Just what kind of assistance do you need?"

Mitch glanced at the clerk's nametag. "Well, Jeff, I thought I might've recognized the couple that just checked in. I'd appreciate a look at their registration card." He winked at the clerk, who smiled back at him.

"No problem, as long as you keep it quiet... if you know what I mean."

"Shua' thang," Mitch said, sliding the bill across the counter.

The clerk glanced around the lobby, eyes darting from doorways to elevators and back again. The bellman had disappeared somewhere, and the room was deserted except for the two of them. Mitch watched him walk over to the back desk and retrieve a card.

"Make it quick," the clerk said in a voice so low it was almost unheard. "The bellman'll be back any minute." He slid the card over the counter to Mitch.

"Mista and Miz Bill Smith, from Dallis," Mitch read out loud. "I see they didn't put down theah car license numba'. Do they come heah offun, Jeff?"

"Could be," the clerk said, looking at Mitch's wallet which was still in his hand.

Mitch pulled out another ten dollars and passed it to the young man.

Jeff leaned across the counter and spoke again in a low voice. "I don't think Smith is their real name. She just calls him "Sweetie" or "Honeybun". They come here just about every weekend and usually stay two nights. Never see 'em in the daytime, though. Always out before sunup. They'll leave here around five in the morning then come back around eleven at night. Out again before daylight again tomorrow. Same thing, near every weekend."

"Much obliged, Jeff." Mitch put his wallet back in his pocket and left the hotel. What he wanted now was the license plate number from the Lexus, but it had been parked by a valet and was out of sight. With the plate number, he could get the identity of Sheila's friend. He looked around for the valet, but no one was in sight. The front of the hotel was deserted.

Mitch considered staying awake in his car until the couple left. However, since he knew about what time they would be leaving, he decided instead to get a few hours of sleep and set the alarm on his wristwatch for four o'clock. Having made that decision, he walked to his car and got in.

Chapter 22

Sheila reclined on the bed in the hotel room, watching television. She sat upright, propped by two pillows against the head of the bed. The top sheet covered her up to the waist. Long, black hair flowed down over both shoulders and onto her bare breasts. There were no tan lines to mar the smooth, light brown skin. She nibbled at a chocolate bar and sipped white wine, both from the rather elaborate minibar in the room. An old movie played on television, but the volume was turned so low the voices were almost inaudible.

The man walked out of the bathroom, naked except for a bath towel around his waist. He dried himself with another towel. He paused, smiling, in front of Sheila, rubbing his chest with the thick cloth.

Sheila looked up at him and moistened her lips with the tip of her tongue. "What's on your mind, Lover?" She slid down in the bed a bit and held out the chocolate bar toward him. "Does Sweetie Pie want some of my candy?"

He walked to the side of the bed and looked down at her. "I sure do." He sat on the edge of the bed. "But I don't care for any of your chocolate bar." He slid into bed beside her, leaving the towels on the floor.

A short time later, they lay back on doubled pillows, sipping wine, watching Jay Leno interview a celebrity neither of them had heard of.

"I'll be glad when all this other business is behind us," Sheila's friend said. "We can come out of hiding and leave this stinking city." He stared at the ceiling. "We can go to Spain, and maybe Italy and Greece. See the world and live like royalty." He turned and winked at her. "Make love ten times a day, if we want to."

Sheila sighed. He annoyed her when he talked like this. "Why don't we do all that right now?" she asked. "Just leave this goddamn place. I'm tired of sneaking around all the time, Sweetie. We could move somewhere else and live like any other normal couple."

"Sheila, we've been through that a dozen times. We're not a 'normal couple'."

He got up and started pacing. "We only have a few good years to be together. I want those years to be special." He stopped pacing and sat on the edge of the bed. "For that, we'll need money -- more money than I've got."

Still annoyed, Sheila slid out of bed and slipped into a short terrycloth robe with the hotel logo on front. "But this fucking lawsuit could take a long time, and we're not even sure we'll win." She began pacing, now that her lover sat on the bed.

"Trust me, we'll win. And it may not take much time either. All we have to do is get them to settle out of court."

The man got up again and walked over to the mini-bar. He opened the door and reached for a bottle of scotch. "Something else to drink?"

"No, I still have some wine." Sheila stopped pacing near a large glass sliding door. She drew back the curtains with one arm and looked out at the night. The city extended as far as she could see, thousands of tiny lights twinkling like Christmas trees. "I like the city," she whispered.

She sipped the wine and looked down at the miniature cars in the street far below. Something in the back of her mind had been bothering her, and now she realized what it was.

"Sweetie, did you notice the man who was sitting in the hotel lobby when we were waiting for an elevator?" she asked.

Her companion busied himself with his scotch, sipping it like a fine wine. "The guy who was reading a newspaper? Yeah, I saw him. Why?"

"He was in Attaboy's too. I noticed him staring at me several times. And he was by himself." She turned her back to the glass door. "Do you think he could be following us?"

He turned to face her, appearing alarmed at this suggestion. "Holy shit! I hope not!" He took a large swallow of his drink and added the rest of the scotch from the small bottle.

Sheila closed the curtains and resumed pacing. "What should we do?"

The man ran his fingers through his hair and sat again on the edge of the bed. "If we're being followed then maybe we'd better not be so predictable. Maybe we shouldn't even see each other for a couple of weeks." He jumped up and reached for his pants. "We'll assume the worst. They may even have your phone tapped, so I won't call you at home either. There's too much at stake."

Sheila stopped pacing and crossed her arms on her ample chest. "You won't even be able to call?" She frowned. "But how'll we talk?"

"You'll come to Attaboy's on weekends. When the coast looks clear, I'll contact you."

Sheila was quiet for a minute before she moved closer to him. She let her robe fall to the floor. "If we're not going to be seeing each other for that long then let's not waste tonight."

Her lover grinned and put his arms around her narrow waist. "You've got that right," he said, tossing his pants back to a chair.

***

At six o'clock, Mitch looked at his watch for the hundredth time. He had parked on the street where he could see the couple when they picked up the Lexus in front of the hotel. He had been back on stake-out since his watch alarm went off at four. Not a single person had left the hotel since he had returned.

Mitch climbed out of the ancient Pontiac and went into the lobby. A few people were stirring, and the same clerk was at the front desk, reading a newspaper.

Mitch slid a five dollar bill onto the newspaper, which lay on the countertop. "Have you seen my friends since I left last night?"

The clerk looked at him with an amused expression, causing Mitch to realize he had forgotten to use his southern drawl when he spoke. The young man quickly covered the bill with his hand and palmed it. "Yeah. They came down around two-thirty, checked out and left."

"At two-thirty? I thought you said they us'lly left a lot lata' than that!" He remembered to use the accent this time.

"Yeah, they do. Mr. Smith said something about having to hit the road early today."

"Did he happen 'ta say if they'd be back t'night?"

"Said they had to change their plans. Won't be back tonight."

Mitch put another five on the countertop. "Much obliged."

Cursing himself for not staying awake all night, Mitch drove back to Sheila's apartment and parked on the street. There were no lights on that he could see, but it was well past sunrise by this time.

Slumping behind the steering wheel, Mitch pondered the situation. Why had the couple left so early? Had they seen him watching? Was Sheila in bed at home? Had they left town together?

Realizing there wasn't much else he could do at the time, he started the engine and pulled into the street. He decided he would have to try picking up the trail again tonight -- and hope they hadn't left town

***

Saturday dawned bright and clear, another beautiful spring day. Brent had been up since well before daylight, however, since he had been unable to get to sleep again after waking around three.

He awoke thinking of all the things he needed to do that day. Over coffee at the kitchen table, he made a list. First, he wanted to let Gary Morgan know what had happened. It looked like there wouldn't be any practice for the young surgeon either to join or take over, in light of the past week's events. Next, he needed to meet with Todd Ward. It wasn't enough that he had to deal with being infected with HIV and all that had happened as a result, but he also had a lawsuit to contend with.

Last, he would make an appointment with someone in the Family Medicine Department at the University of Texas to discuss areas in need of primary care physicians. He might even need to do a short fellowship in primary care somewhere. The reality of having to open another office was depressing, since he couldn't practice surgery, but he didn't know of anything else to do given the current situation. And he knew that small towns in search of doctors commonly made contact with residency training programs.

The Galveston area or the Texas coast south of there should be a good general area for relocation. He and Nichole might even be able to keep *Caribe* if they lived near the Gulf and he was able to find a place to start working in the next few weeks.

Nicole came downstairs just as daylight was breaking. She also had not slept well and had a list of her own to tackle. "After we've taken care of the things we each have to do," she suggested, "why don't we drive down to Kemah and spend the rest of the weekend on the sailboat?"

Brent agreed. Time spent on the boat was revitalizing, and he wanted as much of it as he could get.

***

Gary Morgan answered the phone on the third ring. "Good morning, Gary Morgan here!" Brent reflected for an instant on what it would be like to have an outlook on life like Gary had.

He tried to sound cheerful. "Morning, Gary. This is Brent. Do you have a little free time this morning?

"Hey, for you? Anytime! Besides, it's Saturday, and I'm not on call. What'd you have in mind?"

"I'd like to talk with you for a few minutes. Could you meet me in my office in about an hour?"

"Sure. It'll take me a few minutes to get there. About eight o'clock?"

"That'll be just fine. I'll leave the side door unlocked. Just let yourself in."

"I'll be there."

"Thanks, Gary... 'bye."

Brent replaced the phone on the receiver and turned to Nicole. "That takes care of the first item on my list."

Next, he called Todd Ward, who answered the phone in the middle of a yawn. "Good grief, man, it's still the middle of the night!" he said after Brent told him what he wanted. He agreed, however, to meet Brent at about ten o'clock.

***

The office was as silent as a tomb when Brent unlocked the side door and went inside. He left the door unlocked so Gary could get in when he arrived.

For the first time in years, Brent lingered and looked around at his office. By most standards, it wasn't very large, occupying about twelve hundred square feet in all. Nicole had selected all the pictures on the walls with a loving touch. Lining the hallway between the four exam rooms were several watercolors of sailboats.

The waiting area up front had also been decorated and furnished by Nicole. The chairs were large and comfortable and had been arranged so that patients wouldn't have to sit facing each other while waiting to be seen. Live plants were placed so they would not get in the way of people going in and out of the room.

Still engrossed in the office setting, Brent inventoried all the machines and equipment in the business office. Three rows of large filing cabinets stood behind the receptionist's glassed-in area. Behind the cabinets were a large copier and central computer terminal with a printer. Two desks stood off to one side of the room. Each had its own computer terminal with monitor and keyboard. A fax machine rested on a separate countertop near a wall. He decided he could use most of the equipment in his new office, assuming he found a place to practice.

He moved down the hall toward the examination rooms. Each of the four rooms was almost identical, with an examination table, two chairs, and a small cabinet for dressings and other supplies. Certificates documenting his training and areas of expertise hung on the walls of each room.

Brent went into his private office and sat at his desk. He was wondering just what he should say to Gary when a loud snap interrupted his thoughts and the side door to the office opened.

Chapter 23

"Hello, anybody here?" a cheerful voice called out.

Brent recognized the voice. "I'm in my office, Gary!" He rose and walked toward the door. Gary Morgan came down the back corridor toward him. They met midway down the hall. Gary wore a pair of old jeans and a knit shirt. A pair of leather moccasins covered his sockless feet.

"I'm glad you're not on call this weekend. And dressed for the occasion too!" Brent said with a grin, gesturing with his arm toward the office. "Come on in."

They went into the office, and Brent sat behind his desk after pointing out a chair to the young, blond man who looked like he was just old enough to be out of high school, let alone practicing surgery.

"Thanks. You're right, I'm off until Monday. Dr. Brown, our Surgery Department chairman, wants to meet with me then. I'm pretty sure he's going to reassign me to work with someone else for the rest of the year."

"Yes, I guess that's inevitable." Brent shifted in his chair and twiddled his thumbs on the desktop. "Gary, have you heard any rumors about me in the surgery lounge?"

Gary looked embarrassed for a couple of beats but recovered with a somber gaze at his former mentor.

"Yes, there was some talk yesterday afternoon." He cleared his throat and leaned back. "They said you had lost your surgery privileges."

Brent concentrated on his hands, thumbs still twiddling. "Is that all they said? They didn't mention why I lost them?"

Gary shifted his weight in the chair and cleared his throat again. "Well, -- I'm not sure, but – "

"I'm sorry, Gary," Brent interrupted. "I didn't ask you here to put you on the spot. It's true. My operating privileges have been withdrawn. I could fight it and might get them back, but the publicity generated would destroy what little is left of my reputation."

Gary looked up. "Is what they said about the Western Blot result true too?"

"If they said the result was positive then it's true. I found out yesterday."

"God, that's terrible." Gary got up from his chair and walked over to a window. "What are you going to do?"

Brent got up and stood beside his young friend. "I wish I knew, Gary. Honest to God, I wish I knew." They gazed at the traffic below, neither of them speaking for several minutes.

At last, Brent broke the silence. "I'm going to close my office on Monday. That's for starters. We've listed our house with a realtor already."

"What about your patients? Has someone agreed to take over for you?"

"Yes, Jim Wilson has agreed to do that. He's pretty busy already, so it was very gracious of him."

Gary walked across the room and appeared to be studying one of the certificates hanging on the wall. "I guess that wipes out our plans to work together, doesn't it?"

"I'm afraid so. There's just no alternative, Gary. I haven't seen a new patient since that story came out in the paper last week. Most of my old patients canceled their office appointments, and Elizabeth resigned yesterday. The other girls are looking for new jobs too, I'm sure."

"But what are you going to do?" You can't just sail off into the sunset and disappear!"

Brent cleared his throat. "I'm considering opening an office for general practice in a rural area. But I'd rather sail off into the sunset and disappear, if I could." He turned back to his chair and took a seat.

"General practice! Brent, you'll never be satisfied doing anything but surgery!" Gary shook his head in disbelief and went back to the window. "I'm hear to tell ya' I think you're making a big mistake."

Brent thought for a minute or two. Earlier, he hadn't appreciated the young man's maturity and insight. Gary's casual outward appearance betrayed his wisdom and genuine concern.

"You're right, of course. There just don't appear to be many choices. Any suggestions?"

"You're a great teacher. Have you considered joining the faculty at one of the medical schools?"

"The thought occurred to me, but that would require me to participate in open procedures. I'd be right back to square one."

"But from what you've told me before, there's no law against practicing medicine or surgery just because you're infected with HIV. Unless there's another bigot like Rudman on the staff wherever you go then there shouldn't be any problem." Gary began to pace the floor.

Brent's eyes lit up as he considered Gary's suggestion. "Of course, I'd love to find a way to continue in surgery. A teaching position might be the way to do it." Relaxing a little, he leaned back in his chair and sighed. "For heaven's sake, Gary, stop pacing and sit down! You're driving me crazy!"

Gary laughed and sat down. "So what are your plans for the rest of the weekend?"

"Nicole and I thought we'd spend some time on *Caribe*. But first, I need to run by my attorney's office and review some things with him." He considered inviting Gary to join them sailing but decided he and Nicole needed the time alone.

Gary got up and stretched. "I need to get moving, myself. The morning's half gone, and I have several things to do. I want you to know how much I appreciate you meeting with me to let me know what's happened."

Brent smiled. "I felt like I owed you that much, to say the least. What are you thinking you'll do when you finish your residency?"

Gary scratched his head and looked at the ceiling. "There's still the surgeon in Austin.... I don't think he's found anybody yet. I'd rather stay in Houston though."

Brent stood and walked around the desk to face his friend. "You won't have any trouble finding a good opportunity. You're a very talented young surgeon."

"Thanks, Brent. Please let me know if I can be of any help to you, whatever you decide to do." The two men shook hands then Gary left Brent alone in the office once more.

Resuming his place by the window, Brent pondered Gary's advice. A position on the teaching staff at one of the University Hospitals sounded attractive. He was well-trained and had stayed current with new developments over the years. He also had given lectures and published several papers. So teaching was a possibility, at least.

Leaving the office, Brent locked the door behind him and took the stair steps two at a time on his way out. A few minutes later, he pulled out of the clinic parking lot and pointed his Suburban toward downtown Houston and Todd Ward's office.

***

Saturday morning traffic was light, and Brent had no difficulty finding a parking place on the street near Todd's office. He locked his car doors and walked the last few feet to the office entrance.

Todd sat at his desk, dwarfed by stacks of legal books and papers. His gray hair appeared disheveled, and he looked up at Brent through his wire-rimmed glasses with bloodshot eyes.

"Brent! Now that I'm out of bed, I'm glad you called this morning," the lanky attorney chuckled. "I have plenty of work to do, so have a seat." He stood and gestured toward a plush, leather chair that was centered in front of his desk. "How have you been doing?"

"Oh, I can't complain, I guess. Truth is, I feel fine." Brent took a seat.

The attorney sat down again. "Weren't you supposed to have the results of your Western Blot back by now?"

"That's why I'm here, Todd. Bad news, I'm afraid." Brent hesitated then lowered his voice a little. "It looks like I do have the virus."

Todd leaned back. "I'm sorry, Brent. That's terrible news of course. When did you find out?"

"Late yesterday. My mind has been in a state of turmoil ever since, even though I thought I was prepared for this turn of events."

"I think I understand. Will you continue to practice?"

"No, I don't think that will be possible."

"For the reasons we discussed earlier?"

"Within minutes of getting the result of the test, I was notified that my surgical privileges had been withdrawn. I can't operate."

Todd scratched a place behind his ear and was silent for a few beats. "Do you want to fight that decision? Legal odds are in your favor, you know."

Brent looked at the ceiling and sighed. "Getting my privileges back wouldn't equate with winning, I'm afraid."

"Because of the things we talked about last time?"

Brent sighed, weary of having to explain what seemed obvious to him. "Come on, Todd! It would be a moot point to get my surgical privileges back in court. With all the publicity, I wouldn't be able to attract any patients. And my office staff is leaving me too."

Todd resumed scratching behind his ear. "That's your decision to make, of course. And you're probably right, all things considered."

"So, that's settled. What are we going to do about the Walters' suit?"

"During the last week, I've spent quite a bit of time researching this case. There's not another one quite like it, which means we're breaking new ground."

"What does that mean to me?"

"It means that going to court to try to fight this suit would be a roll of the dice. The decision could go either way. The jury won't be made up of doctors and scientists. They'll be people off the street. If they decide in favor of the Walters girl, and they well might do that, I'd guess the award would be in the millions of dollars."

"Couldn't we appeal?"

"Sure we could. We could drag this out for years, if you want to do that. How much of the rest of your life do you want to spend trying to fight this?"

"Are you suggesting we settle?"

"You have excellent coverage. Your twenty million dollar umbrella makes a very attractive target to a plaintiff attorney, so I doubt they'll take a small settlement."

"Do they know how much coverage I have?"

"Don't be naive, Brent. Of course they know. These guys are professionals."

"What will my insurer say about settling?"

"As a matter of fact, I had a discussion with the risk management department at Texas Mutual a couple of days ago. They're pretty worried. They want us to make an offer to see if we can settle this case."

"Why do they feel that there's such a great chance of losing? I know I didn't infect that girl!" He felt agitated with the turn of events.

"Knowing something in your own mind and being able to prove it in a court of law are two different things, Brent. The fact that you knew about your positive HIV screening test before you operated on the girl the second time could be difficult to defend. Considering your circumstances, settling now might be the wisest thing for us to do."

"Will the choice be mine?"

Todd removed his glasses and rubbed his eyes for a minute. "According to the terms of your policy, the insurer has final say-so on the decision. They would like for you to be in agreement, if possible."

"Does that mean they have made up their minds?"

"I'm afraid so. They have authorized me to make an initial offer of five hundred thousand."

"And what if they won't accept?"

"I can go up to two million, if necessary."

Brent looked toward the window and took a deep breath. "They're that afraid to go to court?"

"Historically, in liability cases such as this one, jury awards tend to be astronomical if the decision is in favor of the plaintiff. If that young girl gets on the stand and pulls on some heartstrings, things could get pretty bad."

Brent stood up and took a couple of steps toward the door then turned back to face the attorney. "If the decision has been made then I guess that's about all we have to talk about, Todd."

"I'm sorry you don't agree, Brent. Think about it some more, and I'm sure you'll see things our way."

Chapter 24

Nicole cleared the galley after a light breakfast of toast, jelly, and coffee, and Brent motored out of the marina. The sun appeared as a bright red disc behind a long, low bank of orange-red clouds on the eastern horizon. A brisk, southwesterly breeze promised good wind.

Following the disappointing news from Todd Ward regarding the intention of the insurance company to settle the lawsuit, Brent had gone straight home and told Nicole. After talking, they decided to spend several days on *Caribe* rather than just staying the weekend.

Before leaving home, Brent had called one of the two employees who still worked for him and told her that he would be closing the office. Records and continuing care for his patients would be turned over to Dr. Wilson. He told her he would mail the final paychecks plus two weeks severance pay on the next payday. She wished him good luck and agreed to call the newspaper on Monday morning and have an announcement run. He sensed that she had been secretly relieved to learn of the closing.

Nicole had already given a house key to the realtor, and he had permission to show the house in their absence. All they had had to do then was pack a few clothes and pick up some groceries and ice on their way to the marina.

They arrived just after sunset but stayed up late Saturday night, sitting in the cockpit and talking late into the evening. Brent always felt he could get things into a better perspective while on the boat like this, smelling the salty air and feeling the cool, night breeze in his face.

To their disappointment, no new solutions presented themselves that evening, and they went to bed still unsure of the course they would follow.

***

Leaving Clear Lake and Kemah Sunday morning, Brent gave the helm to Nicole when *Caribe* cleared the number three channel marker. They tacked to the southeast, and Brent trimmed the sails as they headed down into Galveston Bay.

In short order, sail covers were stowed below and both mainsail and genoa pulled them along at a steady seven knots on a starboard tack. Brent busied himself coiling halyards and other lines. Finding himself in a lighter mood, he reflected on what it would be like to be able to spend months or even years on a sailboat, cruising from port to port and moving when the mood struck. Perhaps to see the Caribbean and then move over to the South Pacific via the Panama Canal. He had always wanted to see Tahiti and the Fiji Islands, maybe spend a few months at each place.

Stepping around a deck winch and ducking under the Bimini, he climbed down into the cockpit. "How's she handling, Nikki?"

"Like a dream! Just like always!" Nicole glowed in the early morning sunlight. Her long, brown hair blew back over her left shoulder, and she gazed straight ahead while holding *Caribe* on course. She wore a light blue windbreaker over a white cotton shirt and shorts, and Brent realized, when he looked at her, that he had made a big mistake by not spending more time like this before all his trouble started.

"How far do you want to go today?" Nicole asked, interrupting his thoughts. She spoke in soft tones, since it was possible to converse in a normal voice in the absence of competition from engine noise. They could hear the lapping of waves against the hull and an occasional flap of a sail. The breeze in their faces and motion of the boat as it loped across the seas delighted them. Gulls circled and called in the distance, searching Bay waters for bait fish.

174

"If the weather forecast is right, the wind should stay at about fifteen knots out of the southwest today then shift to the southeast tomorrow. And there's just a slight chance of thundershowers. We should be able to get into open water outside Galveston Island and sail down the coast another twenty or thirty miles before dark."

"Will we be able to find a sheltered place to anchor for the night? You know I don't enjoy night sailing all that much. We'd have to take turns napping."

"The chart shows some sheltered water just below the tip of Galveston Island. We can spend the night there."

The steady breeze promised good sailing.

***

Back in Houston, Mitchell Jackson puzzled over his next move. After catching a few hours of sleep during the day Saturday, he had staked out Sheila's apartment all night. A dim light shown through a front window, but no one had entered or left.

He looked at his watch. It was one o'clock in the afternoon, and he doubted that Sheila would be going anywhere soon, provided that she was even at home. And he was getting hungry. He considered calling her on the phone but knew that an unrecognized male voice would confirm her suspicion that she was being watched -- if she had, as he suspected, figured that out.

Then he remembered Molly, a pert little gray-haired lady who did some occasional typing for him. She had volunteered on more than one occasion to help out if ever the need arose. His stomach growled as he started the engine and pulled into the street.

Cellular phones were a godsend, but they lacked the security Mitch needed. He drove to the nearest service station and used a public phone there.

"Hi, Mitch!" Molly answered in her usual cheerful manner. "What a pleasant surprise to hear from you. Do you have some more typing?"

"Not today, Molly, but I do need a little favor. Could you make a phone call for me?"

"Well sure! But why do you want me to call? Break your finger or something?" She laughed.

Using as few words as possible, Mitch explained the situation. Molly giggled even more at the prospect of doing something of a clandestine nature to assist with a case. She agreed to call him back on the pay phone just as soon as she had made the call to Sheila's apartment.

Mitch walked into the service station, which also doubled as a deli of sorts. He looked through the selection of cellophane-wrapped sandwiches on display. Selecting a ham and cheese on rye and a tuna salad on white bread, he grabbed a bag of chips and a Coke, paid for his lunch, and went back outside to wait for Molly's return call.

After resting the drink on top of the telephone cover, Mitch almost dropped his sandwich when the phone rang. He hadn't expected it to be so loud. He answered before it could ring again.

"Hello, Mitch?"

"Yeah, it's me. What'd you find out?"

"Oh, this is so exciting! I'm just thrilled you decided to let me help on a case, Mitch. Now, maybe you will let me help more often."

"Sure, Molly, sure. What did you find out?" he asked while fumbling with the cellophane wrapper on the sandwich.

"Well, I called the number you gave me, and a woman answered. I just tried to sound real casual-like. I said, 'Is Sheila there?', and the woman said, 'Speaking.' Then, I said, 'Oh, someone's at the door. I'll call back later.' Then I just hung up. How's that for being cool? Pretty good, huh?"

Mitch rolled his eyes skyward. "That's great, Molly. You're a natural born detective if I ever met one. Thanks a million." He took a large bite of the sandwich and started to hang up the phone.

"Don't forget to call if I can do anything else now, Mitch."

"I won't," he mumbled through the sandwich. "Thanks again, Molly. Bye now." This time, he put the phone back on the receiver before she could say anything else.

Mitch grabbed the drink and chips and tucked the remainder of the sandwiches under his elbow while he opened the car door. Tossing the food onto the seat beside him, he dropped the drink into a holder on the center console and cranked the engine. A few minutes later, he was back on stakeout down the street a little way from Sheila's apartment. Now, at least, he knew she was home. He just hoped that Molly's little phone trick hadn't tipped her off.

***

Brent and Nicole spent a comfortable Sunday night at anchor in quiet water on the northeast end of Follet's Island, a few miles south of Galveston. Monday was a repeat of the beautiful day before, in spite of scattered thunderstorms nearby. Marinas were scattered along the coast, and they found sheltered water south of the Brazos River on Monday night. They experienced rare, short thundershowers at night, and the days were beautiful in spite of the ominous red skies each morning.

Early Tuesday morning, Brent finished putting the anchor in its chocks and stuffed rope down into the anchor compartment at the bow. He inhaled the fresh, salt air deep into his lungs and savored the smell, even though it was somewhat reminiscent of rotten eggs as a result of marsh gas. He looked up into the clear sky and tried to gain a better perspective on his situation.

Two full days on open water had given Brent time to think about plans for the future. The cold fact that loomed largest in his mind was that, at the present time, infection with HIV was tantamount to a death sentence. He recognized and acknowledged that he had no real desire to open another office in a small town somewhere and go into general practice. In addition, he had thought about Gary Morgan's advice and came to the realization also that he didn't want to join the teaching staff at the University and spend his final years that way either. He just wanted to be left alone with Nicole on their boat. That was what it all boiled down to -- he just wanted to be left alone to enjoy the life he had remaining.

They owned the boat and had enough money saved, along with the equity in the house, to continue in this lifestyle for several years. He thought again about the fact that he might have just a few years to live. Some of those years might not be of very good quality. He wanted to live life to the fullest while he could. Up to this point, he had devoted himself to his work, taking little time off for himself or Nicole. But now it could be different. He also had a decent amount of life insurance, so Nicole would be in pretty good financial condition after he was gone, if they could afford to keep the premiums paid.

A fresh breeze stirred and the pungent smell of swamp gas, mixed with the familiar odor of decaying marsh grass, drifted across them while Nicole steered *Caribe* out of the anchorage and into open water. Brent raised the sails, and Nicole stretched while yawning behind the helm as *Caribe* pushed at a steady pace through the choppy seas on a southwesterly heading.

"I could learn to like this kind of living," she laughed. Brent knew she had always loved sailing. He wondered what she might think about a much longer trip in the immediate future.

After a few minutes of idle chores, Brent sat down and leaned back against the cockpit cushions. He sighed. "I guess if the insurance company insists on a quick settlement of the lawsuit, we could find ourselves without any strong commitments for our time. What would you think about spending a few months sailing in the Caribbean?"

Nicole showed little reaction, which disappointed him. "Wouldn't that be the same as running away?"

Brent shifted his weight on the cushioned seat. "I don't think so, but what difference does it make? Is there some kind of penalty for doing what you really want to in life? Whose standards are we trying to live up to -- our own, or somebody else's?"

"Do you think we can afford to break away just like that?"

Brent reflected for a minute. "You mean, do we have the money?"

"That, and the mental part of it. It'd be a big change."

Brent closed his eyes, searching for an answer. "Who knows what we really need?" We could do it." He recognized the tension in his own voice.

Nicole remained silent for a minute. "I don't think it would work, Brent. That would be running away, and it's not like you to do that. You need to continue practicing medicine, one way or the other."

At that moment, a fresh breeze breathed new life into the sails, and *Caribe* surged forward as though released from bondage. Brent looked up into the cloudless, morning sky and sighed again. "I don't care if it's running away or not, it's something I've decided to do. I'm sick of practicing medicine."

Nicole didn't answer right away. The warm breeze blew her hair back off her shoulders, and she stared straight ahead, gripping the wheel with both hands.

"So, what do you think?" he asked after a few minutes.

"I've told you what I think, Brent." Her mouth had a determined set, and she didn't smile as she spoke. "If you do any extended cruising, it won't be with me. I won't help you run away from your life."

Chapter 25

Mitch poured himself another cup of coffee from the pot in the corner of Todd Ward's office and stirred in a spoonful of sugar. "I usually drink this stuff straight and black, but I need energy. Been camped out on that damn girl's front doorstep twenty four seven all week." He stretched and rubbed the back of his neck then glanced over at Todd to see how he was receiving this bit of information.

Todd leaned back in his chair. "It's a good thing you found her again after losing the trail over the weekend. Where is she now?"

"In class. She's been as predictable as clockwork. Leaves the house at seven-thirty every morning and drives to school. Stays in class or at the library 'til two in the afternoon. Never eats lunch. She works at a department store from three to seven on Monday, Tuesday, and Thursday. Gets home around eight and stays in her apartment all night. Pretty dull, except for the weekends."

"Have you bugged her place?"

"Yeah, and tapped her phone too. The only person she's talked to is her mom -- calls her at night when she gets in from work."

"Why do you think she has to sneak around to see this guy she was with last weekend? If she lives alone, why don't they just go to her place?"

"I haven't figured that out yet. He's quite a bit older than she is. Probably married. I don't know what's going on between them at this point, but the hotel clerk told me they show up there most weekends."

"What about drugs?"

Mitch walked over to one of the large, leather chairs and stretched out on it. "Yeah, she's into that too. I watched her buy a stash of something before she met her boyfriend last Friday. Took a hit in the bathroom right away."

"Is she mainlining it?"

"Don't know. I doubt it though, since the Doc didn't see any tracks on her arms when he did her surgery. I haven't been close enough to her to see for myself."

"That doesn't mean she's not mainlining. Some of them are good at hiding it."

"She was in the bathroom just a couple of minutes. Maybe she took a snort."

"Sounds like it. Anyway, I'm not sure this is getting us anywhere. The insurance company is pushing me to settle on this case. It's going to be almost impossible to prove how the girl caught the virus, and her only known contact with an infected person has been her surgeon." Todd scratched his head and looked at the ceiling. "If you could get a picture of her shooting up, that would be a different story. Short of that, I'm afraid we're in a pretty bad spot."

Mitch sipped his coffee. "What do you think about the boyfriend? Are we barking up the wrong tree, or can he be a major player in all this?"

"I can't imagine how he can be of any real importance in the defense of the doctor. Can you?"

"Not unless she caught the virus from him."

Todd frowned. "That's an interesting proposition. Think you can figure out a way to find that out? You can't just walk up to the guy and ask him for a blood sample, you know."

Mitch chuckled. "Hell, I can't just walk up to the guy and ask him anything! I don't even know who the bastard is!"

"Maybe you should stay on the case through the weekend, at least. There's a chance you might stumble onto something. There appear to be two possibilities that could be of real value to us."

"Right. She could be mainlining drugs, for one."

"or she could be sleeping with a guy who has HIV, for the other – or hooking."

"That's three."

"Whatever. So I'll stay on it. I'm getting real fond of cat-napping behind the wheel of that old car."

"The weekend is coming up again, so maybe you'll get lucky."

***

Friday night typically was the high point of Sheila's week. She endured the remainder of the days just so she could get to the weekend and meet her lover for a few hours in paradise.

They had met in Attaboy's two summers ago. Sheila was a sophomore in college and worked part-time in the cosmetics section of a department store. Evenings, she frequented various nightclubs but had settled on Attaboy's as the best place to meet older men, which she preferred over the immature children with whom she attended class every day.

Her "friend" showed up in Attaboy's quite a bit back then. It hadn't taken them long to become acquainted and discover that they were fantastic together in bed. He knew how to do things for her that she had never even dreamed of, and Sheila learned that she could be pretty imaginative herself.

That first summer passed, and Sheila found herself back in class during the week. In spite of their close liaison, she knew very little about Mr. Bill Smith, or "Sweetie" as he preferred to be called. Because of his secretiveness, she suspected that he was married. He denied this for awhile but finally admitted that she was right.

He had avoided going anyplace very public with her from the beginning. He had told her that he worked for a pharmaceutical company calling on doctors to promote new drugs. This was the reason he gave for having to be careful about being seen in nightclubs. He gave her the money she needed to move into her own apartment, and they had been able to meet there until the business with the lawsuit came up.

As time passed, Sheila grew even fonder of her boyfriend, but she was unsure if he felt anything special for her -- even though he said he did. She felt that she was in love and wanted more from their strange relationship. When they met on weekends and got high on cocaine and wine, she had begun to fantasize about traveling to exotic places. Her lover went along with the fantasies and even made up a few of his own. Sometimes, she pretended they were making love in Buckingham Palace, in Scarlet O'Hara's bed, or in a back room of the Louve, surrounded by centuries-old paintings worth millions of dollars. Sometimes, they would pretend to be on a moonlit, tropical beach somewhere in the South Pacific with palm trees swaying overhead in the gentle night breeze.

Sheila had begun to push him a little. All she wanted was to be picked up at home when they went out and to go places other than the same nightclub and hotel weekend after weekend. He had balked, admitting to her that he was married and had children. He intended to get a divorce though, when the time was right. Then he and Sheila would get married and live out their fantasies.

Weeks and months went by, and her lover lost some weight. Sheila noticed that he didn't have as much stamina as he had when they first met, and he sometimes didn't show up at all for their weekend rendezvous.

Then, one beautiful weekend in early October after spending a wonderful night together, he confessed he had a serious health problem. It was something that she needed to know about and be tested for herself, since they had never practiced safe sex.

Sheila had suspected that he was telling her he had HIV, even before he spoke the words. Somehow, the news had not devastated her. It seemed to bind them closer, and all she wanted at this point was to spend more time with him, at any price.

He had told her that he had a little money, but not enough for the things they wanted to do. He had promised he would find a way to get a lot of money, somehow, and they would be able to run away together and do anything they wanted for the rest of their lives. It had all seemed so romantic, almost like Romeo and Juliet. But he continued to insist they meet secretly.

They discussed getting another apartment, a place where they could rendezvous but not live, so they could meet more often. Money was the problem. He didn't have unlimited funds. She had even offered to drop out of school and get a full-time job, but he had refused to consider this, saying she wouldn't be able to make enough money to make a difference, and he would work something out soon. Then, they could be together all they wanted.

Sheila had gotten careless at one point and neglected to take her birth control pills. He arranged for her to have an abortion and paid all the bills. She had missed just one day of classes, and her parents never suspected a thing. A few weeks after the abortion, she had required an appendectomy. Again, he offered her money for the bills, but her parents had insurance which covered her.

A few weeks after the appendectomy, he told her one night that he had figured out how they were going to get the money they needed. He was excited. He told her that the surgeon who had removed her appendix, Dr. Dalton, had been found to be infected with HIV. Since no one knew yet of Sheila's infection, she could claim to have caught the virus from him.

Dalton would be even more vulnerable because Sheila had developed an infection in her incision following surgery. The infection could be cited as evidence for a lapse in sterile technique during the case. Because they had been so secretive in their love affair, it would be almost impossible for the doctor to prove that she did not acquire the infection as a result of the surgery.

It had all sounded so easy, but now that they were being watched, things were getting scary. He had warned Sheila that the whole thing could fall through, and he would not be able to see her again if they were seen together by the wrong people. She had asked why that was so, but he just said it would happen because the doctor knew him and would be able to figure out that he was the one who had given her the infection. That sounded reasonable, and she believed him.

But now it was Friday night, and Sheila felt lonesome. Her lover usually called her every couple of days, but she hadn't spoken with him now in a week. She needed to talk to him, but he had refused to tell her how to contact him. She remembered that he had told her to go to Attaboy's on weekends. She would go there. Maybe he would show up.

Chapter 26

The week had been a long one for Mitch. With few exceptions, he had not left Sheila's trail for more than a few minutes at a time, even when she was home at night. He ate in his car and slept there too, fearful of missing her again if she did something unpredictable.

Friday night about nine thirty, Sheila emerged from the front door of her apartment building, looked briefly in his direction then climbed into her red Mustang and drove away.

Mitch followed her without headlights for a short distance, since he suspected that she knew he was behind her. She went straight to Montrose Street and parked in almost the same place she had used the previous weekend.

Sheila stopped by the same seedy little bar before going on to Attaboy's, and Mitch noticed that she rubbed her nose a few times after coming out of the restroom. *Looks like she's snortin', not poppin'*, he thought to himself. *That makes it more likely that she caught her infection from her boyfriend -- or from some other boyfriend before him.*

Mitch made a special effort to blend well into the background so as not to be seen. He didn't even go into the nightclub for almost half an hour, and then he made sure he stayed behind groups of people and kept his cap pulled down low over his eyes.

Sheila sat at the bar, sipping a tall, pink drink and talking to a chubby, balding, fiftiesh-appearing man who appeared to find her quite attractive. Mitch made a mental note to be careful whom he talked to the next time he went nightclubbing. To look at Sheila, no one would suspect her of having HIV. She could be a beauty queen or a model.

A trio of band members played country music, and Sheila's black hair swirled as she twirled on the dance floor. The bass guitar was turned up too loud, but the singer had a nice voice, so the band sounded pretty good overall. Sheila's chubby friend struggled to keep up with her but was wringing wet with sweat by the end of the second dance.

Mitch sat so far away that he could not use his lip reading skills to any advantage. He felt lucky just staying with Sheila, but where was her regular boyfriend?

By one o'clock, the crowd had dwindled, and Mitch found it more difficult to hide in the corner. He had nursed his way through three beers and had rejected as many propositions, two from men and the other from a plumpish woman in her late thirties who had a pretty face. *You better watch out for yourself old boy,* Mitch thought to himself*, or you'll wind up trying to figure out how you picked up an HIV infection yourself.*

Mitch knew Sheila would be leaving soon, and he didn't want to risk being spotted by her. He left a few dollars on the table and left the bar while Sheila and her companion labored on the dance floor through the last band number.

Blending into the shadows, Mitch waited in a dark doorway up the street a little way from the nightclub. His instincts paid off, and a few minutes later Sheila and her persistent friend came walking up the street.

"We could run over to my place for a little nightcap," the man puffed, stumbling along beside her. "It's too early to go home."

"Yeah, I know it is, Sweetheart. But, I told you my fiancé is a very jealous man. He'd get real mad if I went over to your place."

"What he don't know won't hurt him," the sweaty man replied. "I've got some good music, too."

"It sounds like fun, but I'd better not. Not tonight."

Mitch slipped along the dark street a short distance behind the couple and had little difficulty in hearing what they said. He hoped Sheila would not go home with the man, since that would mean spending a few more hours on her trail. But, if she did go with him, it would introduce a significant question about how she became infected, and if she were hooking, this could be the break they were hoping for.

Sheila and her companion reached the Mustang, and Mitch ducked behind a parked van when they paused in the dark beside her vehicle.

The fat man put his arm around Sheila's shoulders when she opened her small handbag and searched for keys. "I told you, not tonight!" she exclaimed, thrusting his arm aside.

"Look, Babe, if it's a matter of money -- I've got plenty here." He reached into his pocket and pulled out a wad of bills. Holding the money up in Sheila's face, he stepped closer. "Just name your price, Sweetheart -- is five hundred enough?"

"You can take your money and stick it where the sun don't shine, Tubby. I'm not interested!" She backed up a step toward the car and reached into her handbag, coming out with the keys.

"At least, you could let me have a little goodnight kiss," he pleaded. "I spent a bundle on drinks for you tonight."

"Tough shit, Fatso. You're old enough to know better." Sheila turned to open her door, but the man grabbed her and pulled her to him.

"I'm gonna get something for the money I spent tonight, Babe." He reached for the front of her dress, and Mitch saw Sheila's knee come up in a blur, thudding into her attacker's groin. He howled in agony and doubled over with pain.

Sheila's hand went into her bag again and this time came out with a small, dark cylinder, which she pointed at the man's face. "Remember me the next time you try something like that, dickhead!"

Mitch heard a brief hissing sound just before the fat man screamed again and clapped his hands over his eyes and face, coughing and retching as he went to his knees. *Serves the som'bitch right*, he thought to himself, chuckling.

Sheila turned back to her car and unlocked the door, leaving the man now lying on his side in the dirt beside the car. Speech was impossible as he gasped for air and spluttered, struggling to get up again.

I guess that settles the question about whether she's a hooker, Mitch thought, running to his car.

***

Brent and Nicole sailed back up the coast without incident and arrived home late Friday. They both were tired after spending almost a week on the boat. Nicole remained steadfast about not taking an extended sailing trip, and Brent grew more determined that he would leave on the trip as soon as possible. They had reached a critical point in their lives. At home, Brent moved to the guest bedroom. He and Nicole were speaking to each other only when forced to do so.

Brent had daydreamed about his trip all the way back to Kemah. He estimated it would take no longer than a month to prepare for departure. The boat would need to be surveyed for any hidden problems that should be fixed, and the engine needed to be checked out. Charts had to be purchased and courses plotted. Provisions would have to be purchased and stowed aboard, and he needed to buy an inflatable life raft. He also wanted to sell their old dingy and replace it with a newer, larger one with an outboard motor.

Monday morning, Brent left the house early. He had been postponing a follow-up visit with Jim Shubert until the final test result returned, and now seemed to be a good time to take care of that little necessity. He also needed to move out of his office and sell or donate his furniture and equipment.

Shubert had just arrived at his office after completing hospital rounds. He greeted Brent with a smile, and they went into the internist's private office where Brent took a seat in a chair beside Shubert's desk. Shubert acknowledged that he had received a copy of the latest test result, so he knew why Brent had come.

After the customary small talk, Brent got right to the point. "Jim, what do I need to do now that this has happened? Do I need to start taking medication or anything?"

Shubert looked very professional in his starched, stiff white coat. He sat behind his desk and took off his glasses then rubbed his eyes. "No, you don't need to start taking anything until we detect a significant drop in your T-cell count, and that could take years if you're lucky."

"What if I'm not lucky?"

"Your count could begin to drop at almost any time."

"Meaning what?"

"Meaning that you would be susceptible to various kinds of infections. When that happens, you should plan to stay pretty close to good medical facilities so you can get prompt treatment when necessary."

Brent noticed that Jim had said, "When that happens," and not, "If that happens." He thought about the implications for a few seconds then got up and began pacing the floor.

"Let's hope I'm one of the lucky ones. When do I start monitoring the T-cell counts?"

"Today's as good a time as any. I'll call the lab and tell them you'll be coming by later this morning. Assuming your count is in the normal range, and it should be at this point, we'll repeat it every six months for an indefinite period."

"You mean repeat the count every six months until it starts to drop. Is that the point I will be considered to have AIDS?"

"Not necessarily. You will cross that somewhat fuzzy line when you begin to have problems with the infections I just mentioned. Prior to that time, you will go through a series of milder symptoms known as ARC, short for AIDS Related Complex."

"What sort of 'milder symptoms' do you mean?"

"Oh, things like weight loss, low-grade fever, swollen lymph nodes. That sort of thing."

"Does the ARC phase last very long?"

"Again, like everything else with this illness, it's variable. It can last years in some cases."

"In the meantime, we hope for a cure -- right, Jim?"

"Of course. But it's also important to take good care of yourself. Eat right and stay in shape. Avoid stress. That sort of thing."

"Eating right and staying in shape have been habits of mine for a long time. And I've just come up with a great plan to take most of the stress out of my life."

Shubert smiled and leaned back. "Is that so! Why don't you tell me about it. I could use a good stress-reduction plan myself."

Brent sat back down and folded his arms across his chest. "The truth is, Jim, I'm tired of practicing medicine. In addition to the fact that I've lost my surgical privileges, which I know you have heard, there are just too many hassles -- too much interference by the HMO's and third party payers. It's not fun anymore, and it's not worth fighting for. I'd rather do something else with the rest of my life."

Shubert looked at him with a shocked expression. "So that's your plan for stress reduction -- giving up the practice of medicine." He shook his head. "How else can you make a living? Won't you have to do something?"

"I don't know. I'm not sure I'll have to work, at least not full time. Nicole has a good job, and we don't have any kids. She'll be okay. I'd just like to spend a long time sailing my boat. Maybe go to the South Pacific."

The internist looked doubtful. "Do you think that's realistic, Brent? Don't you think you're reacting emotionally to this situation and just trying to run away from it?"

"No, goddammit!" Brent got up again and faced his friend. "How can you say that? How many options do you think I have? This is something I've always wanted to do, and now there's not much else I can do! I don't have unlimited time left, and I'm going to do it while I still can."

Shubert didn't respond for a few seconds. Then he rose from his chair and stuck out his hand. "Then I wish you the best of luck, my friend. If there's anything I can do to be of help, just let me know."

Brent took a deep breath. "Thanks, Jim. You've already been a lot of help, and I appreciate it. I'm sorry if I sounded angry."

"I understand. Don't worry about it. And don't forget to drop by the lab for the baseline T-cell count."

Brent headed for the door. "I won't. Thanks again."

***

Relaxing in a recliner that evening after a satisfying supper of shrimp scampi with a small Caesar salad and a glass of white wine, Brent jotted an occasional note while browsing through a copy of

Hiscock's <u>Cruising Under Sail</u>. It seemed, now that he had made the decision to go, he could think about nothing else.

Nicole busied herself in the kitchen. They had spoken little after arriving home from their trip. At supper, Nicole had told him she might not remain in Houston when he left on his long voyage. She was thinking of moving back to south Louisiana in order to be closer to her parents.

A short time later, Brent found himself back in the operating room. Gary Morgan assisted him. They were in the process of removing the right lobe of a patient's liver, which contained a cancerous growth.

"You ain't seen nothin' yet, Kid," Brent said in his best Bogart imitation while dissecting out the blood supply to the portion of liver to be removed.

"I'm impressed!" Gary said in his usual modest fashion. That was one of the things Brent liked about Gary, his modesty.

"Now, if you'll put a couple of silk ties around these vessels, we'll get on with the case." The operating field was almost bloodless, characteristic of the meticulous technique Brent always used. Skillfully, they tied off branches of the hepatic artery and portal vein then the right half of the main bile duct. "Now, all we've got to worry about are the hepatic veins on the back side."

"Brent! Brent!" Nicole's voice came to his ears from a distance. *What was she doing here?* "Brent, you're dreaming! Wake up!"

With deliberate slowness, he opened his eyes and realized he still had the copy of Hiscock on his lap. Glancing at his watch, he saw that it was only nine o'clock.

"What were you dreaming about? I was afraid you would tear your book, the way you were moving your hands around."

Brent rubbed his eyes. "Oh, nothing of any importance. I was just tying a few knots in my sleep." He closed the book and stood up. "I think I'll drive down to Kemah tomorrow. There are several things that need to be done before I can leave on my trip."

Nicole walked back to the kitchen without replying.

Chapter 27

The next three weeks passed in a blur. *Caribe* was hauled out and placed on blocks for a fresh bottom-paint job, and a mechanic went through the engine and tuned it up. When he had finished, it started and ran "smooth as chocolate syrup", as Brent put it.

Mitch now trailed Sheila just on weekends, in view of what he had observed the night she rejected her would-be suitor. He and Todd Ward had agreed it would be best to let the trail cool off a bit in hopes of bringing Sheila's boyfriend out of hiding.

Sheila continued to go out on Friday nights, but her boyfriend had not shown up again, much to Mitch's disappointment. She followed the same routine every time she went out: park on Montrose Street, drop by the small bar for a purchase then go to Attaboy's for dancing and drinks with whomever offered to buy them for her.

Mitch was careful not to be observed and even went so far as to wear a disguise and drive different cars when he followed the girl. Reluctantly, after reviewing Mitch's growing expense list, Todd had authorized the car rentals.

***

Sheila parked her red Mustang under a large oak tree about half a block from the corner of Montrose and France Streets. It was a little after ten o'clock, and the neighborhood was beginning to come alive.

Locking her car door, Sheila glanced down the street behind her. Seeing no sign of the man whom she suspected of following her, her thoughts drifted to her lover. She missed him and felt angry with him for not leaving her with any means of contacting him. She knew he would look for her in Attaboy's when he felt things were safe, but she was growing more impatient by the day.

Sheila walked to the corner and turned down France Street. An occasional streetlight glowed against a backdrop of dark buildings and distant skyline. Lights from the small bars along the sidewalk also shown out into the street, but shadowy doorways and dark sections of sidewalk dominated the scene.

"Sheila!" called a voice from a black doorway.

Startled, Sheila paused and glared at a dark outline she could just make out in the recessed entry.

"Sweetheart! Is that you?"

"Quiet!" the voice whispered. "He might be following you. Step in here."

Like a fleeting shadow, Sheila ducked into the dim alcove. "Oh, Honey Bun! I'm so glad you came back!"

They embraced and kissed then he pushed her back a few inches. "We can't stay here. He might still be following you."

"I don't think so. I haven't seen him in almost three weeks. He must have lost interest or just gave up."

"Don't count on it. He may have just gotten smarter. I want you to meet me at the White Rose Motel at one o'clock. Go on to Attaboy's, just like it's a regular Friday night, but when you leave, meet me at the motel. Drive by your apartment on the way, and maybe he'll drop off your trail thinking you're going home for the night."

"Okay. But where is the motel?"

"It's on the north side of Pasadena at the intersection of Baytown Freeway and Sam Houston Parkway."

"Yes, I remember seeing it. Do we have to wait until it's so late? I've missed you somethin' awful." She wrapped her arms around him and put her head on his chest.

He stroked her long hair. "I wish it was okay for us to go right now, but I'm still afraid we're being watched. There's too much at stake to risk everything. Now go!" He eased her back out of the doorway and swatted her on the fanny.

***

Mitch had asked Molly to join him, thinking he would be less conspicuous with a female companion, even if she did look more like his mother than a girlfriend. He felt like barbecued pork under the hot wig and fake mustache, and Molly squirmed in her old party dress. But they had to wait less than an hour in the hot, rented Taurus before Sheila left home and drove to Montrose Street. They were able to follow from a safe distance, since Mitch knew where she was going.

Molly had accompanied Mitch for the last two weekends, and he believed that the ploy was working. They wore a different disguise each time they followed her and even took the extra precaution of using a different color rental car every weekend.

After parking, the couple left the Taurus near Sheila's Mustang and followed her from a distance toward Attaboy's. Molly gasped when she saw the young girl disappear into the darkened doorway. They paused, trying to look occupied while deciding what to do.

"What's happening?" Molly asked, adjusting her skirt and checking the buttons on her blouse.

"I'm not sure," Mitch replied. "I can just make out the back of her outline, and it looks like she's standing there talking to somebody. Let's cross the street and get a better look without getting too close."

They crossed the street, arm in arm, taking casual steps. On the other side, they chatted and looked around, looking as much as they could like a couple just out for the evening. Mitch's bald patch was well-concealed under a medium brown toupee' which blended into his natural gray hair on the sides. Fake glasses with plain lenses and heavy, dark frames rested on his nose, and a dark mustache had been glued to his upper lip.

Molly had put a dark rinse in her hair, which made her look much younger from a distance, but she had no need for a disguise. After all, Sheila had never even seen her.

Once on the other side, Mitch let Molly walk next to the street. That way, she would be between Sheila and him when they passed her.

"Don't look straight into the doorway, Molly. Try to look straight ahead. When we are just past the opening of the doorway, drop your handbag then turn your back to the street. I'll pick up your bag and be able to look into the doorway from behind you."

"Mitch, this is so exciting! I could do this every night of the week!"

On cue, Molly dropped her bag and turned her back to the street. Mitch stooped to pick it up and looked past her at the dark figures in the doorway.

"Now, let's continue our stroll down the street, Molly."

"Did you see her?"

"Yep. An' she sure wasn't lookin' at me."

"What do you mean?"

"She was wrapped up in somebody's arms. Looked like they hadn't seen each other in a long time!"

"Could you see who it was?"

"Nope. But I can make a pretty good guess that it's our boy. I haven't seen her kiss a single person the whole time I've been tailing her. It's got to be him!"

"Well, what'll we do now?"

"Stop in front of the next building. We'll stand there for a few minutes and see what happens. We can act like we're trying to decide where to go." Mitch stopped by the next doorway, which was unlit, and reached into his shirt pocket for a cigarette. "Smoke?"

"You know I have better sense than that, Mitchell Jackson. And don't you be blowin' any smoke in my direction!"

Mitch chuckled and lit the cigarette then exhaled over his shoulder, away from Molly. "Don't tell me you believe all that stuff about second-hand smoke now, Molly." He turned a little so as to be able to see the doorway where Sheila's backside was still visible.

"Yes, I sure do. And this is one of my best dresses. I don't want it stinking like cigarette smoke! …can you still see her?"

Mitch turned a bit more. "Yep, still there. Looks like they're talking now. Boy, I'd sure like to know what they're saying." He took another drag on his cigarette.

Molly turned somewhat and glanced in Sheila's direction. "Here she comes, Mitch! She's walking out of the doorway."

Grabbing Molly's arm, Mitch began walking toward Attaboy's once more. "It looks like her friend stayed behind, Molly. Unless she changes her pattern, she'll duck into that small bar just ahead and pick up some drugs. Then she'll go to the nightclub."

Mitch dropped his cigarette on the ground and stepped on it, pausing just long enough to let Sheila pass them on the other side of the street. As predicted, she went into the small bar. The other figure still hadn't emerged from the dark doorway.

"What'll we do now, Mitch?"

"Let's continue working our way up the street toward Attaboy's. If we hang around out here too long, he's sure to realize we're following her. I know he's got to be watching her trail from his hiding spot."

"Which one of them should we follow?" Molly slowed her pace even more when the question occurred to her.

"Good question, Molly. I'm pretty sure Sheila will go on into Attaboy's. If her friend was planning to join her there then he prob'ly would have walked there with her or met her there in the first place." He paused, thinking.

"Hell's bells, Molly! He's sure to have seen us by now. If we hang around out here, he'll know we're following her for sure. Come on, let's go to the nightclub. We'll stick with Sheila. Maybe they've planned another rendezvous."

They entered the crowded club and stopped near the door to survey the scene. The air was thick with smoke, and the strong smell of spilled beer mingled with that of cologne and aftershave. The usual weekend band played noisily over the steady drone of conversation and laughter, and several couples danced to the music.

"There's an empty table near the back of the room, Molly. Let's take it before somebody beats us to it."

They made their way through the crowd on the dance floor and sat at the table. "Can I get you something to drink?" a waitress asked almost before they had caught their breath.

"Bring us a couple of longnecks -- Lone Star." Mitch lit another cigarette then leaned back and began to slap the table with the palm of his hand in time to the music. "I'm beginning to like this band. They kinda' grow on you."

The bottles were dripping with condensation when the waitress returned and put them on the table. Mitch poured Molly's beer down the side of a glass mug and passed it to her.

"What a way to make a living," Molly sighed. "Are all your weekends like this?"

Mitch laughed. "No, most nightsI get to spend all hunched down behind the steering wheel of my car, waiting for somebody to make a move so I can follow them."

"Don't look now, but she just came in the door," Molly said out of the corner of her mouth.

Sheila crossed the front of the room and went straight to the bar. In a very short time, she was approached by a middle-aged man who bought her a drink. They danced a couple of times but appeared to be enjoying themselves. Mitch noticed that Sheila glanced at the large clock behind the bar after every sip of her drink.

They nursed their beers, and Mitch tapped his hand on the tabletop until Molly leaned over and asked him if he wanted to dance. "Why not? We can watch her from the dance floor just as easy as from this table."

The next three hours dragged by. Sheila appeared bored with the man who bought her drinks, but she stayed with him as the evening wore on. Mitch sipped at his fourth beer and considered asking Molly if she wanted to dance again when he saw Sheila get up and head for the door.

"Uh-oh, she's making a move. Let's go!" Mitch tossed some money on the table and took Molly's arm. Sheila was already out the door.

Chapter 28

Taking quick, short steps, Sheila made her way down the sidewalk toward her car. Seconds later, she started the engine and pulled into the street, making a tight u-turn.

She took the Gulf Freeway south to 610 then headed east on La Porte to the Pasadena Freeway and home. As planned, she drove by her darkened apartment, slowed, and then sped eastward again to intersect the Sam Houston Parkway.

***

Molly had just gotten into the vehicle when Mitch duplicated Sheila's U-turn maneuver and sped down the street in hot pursuit. They both breathed hard.

"You almost lost me with that one, Mitch!" Molly's face was flushed from the combination of exertion and excitement. She fanned herself with one hand.

"It wouldn't do to lose her at this point. If we're in luck, she may be going to meet lover-boy." Mitch slowed a bit when Sheila's tail lights came into view.

Fifteen minutes later, he groaned when he saw the red Mustang turn down an exit off the Pasadena Freeway. "Damn it! Looks like she's heading for home." He exited behind her but stayed a safe distance back, keeping a couple of cars between them at all times.

"We might as well go home ourselves," Molly said, stifling a yawn. "If she was going to meet anybody, she wouldn't go home first, would she?"

Mitch turned off his headlights and pulled into a dark shadow near a tree when he approached the corner adjacent to Sheila's apartment complex. "You just never know about these things, Molly. Maybe he's waiting for her at the apartment or something." They watched the Mustang slow down in front of the apartment complex.

"Look, Mitch! She's not stopping! She drove right by the place!"

***

Sheila wondered how she would locate his room, but she didn't have to worry for long. He had been waiting for her and stepped out of the front lobby when she pulled into a parking spot. Pausing for a minute to look around, he seemed satisfied that she hadn't been followed. He trotted over to the red Mustang and tapped on the driver's window.

Sheila stepped out of the vehicle, and they embraced and kissed once more. Then he took her hand and led her to a room on the first floor.

Entering the room, Sheila paused. "I thought you were never going to meet me! Why did you wait so long? You could at least have called!"

"Whoa, Babe. First things first! Get out of those clothes, and we'll talk later." He pulled her to him and kissed her again, this time with more feeling.

"I can tell you've missed me!" she breathed into his ear. She stepped back and smiled up at him. "Help me with my buttons."

A while later, they both lay exhausted on the rumpled sheets. "Did you miss me, lover?" Sheila asked, almost breathless.

His eyes were closed. "Did I ever! Couldn't you tell?"

"I don't mean just that way. Did you miss being with me?"

He opened one eye and looked over at her. "Of course I did. I thought about you all the time. You were on my mind every minute."

"You're not just saying that? You really mean it?"

He raised himself up on one elbow and kissed her again. "Yes, I mean it! I love you! Don't you believe me?"

"If you do love me, why don't we stay together and forget all this other crap. We may not have much time left, and I don't like wasting any of it."

"Now, don't start talking like that again! We agreed not to talk about that until we start getting sick. It could take years."

"Yes, but this damned lawsuit could take years too. What good is the money going to be to us if we don't get it soon? We'll have pissed away the only good time we had left!"

He got out of bed and went over to the sink at the end of the room where he had left a bucket of ice and a bottle of twelve year old scotch. Sheila pulled the top sheet up to her waist and fluffed her pillow against the head of the bed so she reclined at a more comfortable angle.

"Want a glass of scotch?" he asked, pouring himself a glass.

"Sure. Unless you have something better."

He laughed. "I haven't been able to get any of that since we were together last time. You're the one with the source, and I'm not sure if I'm being watched."

"You keep saying that! So what if we're seen together. You're going to get a divorce anyway!"

"It's not my wife I'm worried about," he said, stirring the scotch. "It's Dalton."

"But I still don't understand why."

He handed her the glass and took a long drink from his own then sat on the bed next to her. "Okay, I'll explain it to you again. There are just some things that you wouldn't understand about what is going on. A lot of the doctors in this city know me because of my job."

"So, tell me again – what is your job?"

"I work for a drug company and call on doctors in their offices. Is that so hard to remember?"

"No, it's not. But do they know your wife? So what if they see you out with me at night?"

He sighed and shifted his weight. "Some of them may know I have the virus. Seeing me out with you could blow your chances for suing Dalton. They'd tell him for sure."

He leaned back and took a large drink from his glass. "So you have to keep trusting me and do as I say." He dipped his fingertip in the scotch then reached out and began to make small circles around one of her nipples with the cold liquid. He smiled in appreciation when the nipple began to harden.

Sheila took a sip from her glass and pulled the sheet higher, covering her breasts. "You must think I'm pretty stupid, loverboy. Why didn't you explain this before? Didn't I understand when you explained how I got infected? I've never blamed you for that."

He got up and walked over to the makeshift bar and refreshed his drink. He stirred it again with his finger. "Let's not quarrel, love. We only have a few hours together tonight, but if we can get Dalton's lawyer to settle the case for a decent amount of money, we'll have all the time we want. I know we can do it, and it won't take much longer. Then we'll be able to disappear together."

"But that's what I don't understand! Why do we have to disappear? It's not like we're stealing the money!"

The man stepped into his boxer shorts and turned to face her again. "It's not that you wouldn't understand if I told you everything. It's more like there are things that you are better off not knowing. Does that make sense?"

"No, it doesn't. I'm just as involved in all this as you are, and I have a right to know everything!"

Sheila became more impatient and turned her back to him.

"Sheila, if Dalton learns about me, your case against him will be down the drain! Too many people know I'm infected!"

"But, Sweetie, don't you see? We could claim that you caught the infection from me! Then you could sue him too!"

He got up and began to pace the floor. "No, it wouldn't work. Believe me, it just wouldn't work. Our only reasonable course is to continue with our present plans and push for a quick settlement."

Sheila felt better but still was disturbed about not being able to see him more often. "If we can't see each other in the open, can we still meet like this? At least on weekends?"

"Maybe so. We'll have to be real careful. I wish it was easier for us to talk on the phone."

"Can't we just have the Phone Company check for a phone tap? Aren't they against the law?"

He rubbed his chin. "That might work. But it'll be risky. He could slip in and tap the phone again, so we'll have to be very careful not to get caught." He put his glass on the dresser and went back to the bed, where he stood looking at her. "Are you trying to get bashful on me? What's all this business with the sheet?"

He reached down and pulled the sheet an inch at a time toward the foot of the bed. "My, but you are one beautiful lady!" Her long, black hair flowed around her head and shoulders and hung down over her full, tan breasts, almost hiding them.

He climbed into the bed beside her, pulling her closer. "Let's not talk any more for a little while, okay?"

***

The eastern sky glowed a rosy pink, but headlights still glared in the early morning when the couple walked, side-by-side with arms around each other, to Sheila's car. They kissed one last time through the open window of the Mustang before she drove off. He watched the tail lights disappear down the highway and took great satisfaction with the realization that he didn't see a single vehicle leave the parking lot behind her. *Maybe they have quit following us,* he mused as he walked back to his room and called for a cab.

Chapter 29

A little before four thirty that morning, Molly had walked back to the white Taurus with two more cups of coffee she had gotten from the White Rose Motel office. Mitch slid across the seat and opened the door for her.

"Molly, I told you to call a cab and go home. They could stay in that room for days!"

"Mitchell Jackson, I wouldn't miss this for anything. I'm as anxious as you are to find out who she's with." Molly blew across the surface of her coffee and took a sip. "My, that's hot coffee!"

"If we had gotten here a little sooner, I might have been able to get a picture of him when he came out to meet her, but I was afraid to drive in right behind the Mustang." Mitch took a gulp of coffee. The hot liquid felt good in his throat.

"Did you get a look at him?"

"Not much of one. He's about five-ten, a hundred and eighty pounds and dark complected, with either black or dark brown hair. No mustache or beard. Well-dressed and well-groomed."

"Sounds like a professional man of some sort."

"Could be. Maybe he'll come out for a breather in a little while, and I'll have another chance for a shot with the camera."

"Aren't we kind of far away for a picture? This parking lot is pretty dark."

"Yeah, but I'm using fast film and a telephoto lens. It should work."

The next hour ticked by like ice melting on a winter day, and the two passed the time chatting about whatever came to mind in order to stay awake. Mitch yawned. "This is the worst part of my work, sitting in a parked car for hours on end, trying to hide and stay awake. God, I'd like to get out of this seat and run around the parking lot a few times!"

Their Taurus was parked at the far end of the lot with the back of the vehicle toward the rear of the Mustang, about fifty yards apart. The room they watched was off to one side, about halfway between the two vehicles. Mitch had adjusted his side mirror so he could watch the door to the couple's room through it and had moved the rear view mirror in the center of the windshield so that he could see Sheila's car. The camera rested on the seat beside him.

Molly dozed with her head resting on the half-raised window, and Mitch noticed his vision growing blurry at times while he stared at the door through the side-view mirror. He shook his head and pinched himself to stay awake.

With no sound, a slight movement caught Mitch's attention, snapping him awake like a jolt of electricity. The door to the room opened, and Sheila and her friend walked toward her car.

Mitch reached for the camera with his right hand and kept his eyes on the couple in the mirror. "Damn it all!" he whispered, bringing the camera up to his eye.

"What's wrong?" Molly asked, stirring.

"They're walking toward her car, but it's on the opposite side of the lot from us!"

"So what?" Molly was still half asleep.

"So they have their backs to us, that's what!"

Mitch had the camera pointed at the mirror, waiting for the right moment. He watched through the lens while the couple kissed then watched Sheila climb into the Mustang. Her male friend still had his back to Mitch but had to turn soon in order to walk back to the room or go around the car to get in on the other side, whichever he was going to do.

"Aha! She just started the engine! He'll turn now!" Mitch held his breath, finger resting on the shutter release.

After another quick kiss, the man turned away from the Mustang for a brief instant then walked backward a few steps toward the room while waving good-bye. His back remained all Mitch could see. The detective exhaled then took another deep breath and held it again.

After Sheila's tail lights disappeared down the highway, the man turned and walked back toward the room. Perfect! Mitch squeezed the shutter release. Nothing happened.

"Goddamn it!" He pulled the camera away from his face and fumbled with it for a second.

"What's wrong now?" Molly, eyes now wide, struggled to keep low in her seat.

"Goddamn switch was turned off!" Mitch stabbed at the shutter release once more, just as the figure disappeared into the room and closed the door.

"Did you get it?" Molly's eyes looked like saucers at this point. "Could you see his face?"

Mitch glared at her for a minute then looked down at the camera. "I don't know. He kind of had his side turned to me. I'm not sure if I got his face."

"Well, Mitchell Jackson! If that doesn't take the cake! We sit out here all night, waiting for him to show his face, and when he finally does, you don't have the camera turned on! Some detective! How much are they paying you to do this?"

Mitch could feel the heat in his face and knew he had turned red as a beet. "Now be careful, Molly! You're a novice at this. Don't be getting too cocky about a simple little mistake."

"What are you going to do now?" Molly sounded annoyed. Mitch noticed that she had said, "What are YOU going to do now?" and not "WE".

"Just sit here and wait. That's the name of the game. He has to come out sooner or later."

"Well, I think I've had enough of this for one night. I'm tired of sitting and waiting! I'm calling a cab." She opened the door and got out then slammed it behind her and stomped toward the office.

"I told you to do that two hours ago," Mitch mumbled under his breath. He dropped down low in his seat and resumed his vigil.

About ten minutes later, Mitch saw a cab turn off the Parkway and drive toward the motel. *Good. Now I can concentrate on my job without her asking me any more questions*, he thought.

The cab pulled into the parking lot and cruised like a snail along the front of the rooms. Mitch watched. *You'd think the dumb bastard would know where the office is*, he mused.

Before Mitch realized what was happening, the man he had been waiting for all night walked from his room with a small bag in his hand and jumped into the cab.

Mitch raised the camera, banging the lens on the steering wheel. The cab exited the lot in a cloud of dust while the detective struggled to disentangle the camera strap from his arm and start the engine.

Cursing under his breath, Mitch backed out of the parking spot and sped off down the service road in pursuit of the cab. He saw Molly standing in front of the office, hands on her hips and mouth wide open, the expression on her face saying, "What the hell is going on?"

The cab proved rather easy to follow in the light, morning traffic. Mitch stayed several car lengths back but kept the vehicle in view. They headed back down the Sam Houston Parkway then turned right onto the Pasadena Freeway, moving toward the heart of the big city.

A few minutes later, the cab headed west on the Old Spanish Trail, moving in the direction of the Texas Medical Center, Rice University, and Montrose Street. At last, they turned up Main Street and slowed in front of Graham Memorial Hospital.

Mitch stayed as close as he dared at this juncture, not wanting to risk being seen just when it looked like he might be able to learn whom was Sheila's mysterious lover. He watched the cab pull to the main entrance and stop. The passenger handed some bills to the driver and climbed out of the rear door.

Mitch pulled into the first open parking spot and jumped out of the front seat with camera in hand. The cab pulled away from the entrance, and the detective saw the man disappear into the front of the hospital.

Cursing the slow, revolving door while pushing it as fast as he could, Mitch burst into the front lobby. A dozen or so people walked in various directions in the large room where several corridors opened.

Frantic, Mitch crossed to the back of the room and looked down each of three long halls. It was Saturday morning and not quite seven o'clock, but the place bustled with activity. People were everywhere -- visitors, nurses in uniform, a lab tech carrying a tray loaded with syringes and small glass tubes, an orderly pushing a gurney, two doctors in scrub suits -- but the one person Mitch sought was nowhere in sight!

He went to the elevators and looked inside the one which had an open door. Empty. With strides as long as an ostrich's, he walked the length of the first hallway to the right and noted that the area contained just administrative offices. It was the least crowded of the three corridors.

The center hallway led to the cafeteria and gift shop. Mitch went into the cafeteria and walked the perimeter of the room. Still, nothing. The man had disappeared!

The third corridor led to the radiology department and to the laboratory then to another bank of elevators. Stretchers bearing patients waiting for x-rays lined the hall on one side, and laboratory personnel moved up and down the busy passageway. A steady hum of conversation filled the space, and Mitch wrinkled his nose at the antiseptic smell.

The toupee still rested on top of his balding pate, and Mitch noticed it growing uncomfortable. It had been a long night. He decided to make one more pass up and down each corridor then call it quits if he couldn't pick up the trail again. Ten minutes later, he walked with head hanging out the front entrance and trudged back to his parked car.

Where had the man gone? Did he work at the hospital? Did he go there just to lose anyone who might be following him? Mitch decided to get some sleep then talk to Todd Ward and see what they could piece together. Maybe the single photo he had gotten would prove useful.

Mitch felt his spirits lift somewhat at the thought of the photo being of value. He started the engine and drove back down Main Street, looking for a one-hour photo lab.

An hour and a half later, Mitch examined his photo at the counter of a drugstore in a shopping mall near the South Loop. The picture appeared a bit blurry from motion and also was a little dark, but he could make out the man's profile, he thought. But the face was turned away from the camera.

He drove home and parked the Taurus, thinking that he would need to return it later that day and rent a different car for tonight's vigil. He opened the door to his small apartment and walked in, closing the door behind him. The air had a stale, musty smell, and the room felt warm, so he turned the thermostat down several degrees.

Although he felt tired, Mitch knew that he would not be able to sleep right away. Years ago, he could drop off to sleep anywhere, anytime, but as he grew older he had developed a problem "shutting things down". His mind continued to work on a case long after his body begged for rest.

He poured himself a large glass of milk and laced it with a generous measure of scotch then sat at the small dinette table. He took the picture out of his pocket and stared at it. *Why did the man go to the hospital? And why that particular hospital?* It just didn't make sense. *Graham Memorial. There's something about that name. It sounds too familiar. Wasn't that the same hospital where Brent Dalton had worked and had gotten infected with the HIV virus? That's it! Bingo!*

Almost spilling his milk in the process, the detective bolted from the table, grabbed the telephone book and looked up Todd Ward's number. He dialed and let the phone ring a dozen times before hanging up. It was now a little after nine o'clock. *Maybe Todd doesn't come to his office on Saturday. Try the house.*

Todd answered, yawning, on the fourth ring.

"Todd, this is Mitch. Good news. I may have something for you on the Dalton case."

"Well, it's about time. I've been wondering if all those car and costume rentals were worth the expense. What have you got?"

"Sheila met loverboy last night, and they had a little rendezvous at a motel. After she left around daylight this morning, he took a cab. You'll never guess where it took him." Mitch felt pretty smug at this point and smiled into the telephone.

"How the hell would I know where it took him? Hobby Airport! The Astrodome! Timbuktu!"

"Just calm yourself, Big Guy. He went to a hospital. Know which one?" Mitch smirked at his cleverness.

"Goddamn it, Mitch! Stop with the guessing games! Just tell me what you've got!"

Mitch shifted the phone to his other ear. "Okay, Todd, he went to Gra-ham Mee-mor-i-al Hos-pital."

"Graham Memorial! Now that is interesting! What did he do there?"

Mitch hesitated. "I'm not real sure."

"Well, where did he go in the hospital?"

Mitch hesitated again. "I don't know. He disappeared down one of the halls before I could get in the front door. I walked all over the friggin' hospital, but I couldn't find him."

"Do you know who he is?"

"No, but I got a picture of him." Mitch paused. "It's not very good though, because you can't see his face."

"If you can't see his face, it's definitely not very good. What about his profile?"

"You can tell something about that. I caught him sort of quartering away from me."

"Why don't you meet me at the office in an hour. I'll call Dalton and have him come too. Maybe he'll recognize the guy in the picture."

"Fine. I'll see you there in an hour."

Mitch hung up and refilled his glass with milk and scotch before going into the bathroom for a shower and shave. Thirty minutes later, he locked his front door and left for Todd Ward's office.

***

Brent had made most of the final arrangements for departure on *Caribe*, lacking only a trip to the grocery store for a few fresh food items such as vegetables and meat. The boat had been serviced, and the fuel and water tanks were topped off. Charts and navigation equipment were in their places, and clothing and dry goods had been stored. He planned to leave on Monday, work his way across the

Gulf Coast and down to Key Westthen cross the Gulf Stream to the Bahamas. From there, he would continue down to the Virgin Islands. First port of call, Biloxi, Mississippi. He wished Nicole were going with him, but they still were not speaking to each other except out of necessity. Nicole had refused to approve of his plans for an extended cruise, maintaining that he was running away from reality.

The jangle of the phone startled Brent, and he jumped to answer it. Todd Ward greeted him from the other end of the line.

"Brent, I may have something of use to you. Mitch followed the Walters girl last night. She met her boyfriend again, and Mitch got a picture of him. Says the guy took a cab from the motel after the girl left. And get this, he went to Graham Memorial."

"No kidding! …and a picture!" Brent's mind raced at the prospect of learning the mysterious man's identity. "Where did he go when he got to the hospital?"

"We don't know. Mitch lost him after he went inside."

"Damn! What luck." Brent was just a little disappointed with that bit of news, since they had a photograph now. "When can I see the picture?"

"Mitch is going to meet me at my office in an hour. He'll have it with him."

"I'll be there too. Thanks, Todd," he said, already heading for the door. This could be the break he needed.

Chapter 30

Brent stood waiting by the door when Todd arrived at his office. They went in, and Todd flicked on the lights. The rich smell of leather and old books filled the room like fine perfume.

They moved through the reception area and entered Todd's private office.

The attorney waved his hand toward one of the leather chairs. "Have a seat. I'll put on a pot of coffee while we wait for Mitch."

"Thanks," Brent said, taking a seat in the comfortable old wingback chair. "It's a good thing this happened when it did, or I would have been hard to reach."

Todd reached into a cabinet and pulled out a canister of coffee. "Hard to reach? Why?"

Brent cringed at his *faux pas*, knowing that the attorney would not approve of his plans for an extended cruise. He shouldn't even have mentioned it, he reflected. "I'm leaving Monday on a sailing trip. Not sure when I'll be back."

Todd measured water in the coffee carafe and looked over his shoulder at Brent. "Do you think it's a good idea to do that right now? The Walters girl's attorney has requested an expedited settlement. That sometimes means they won't be as greedy as they might get if we go to court. And Mitch is still working on the case. Things are happening, Brent. We can't proceed very well in your absence."

Brent again regretted that he had mentioned the sailing trip. "I'm sorry about that, Todd. I'll keep in touch, and we can make decisions over the phone."

Todd finished the coffee preparation and took a seat behind his desk. He leaned back and folded his arms across his chest. "I don't like that idea, Brent. It's going to slow things down."

"None the less, it's something I'm going to do. Don't forget, I have the HIV virus too. The person who'll benefit from an expedited settlement is Sheila Walters -- not me. It's not my fault that she has the virus, but it looks like I'll have to take the blame. At this point, I don't care how slow things go." He had forgotten about the picture for the moment.

Just as Todd opened his mouth to answer, the front door slammed, and Mitch called out from the reception room, "Anybody here?"

"We're in my office, Mitch," Todd said, rising to open the door.

The private eye entered the room and went straight to the coffee pot. "Boy, I can use a cup of this stuff. Been up since six yesterday morning."

"Help yourself," Todd said, returning to his seat. "I've briefed the doctor about last night. Do you have the picture?"

Mitch looked around, sloshing coffee over the top of his cup in the process. "Oh, hello, Doc. I almost didn't see you there in that big ol' chair. How are you?"

"To tell the truth, I'm most anxious to see that picture," Brent responded, rising from the chair. "Do you have any idea who the man is at this point?"

"No, I don't. Not yet, anyway. If he doesn't disappear again, I should be able to figure that out pretty soon though." Mitch put his cup on Todd's desk and reached into his inside jacket pocket. Brent and Todd both rushed to his side to get their first glimpse of the mysterious lover whose identity remained such an enigma.

Brent was disappointed at his first glimpse of the likeness. "I can't see his face at all," he commented, staring hard at the photo. "This is not very good. Is that the only picture you were able to get?"

"Yeah, I'm afraid so." Mitch's face reddened a bit. "He had his back to me most of the time."

"Looks like he is about medium height and build," Todd suggested. "Can you describe him?"

Mitch looked toward the ceiling and closed his eyes. "He's about five foot ten, medium build and dark complected... has dark brown or black hair. Trim. Sharp features. The kind of guy most ladies would probably find attractive."

"Does that ring any bells for you, Brent?"

"H-m-m. When you told me he went to Graham, I tried to imagine who he might be. The only person I can think of, and he could fit your description, Mitch, is Bill Rudman."

"Who is he?" Todd went back to his chair, leaving Brent with the photo in his hand.

"He works in administration. Vice-president in charge of something or other."

"Why did you think it might be him?"

"I guess because he is the single person at the hospital who has demonstrated the most paranoia about my continuing to practice." Brent wandered back to the wingback chair, still staring at the picture. "I've wondered about the reason for his attitude."

"If this guy -- Rudman? – turns out to be the person we're looking for, will that help your case in any way you can imagine?" Todd looked at his coffee and stirred it while he talked.

Brent scratched his head. "Not unless we can prove he has the HIV virus. I guess that would explain some of his paranoia, too -- if he is infected, I mean."

Mitch had remained silent during the conversation but now appeared confused. "I'm not sure I follow that, Doc."

"Well, if he is Sheila's lover, and they both have the virus and know that she didn't catch it from me then he would want to make a big production out of my infection as a smoke screen. That could also help her case against me."

Todd tweaked his ear and grimaced. "That seems kind of weak, but I guess stranger things have happened. Did you take my advice and have your blood test repeated at a different lab?"

Brent hesitated. "No, I didn't. Tell me again why you think that's necessary."

"Like I told you before, it seems that all of your trouble is focused in one place -- Graham Memorial Hospital. It just makes sense to have your test done somewhere else."

"Maybe so, but I doubt it."

"When had you planned to leave on your trip?"

"Monday morning."

Todd took a sip of coffee and looked at his wristwatch. "That's about forty-eight hours from now," he commented, putting his cup back on the desktop. "Maybe you could have a blood sample taken before you leave. Would that be possible?"

Brent was annoyed at the request to delay his departure but realized the attorney was right. "Sure, why not," he agreed, looking out the window.

Mitch moved over to the coffee pot and poured himself another cup. "I guess you want me to stay on the trail for now, don't you?"

"Yes, for sure," Todd answered. "We want to know who this guy is and what his real relationship is to Sheila. Is he more than just her lover? And the most important question, does he have HIV?"

"Okay, I'll stay with it. That means another night up, so I think I'll say adios and grab some shuteye." Mitch drained his cup in one gulp and headed for the door.

"I'll be at home tomorrow," Brent said. "Give me a call if you find out anything tonight."

"I'll do that." Mitch opened the door to the reception room and left the office.

"The photo isn't a lot of help," Brent said. "Are you sure Mitch is worth the money we're paying him? He seems to be a bit of a klutz." He stroked his chin. "But at least, the description he gave us might be useful."

Todd grinned. "Yeah, he is a klutz, but he comes through most of the time. And remember, he doesn't charge much."

"If you say so," Brent said, shaking his head. "But I'm not so sure."

"Is there any way you can find out more on your own?" Todd asked. "Maybe ask around the hospital about this guy Rudman and see what people say."

"You're forgetting that I'm *persona non grata* at the hospital," Brent replied. "I'm afraid I'm not going to succeed at snooping around Graham and coming up with anything useful."

"You must have friends there you can call on. See if you can get one of them to dig a bit for you."

"Yes, I could do that." Brent got up, dejected, and moved toward the door. "I'll talk to somebody and see what I can do."

"Good. And don't forget to have your blood test repeated Monday morning."

Brent ran his fingers through his hair and looked at the floor. "Sure. One more time. I guess there's nothing to lose by having it done one more time."

"And think about that trip you've planned. If you could just delay it for a couple of weeks, it would be a big help."

Brent moved toward the door. "I'll think about it."

"Keep in touch," Todd said, still reclining in his chair with arms folded across his chest.

"I'll do that." Brent paused before opening the door to the reception area as though he might have something else to say then opened the door and left.

***

Brent felt unhappy with the way things had ended in the attorney's office. He knew Todd wanted to bring the lawsuit to a rapid conclusion. What distressed him most was the advice to postpone his trip. Now there was one more significant person who objected to his going away.

Mid-day Saturday traffic moved along like a galloping horse, and Brent again found himself driving toward Kemah. The day was cool, breezy and a little overcast. A few dark clouds floated across the sky from the northwest.

Less than an hour after leaving Todd's office, Brent parked near *Caribe*'s slip and walked out to the dock. He adjusted some lines and pulled the boat closer to the wooden platform then stepped aboard and slid back the hatch to the companionway. A distant boom of thunder sounded far away.

The main cabin had a familiar smell of mahogany and fiberglass, and light filtered through curtains covering portholes along each side of the cabin. Brent opened hatches over the salon and in the forward stateroom and took a deep breath of salty air when a cool breeze wafted through the cabin.

The refrigerator, which operated off shore power when the boat was at the marina, had a good supply of cold beer. He opened a can and sat at the dinette table.

Brent had difficulty thinking about anything in particular because his thoughts kept skipping back to Nicole. Truth be known, he was heartbroken that she had refused to go with him, and he missed her already. Nonetheless, he was hopeful she would change her mind and join him later, perhaps in the Keys or the Virgin Islands. He had not decided whether he would postpone the trip as Todd wanted him to.

He reclined on the comfortable seat and propped his feet on the opposite cushion. Outside, boats moved in and out of the marina, creating gentle waves, and *Caribe* rocked slightly. The setting was familiar and comfortable. It soothed him.

He wondered about the strange man that Mitch had followed to Graham Memorial. If it was Rudman, and even if they could prove a liaison between him and Sheila, what would that mean as far as proving Brent had not been responsible for Sheila's HIV infection?

Of course, if they could prove Sheila had a lover who had the virus also, that should be enough to convince even the most skeptical of people that Brent was innocent. It should be just a short time until they discovered the identity of the man. The tricky part would be how to go about learning his HIV status.

Brent yawned and stretched. He drained the last swallow from the beer and decided to grab some lunch at The Green Parrot then take the boat out for the afternoon. He closed the companionway and jumped over to the dock just as Walter Heathrow, the harbormaster, walked past.

"Hello, Doc! Looks like you've about got things ready for the big trip. Not leavin' today, are you?"

"Hi, Walt. No, I'm not leaving on the big trip today, but I thought I'd take her out this afternoon and get some practice handling her single-handed."

"Got an autopilot?"

"Yep. One of the best."

"How long you plannin' to stay out?"

"Walt, the way things have been going, I might just stay out there all weekend, if the mood strikes me. I can anchor just about anywhere in the bay."

"Well, stay clear of the ship channel, and don't forget to turn on your anchor light tonight. The forecast calls for scattered thunderstorms, so be careful."

"I will. Take care, Walt."

"So long, Doc. If you have any problems, I monitor channel sixty-eight on the radio."

"I'll remember that. Thanks." Brent walked across the parking area to his Suburban and called Nicole on his car phone. She didn't seem surprised when he told her about his plans. Next, he went over to the lower deck of the Green Parrot and ordered a sandwich, but ate little of it while watching boats going in and out of the harbor.

***

An hour later, Brent throttled back on the diesel and pointed *Caribe*'s nose into the wind. He set the autopilot to hold the course and moved forward to raise the mainsail. When it reached the top of the mast, he cleated the halyard and adjusted course so he sailed on a close reach. The boat breathed with new life and heeled over a few degrees when the sail caught the wind.

Next, he adjusted the mainsheet, letting it out until the sail was full.. Then he killed the engine. They moved forward over the waves in small leaps, he and his boat, and the only sound to be heard was the gentle lapping of waves against the sides and a slight humming from the wire shrouds supporting the mast. His spirits lifted. What a beautiful day!

A few minutes later, Brent had the big genoa pulling in front of the main, and they breezed along at a steady seven knots. "It jus' don't get much betta dan dis," he said out loud in his best Durante style.

That is, unless Nicole's here with me, he reflected.

Brent let the autopilot steer so he would be free to move about on deck. He coiled halyards and dock lines and put them all in their proper places then stepped back and reflected on the good looks of *Caribe* slicing along under her own power. He felt now that the trip to the Caribbean was long overdue. He just didn't know when he would be able to leave.

With the exception of fresh food, the boat had been ready for departure for almost a week. He had already postponed leaving for a few days in the hope that Nicole would change her mind and decide to go with him, but it didn't look as though that were going to happen. Now, this new business about somebody at the hospital who might be Sheila's lover had come up, and Todd wanted him to delay even longer. It seemed that there was always something that prevented him from being free to do as he pleased. So many strings attached to him.

Brent relaxed in the cockpit, reflecting on the current state of affairs, sometimes trimming sails so they caught the wind a little better. Absorbed in his thoughts, he failed to notice a low bank of dark clouds moving toward him from the west.

Chapter 31

At the sound of a loud crack of thunder, Brent spun around and saw the western part of the sky covered with a solid bank of black thunderclouds. It moved steady as a freight train in his direction, a dense line of solid rain on the leading edge.

Leaping to his feet, Brent took over the steering and spun the boat dead into the wind, started the engine, and re-engaged the autopilot. Then, sails luffing with a sound like cracking thunder, he released the jib sheet to allow the big genoa up front to be roller-furled back onto the forestay, but it wouldn't furl. He pulled several times on the furling line, but it was caught on a deck cleat forward of the mast and held the sail in place.

Cursing under his breath, he abandoned the genoa and scrambled onto the deck to release the main halyard then pulled the huge mainsail down. The sail flapped and beat him like a mad dragon as he struggled with it, but he soon had it subdued with a couple of ties.

Large drops of rain began to pelt him, and the wind gusted so strong Brent had difficulty staying on his feet. The genoa popped like a bullwhip as he struggled forward to free the trapped line. Waves crashed over the plunging bow and washed down the deck, making it ever more difficult to stay upright.

After what seemed an eternity, Brent reached the fouled line and freed it then turned to fight his way back down the slick, pitching deck toward the cockpit. Wind screamed through the rigging, and rain mixed with sleet poured down in heavy sheets.

Clinging to lifelines along the outside edge of the deck, Brent inched toward the shelter of the cockpit. The bow behind him pitched and tossed like a wild horse and sleet coated the wet deck, making it more difficult by the second to stay on his feet.

Then, in one split second, it happened. The boat plunged downward just as Brent lifted his foot to take a step. A strong gust of wind hit him full force when he had only one foot planted on the slick deck. The next moment, he hung over the side, clinging with all his strength to the bottom of a stanchion, a small, upright stainless steel post at the edge of the deck. Both legs dragged in the water alongside the wild boat. The loose genoa cracked furiously over him in the driving wind.

Brent gasped for breath. *God, I'm not even wearing a life jacket!* he thought, attempting to pull himself up onto the deck. Straining for all he was worth, he could not hold himself high enough on the side of the pounding boat to throw his leg up onto the deck. Spluttering and choking after several futile attempts, he allowed himself to hang down at arms' length for a few moments in an attempt to rest his aching muscles. His mind raced with the urgency of his situation.

In spite of all that had happened in the last few months, Brent had never in his life felt so close to the possibility of death as he did now. Grim reality closed in as he clung to the boat in the midst of the worst storm he could remember. He knew he could not hold on for much longer, and he did not have a life jacket. He had almost exhausted himself trying to get back into the boat.

He was flooded with despair. There seemed to be no options. He would cling to the boat as long as he could then he would fall into the water and drown. *Maybe this is the best solution after all,* he thought. *If I die out here then it will all be over. No need to worry about what to do with the rest of my life. Nicole will be all right.*

It will be pretty easy. Just let go and drop into the water. No need to struggle, just let it cover me and drift down peacefully. Hold my breath for as long as I can. Then, one big, deep gasp and it'll all be over. Pretty easy. He began to relax his grip on the stanchion. A weary but peaceful feeling replaced the despair he had felt earlier.

Then, as sudden as a flash of lightening, and though death seemed imminent, he knew he was not ready to die. He tightened his grip on the stanchion and held on for his life.

Moments later, he became aware of something bumping against his side at the edge of the churning water. It was an inflatable bumper he had tied over the side of the boat to prevent the boat from rubbing against the dock while in the marina. The bumper was cylindrical, about two feet long and eight inches in diameter. Enough to keep him afloat!

Brent relaxed his grip with one hand and grabbed the bumper with it. He wondered if he should release the bumper from the boat or try to hold on for as long as he could. He needn't have worried, because as soon as he transferred his weight to the bumper, the rubber ring to which the securing line was tied tore through, plunging him into the cold, churning water. His head went under, and the salty liquid burned his eyes and nose. He struggled upward, kicking his legs harder than he had ever done before. Then, all of a sudden, he bobbed back to the surface in the midst of the driving rain and sleet. The bumper kept him afloat! How good the fresh air felt as he breathed it in deep gulps and watched his sailboat leave him behind.

Caribe plowed ahead toward the west with the genoa flailing and cracking over the other sounds of the storm. Brent knew now that he had a chance to survive this ordeal. He would cling to the floating bumper for as long as his strength allowed. If he held on long enough, someone would come by in a passing boat and rescue him. He wanted to talk to Nicole, to tell her how much he loved her and that he never wanted to be away from her again.

Bobbing in the cresting waves, Brent knew he could never have followed through with his thoughts of ending it all by drowning himself. He had too much to live for. The sailing trip was no longer important. Neither was the lawsuit. Nor even the HIV infection. All he wanted now was to be able to spend whatever time he had left with Nicole.

The wind and rain slackened. How he longed to be with Nicole once more. She was like his lifejacket in a sea of trouble, and he was sorry he had left her behind. Things had been said and done that would require some repair. That wouldn't be a problem. He knew

Nicole loved him too, so things would work out. He might also find a way, somehow, to continue practicing surgery. It was too much a part of his life to just give it up now.

Hours passed, and the storm subsided. Brent had watched boats in the distance numerous times and had even attempted to hail a couple of them, but to no avail. Dusk now approached, and the western sky began to take on a dull, red glow. An occasional breeze stirred the air every few minutes, and the bay lay almost flat calm. He shivered in the water and struggled against a great weariness that threatened to overtake him. Gulls mewed in the distance and sometimes flew overhead, but he took no notice.

Several times during the long, dark night, Brent's grip on the boat bumper loosened and he almost separated from it when his head sank beneath the water's surface. Each time this happened, he spluttered and grasped the cylinder tighter, hugging it close to his numb body. Shivering had become violent early in the evening but now was more intermittent. At times, he almost felt warm.

Where are the boats and planes that should be searching for me? he wondered. Then he remembered, he had told both Nicole and the harbormaster that he might stay out all weekend.

Sleep crept up on him like a dense, silent fog, without warning. He knew he had to stay awake and realized he was becoming hypothermic. Still, he dozed and loosened his grip on the bumper at regular intervals.

He thought about what had happened to him. His practice was gone. It would require a lot of work to rebuild because of the publicity he had received. He once had a strong referral base with lots of other doctors and satisfied patients who kept him very busy. *Too bad about Gary Morgan. He would have been a great partner.*

The memory of Julie Sanders came back with startling clarity, shocking him into wakefulness for a few moments. *What a tragedy! She had so much to live for.* He felt sorry for her poor husband and couldn't blame him for trying to place the blame on her doctors for the unexpected event which caused her death. Few people understood the sense of grief doctors felt when they lost a patient because of unexpected complications. But Brent knew in his own mind he had done his best for the woman, and that was all anyone could expect. He no longer blamed himself for what had happened to her.

It became difficult to concentrate, and Brent found himself daydreaming about silly things that made no sense. Things that happened long ago.

Once, he became alarmed with the sudden thought that he needed to study for a physiology exam which would be given the next day. Then he worried because he couldn't remember what time the exam was to be given or where the classroom was. Next, he found himself worrying about the brakes on his old Volkswagen, a car he had sold fifteen years ago. Conversations with friends he hadn't seen in many years drifted through his head until he became so disoriented he had no clue about where he was or what was happening. He talked out loud and tried to sing songs to stay awake.

Deep in his mind, he knew he had to hold on to the bumper and stay awake, but he had difficulty remembering what had happened and couldn't concentrate long enough to put the pieces together. It seemed daylight would never return.

Chapter 32

In Brent's mind, the night seemed it would never end. Hour after hour of bone-chilling, mind-numbing cold... confused thoughts. There was little wind, and the water remained calm all night, or Brent would not have been able to hold on to the bumper. Daybreak came with a light breeze, and soon the sun appeared over the horizon as a huge, orange globe resting on the edge of the water. He dozed at intervals but awoke with a start each time he sensed himself slipping under the surface.

A distant buzzing sound seemed to be growing louder, and he wondered when it had started. Had the sound been there all night? No, he didn't think so. It must be a chainsaw. Somebody's cutting firewood -- out here? He shook his head and realized he was listening to an outboard motor which approached him from behind. With a great effort, he moved his legs and turned to face the direction of the oncoming boat.

"Hello, you in the water!" a figure yelled from the front of the small boat. Brent tried to shout back, but a slight groan was all that escaped his lips. In a matter of seconds, they pulled up beside him, and two men struggled to lift his rigid hulk into the boat.

"Are you okay, fella? How long you been out here like this?" The men eased him down into their fishing boat.

Brent again tried to talk, but found that his jaw and tongue were so thick they just wouldn't work. All he could do was groan. He began shivering again, and within minutes the shivering became violent. He felt a tremendous sense of gratitude for being rescued, but everything now seemed even more confused than when he was alone in the water. He found it difficult to understand what was happening.

One of the men took off his jacket and wrapped it around Brent's chest, and the other man laid his over Brent's midsection and upper legs. "It's okay, guy. You're out of the water now. You'll be alright in a little while," one of them said then added, "Man, he's some kind of cold! Would you look at his skin? … he's bluer 'n my Levi's!"

"We gotta get this guy to a hospital fast!" Brent heard another voice say. "He's got the hypothermia, big time!"

Somewhere in the inner recesses of his mind, Brent heard an outboard engine roar, and he sensed that the boat leaped up in the water. Someone lay beside him in the bottom of the boat and tried to block the cold, morning wind from his body as the boat raced and pounded ahead.

***

The cold boat ride was the first thing Brent remembered when he woke up many hours later. Little by little, he became aware of a nearby beeping sound and recognized it as an alarm from an occluded intravenous line pump. To a person who had spent as many hours in hospital rooms as he had, it was a familiar sound. He opened his eyes to tiny slits, but everything was blurry. He was in a hospital room. Nicole sat in a chair at his bedside, looking at him.

"Brent! Thank goodness you're awake!" she said, breaking into a wide smile and moving quickly to sit on the side of his bed. She fell across him and smothered him with a hug then cradled his face in the palms of her hands and put hers down close, nose to nose. "What in heaven's name were you doing out there in the water in the middle of the Bay -- without a boat or even a life jacket?"

Brent shifted in the bed and started to sit up then lay back again, a little lightheaded. "What? Where am I?"

He looked around the room. It contained standard equipment for an intensive care bed, with a wall-mounted bank of monitors jutting on a bracket from the corner of the room. A tray stand on rollers stood against one wall. A bedside table and the chair in which Nicole had sat completed the furnishings. A heating unit at the foot of the bed was attached to some tubing which ran under the covers. He felt hot.

"Brent, are you all right?" Nicole sounded concerned.

Attempting to rise, he found he was covered with layers of blankets which he threw back as he sat up. "Nikki! How did you find me?" They embraced, and she hugged him again before answering.

"They called me from the hospital. Brent, you were almost dead!"

He was confused. "What happened? I took the boat out for a sail. I remember the storm, it was a bad one, and falling overboard and spending a long time in the water hanging on to a bumper. God, it was cold! Then it got dark, and I had a lot of trouble holding on. I knew I didn't want to die out there. I... I had to get back to you." His eyes became watery when he remembered his thoughts. "Things get a little fuzzy after that. And then -- something about a long, cold boat ride." He shook his head and stared at the wall.

Nicole took his hand in both of hers. "You were rescued by a couple of fishermen who just happened to see you in the water. No one even knew you were in trouble!"

"The boat! What happened to *Caribe*?" He sat bolt upright.

She looked surprised. "I don't know. No one has told me anything about the boat."

Brent climbed out of bed and realized he ached all over. Every muscle in his body felt like it had been beaten to a pulp. Still feeling light-headed, he put one hand on the arm of the chair and sat down.

"I was caught in a thunderstorm. The autopilot was steering, I remember, and I had turned around to head back toward Kemah when the wind picked up and shifted. Then the storm hit in full force. God, did it blow!" Brent paused as he remembered being washed overboard. "Hasn't anyone told you anything about the boat?"

"No, not a thing. How did you get in the water?"

Brent strained his memory and remembered bits and pieces of the accident. It seemed like a dream. "I remember slipping and falling while walking on deck. It was rougher than I've ever seen, storming and raining, with sleet too. Then, next thing I knew, I was hanging on to the side of the boat trying to get back aboard. I grabbed onto a bumper, and it broke free." The memory was becoming clearer in his mind now. "I held onto it in the water. If it hadn't been for that bumper, I would have drowned for sure." He shuddered as the scene came back to him.

Nicole moved to his side and smoothed his tangled hair. "Thank goodness the bumper was there." She kissed his forehead. "You're lucky, you know -- falling overboard in a storm by yourself without your lifejacket on!"

"...and living to tell about it," he added.

A nurse opened the door to the room after a token knock. She smiled. "Good morning, Dr. Dalton. We could tell from the monitors that you must have gotten up. Feeling okay?"

Brent returned the smile. "Pretty well, thanks. What hospital is this?"

"Bayside, in Kemah. Have you heard of it?" The nurse stuck a thermometer in his mouth and wrapped a blood pressure cuff around his arm.

He shifted the thermometer to one side and talked around it. "Yes, I'b hearb ob it. How long hab I been here?" Brent grimaced a little as the pressure in the cuff increased.

The nurse remained silent for a minute while she took his blood pressure. "You were brought in yesterday morning by two fishermen. They found you out in the middle of the Bay, hanging on to a rubber float and so cold you couldn't even talk." She took the cuff off Brent's arm. "You were very hypothermic."

"What day is it?"

"It's Monday morning." Nicole answered. "You've been out of it ever since they brought you in yesterday morning."

Brent stood up. "Monday morning! I've lost a whole day!" He walked over and opened the door to the small hanging clothes locker that was built into the wall. "Where are my clothes?"

Nicole laughed. "Brent! What do you have to do that's so urgent?" She went over to him and pulled his hospital gown together in the back. "I'll have to get you some clothes. They cut yours off when you were brought in yesterday. But I have your wallet and watch."

Brent relaxed when he realized she was right. He had no appointments to keep, since he had planned to leave for his extended cruise at about this time. He moved away from Nicole and sat on the edge of the bed then looked at the nurse again.

"Who is my doctor?"

"Doctor Paul Williams was the internist on city call when you were brought in. You're on his service."

"What time does he make rounds?"

"He's an early bird." She looked at her watch. "...should be here any time now." The nurse folded the blood pressure cuff and put it in a wire basket on the wall. "Would you like me to take off your monitor pads? Dr. Williams left an order to discontinue monitoring when you were awake and stable."

"Yes, that would be nice. Thanks." Brent slipped the hospital gown down to his waist, and the nurse proceeded to pull the sticky pads off his chest along with a few hairs. "Ouch," he complained, rubbing one of the places where a pad had just been removed. "That hurts!"

Just after the nurse opened the lid to the covered waste can and discarded the pads, a short, chubby man dressed in a blue, pinstripe suit entered the room. A stethoscope hung around his neck.

"Good morning! And how are we doing today? Must be pretty good -- I see you're up, and Jill has taken you off the monitor."

"Doctor Williams, I presume." Brent stuck out his hand, and the doctor shook it.

"Yes, that's right. And you're Brent Dalton, a surgeon from Houston."

Brent smiled and leaned back on his elbows. "Ex-surgeon. I'm retired."

Williams grinned at him. "I'm envious! How'd you manage to do that at such a young age?" It was a rhetorical question, and Brent recognized it as such.

"Oh, just lucky, I guess." Brent looked at Nicole, and she rolled her eyes toward the ceiling and shook her head.

Williams laughed and slipped the stethoscope off his neck then proceeded to listen to Brent's chest. "Take a couple of deep breaths for me."

Brent obliged, and the doctor draped the stethoscope around his neck again after he had listened to his satisfaction. "Sounds just fine.

You're a pretty lucky fellow, all right. Your core temp was down to ninety-one degrees when they brought you in. Much lower, and you might have had problems with arrhythmias when we rewarmed you."

Williams studied his fingernails for a few seconds. "By the way, you wouldn't know anything about an abandoned sailboat found stuck in the mud a few miles west of where you were found, would you? I saw something about it on the news before I left the house this morning."

Brent bolted upright in the bed. "A sailboat? Stuck in the mud?"

"That's right. At least that's what they said on TV. Said the Coast Guard was trying to contact the owner, but they didn't say who that was."

Brent stood up and clapped his hands together. "Wow! What a stroke of fortune if that's our boat! It must be! I need to get out of here and check on it. Any problem with discharging me right away?"

"No, none at all, if that's what you want to do. I'd like to see you in a couple of days, just to be sure you haven't developed pneumonia or something. And I'd also like to check your electrolytes and white cell count before you leave."

"Sure, no problem." Brent turned to Nicole. "Sweetheart, could you please run to the nearest store and pick up some clothes for me? The Coast Guard might not approve if I come in wearing nothing but this gown."

Jill, who had been standing in the corner near the monitors, laughed. "I don't know about that. Some of the ladies at the Coast Guard Station might find your visit -- well, entertaining!"

Brent blushed. "You ICU nurses are worse than the ones in the OR!"

Nicole laughed too then she and Jill walked to the door. "I'll go and get you something to wear. Be right back." Jill walked out just ahead of Nicole, leaving the two doctors alone.

"I would like to ask a small favor of you," Brent said to Williams after the women had left.

Williams sat on the edge of the bed. "And what would that be?"

"I need to have a Western Blot for HIV run, and I was wondering if you would order it when you get my blood work this morning."

Williams looked at him with a curious expression. "Do you mind my asking why you need to have it done?"

"No, of course not." Brent, in an abbreviated fashion, explained what had transpired during the months that had passed following his accident in the operating room, ending with the recommendation from his attorney that he have the test repeated at an independent laboratory.

"What a nightmare!" Williams exclaimed. "That's every healthcare worker's worst dream, contracting an HIV infection from a trivial accident with a needle! I'll be glad to order the Western Blot for you, but it sounds like we'll expect the result to be the same as the previous ones."

"I know. But it's something that needs to be done."

Dr. Williams picked up Brent's chart and flipped through it then wrote a few orders. "That should take care of it. Someone will be right up to take a blood sample then you'll be free to leave as soon as your clothes get here."

"Thanks very much. I appreciate your help."

"Don't mention it." Williams stuck out his hand, and Brent shook it. "Good luck, Brent. Don't forget to see me in a couple of days."

"How long does it take to get the Western Blot result back?"

"We send them off, to California I think, so it'll be early next week before we get the result."

"Okay. Thanks again. I'll try to see you later this week, but no later than next Monday, for sure!"

Dr. Williams left the room, and Brent lay back on the bed to wait for the lab tech and his clothes.

Chapter 33

Nicole drove them to the Coast Guard station after Brent changed clothes and was discharged from the hospital. The station consisted of a tall, round, white stone tower resembling a lighthouse. After climbing the spiral staircase to the observation area, they spoke with the Duty Officer, Lt. Stanley Smith. He offered them seats.

Brent recanted the events leading up to their visit, and the lieutenant sat without moving while listening.

Smith sat behind a gray, metal desk and smiled at them from under a handlebar mustache. The young lieutenant twirled one side of his mustache between his index finger and thumb.

"We received a radio message just before dark yesterday that there was a sailboat hard aground off Eagle Point. The boat appeared to have been abandoned. The caller said that she was listing pretty badly and appeared to be at risk for damage if the tide went out and left her on the flats."

"Did you check it out?" Brent asked.

Smith twirled his mustache again. "Yes, we sent our cutter over to investigate. It was apparent no one was on board. When we checked the registration, we found that the owner was the same individual who had been rescued and hospitalized with hypothermia the previous day. That would appear to be you. We tried calling you at the hospital last night, but they told us you were unable to take calls and to try again today. I was just getting ready to call when you came in."

"Did you move the boat?"

237

"Yes, we towed her back to our dock here in Kemah. The harbormaster at the marina told us you were alone when you left Saturday afternoon, so we didn't organize a search. We had been notified earlier that you were in the hospital."

Brent felt both grateful and annoyed. "Why didn't you leave word you had my boat?"

"Like I said, we tried calling your home, but all we could do was leave a message on the answering machine. When we checked with the hospital, they told us you couldn't talk. So we decided to wait until today and try again. You got to us before we got to you, I'm disappointed to say."

"Is the boat okay?"

"Pretty much. The foresail was shredded, but everything else seems to be okay. She had run aground in soft mud, you see. The engine must have died, because the fuel tank was almost full, and the ignition switch was still on."

"Where is the boat now?" Nicole asked.

"She's tied up at our dock, just around the corner from here. Want to go check her out?"

"Yes, please." Brent and Nicole stood and moved toward the door. Lt. Smith took his hat from a rack in the corner and led the way, smoothing the ends of his mustache while he walked.

Nicole gasped when she saw their boat. The big genoa hung in shreds, giving *Caribe* the appearance of a ghost ship. Everything else, at first glance anyway, looked all right.

They climbed aboard, and Brent walked around the deck. The jib sheet which had fouled and caused all the trouble lay tangled along the deck, but everything else seemed to be in place.

Brent opened the companionway and went below. With the exception of a few books and magazines scattered on the floor, the cabin looked just like he had left it when he motored out of the marina on Saturday afternoon. He felt a sudden surge of pride in the boat. She had weathered the storm a lot better than he had.

"What do you think?" Nicole asked.

"I'm relieved. Very relieved. She could have been a total loss. Worse yet, she could have collided with another boat and hurt, even killed someone. We're lucky."

"I need to get back to the station, if that's all right with you two," Lt. Smith announced from up on deck. "And if you don't mind, Dr. Dalton, please stop by before you leave. I'm afraid there's some paperwork that needs to be taken care of."

"Yes, of course," Brent replied. "We'll just be a few more minutes."

A few thuds of the lieutenant's shoes sounded in the cabin then Brent found himself alone with Nicole. He contemplated her for a few moments, studying her curvaceous, feminine profile. He remembered now the emotion he had felt thinking of her while he had floated alone and miserable for those long hours just two days ago.

"Nikki...I, uh... I thought about you a lot while I was in the water Saturday night."

She smiled at him. "You did? I'm glad. I've thought a lot about you too." She spoke in a voice that was almost a whisper and looked into his eyes. "What did you think about?"

Brent moved over to her and slipped his arms around her waist. "I thought about how much I want to be with you for the rest of my life. No matter what. To hell with lawyers and lawsuits, and to hell with hospital administrators and medical staffs. To hell with everybody! The sailing trip isn't as important as I thought it was. You were right, it was just a means of running away. Maybe we'll do it some other time, if you want to. But it's not important right now."

Little puddles appeared in Nicole's eyes, and she blinked, sending them cascading down her cheeks. She leaned into his chest and put her arms around him . "Oh, Brent! Welcome back! I knew you wouldn't leave in the middle of all this mess!"

Then, in the dim cabin of the quiet sailboat, he tilted her head back and kissed her with more feeling than he had kissed her with in a long, long time.

***

There had been less paperwork than Brent anticipated when he stopped by the Lieutenant's office, and he was relieved to learn the boat was not impounded and there were no fines involved. His insurance would cover towing charges, if there were any to be paid.

Nicole helped Brent take down the shredded genoa, and they raised in its place a smaller, working jib which had been stowed below in the sail locker. The diesel engine started and ran as though nothing had ever happened. In just a short while, they had *Caribe* secured in her own slip at the marina.

Since they were in separate vehicles, Nicole followed Brent back to their house. The late afternoon sun hung low in the western sky by the time they arrived. After parking the cars in the garage, they paused to look at their house and yard before going in.

Brent put his arm around her shoulders. "Nikki, I did some more thinking while we were driving home. We've gotten used to this place. I don't believe we should go anywhere else to start over."

She smiled up at him. "You mean you don't want a new 'view out the back window'? You used to say it could always get better, if a person wasn't too complacent."

"I was wrong. The view might get better, but a different view doesn't always mean things are better. Everything I want or need is right here, as long as you're here too."

They walked side by side, each with an arm around the other, to the front yard. Brent pulled up the "for sale" sign and threw it in the trash bin behind the garage. "I'll call the realtor first thing in the morning and give her the news," Nicole said when they entered the semi-darkened kitchen.

Brent flicked the light switch and went to the wine rack. "What'll it be? Something to celebrate the occasion?"

Nicole paused in the midst of taking off her shoes and put her finger to her chin. "Do we still have some Merlot?"

"Yep, right here." He removed the lead from the top of the bottle and pulled the cork. He poured them each a glass and gave Nicole's to her.

They stood together for a minute in silence, savoring the wine's bouquet and enjoying the quietness. Brent raised his glass. "Here's to us, kid." Their glasses clinked as they touched, and they drank to each other.

***

Tuesday morning, Brent rose at daybreak and prepared a breakfast feast of eggs, bacon, and pancakes, with coffee and juice. Nicole came downstairs in her robe just as he took up the last egg and put the plates on the table. "I don't know why I'm so hungry!" she said, drinking her juice before being seated.

He laughed. "I have a pretty good idea why, and it's probably the same reason I'm starving to death!"

She giggled, and they proceeded to devour every morsel on the table. Nicole leaned back in her chair and put her hand on his. "My, that was good." Then she winked at him and faked a yawn. "How about a nap?"

He winked back. "How about an encore?"

***

Later that morning, Brent called Todd and learned that Sheila had stayed home the remainder of the weekend. There was nothing new to report.

Mitch had gone to Graham Memorial a couple of times and walked the halls looking for their man but hadn't seen him.

Sheila's attorneys had sent Todd a new letter offering to settle the case for three and a half million dollars if that amount was agreed to within two weeks. Otherwise, the offer would be withdrawn.

"That's ridiculous," Brent said when he heard the amount. "Let's go ahead and fight this in court. I know it's a gamble, but I also know we're right. The burden of proof would be on them!"

"It's a risky case, Brent. If they get a sympathetic judge and jury, the insurance company could lose up to twenty million, and they could still go after your personal assets if the award is more than that."

"That wouldn't do them much good, would it? I have a little money in the bank and in some investments, but most of my net worth is in my retirement fund and my home. Can they take that away?"

"They could force you into bankruptcy, take everything you have -- except, as you said, your home and retirement account. They could even garnish your future earnings."

Brent thought about that for a minute. "I still say 'let's fight it'. Don't you think a jury will believe us rather than her?"

"That's not a given, Brent. The insurance company won't approve a settlement of three and a half million anyway, so we have some time to work with. Why don't you take a walk around the hospital with Mitch? If you see our friend, you might be able to identify him."

"Yeah, I thought about that earlier. Sounds like a good idea to me. I want to be sure he sees Bill Rudman, since he's still the best suspect in my book."

"Fine. I'll call Mitch. What time do you want him to meet you?"

"This afternoon will be okay. Tell him to meet me in the front lobby at two o'clock."

"Consider it done. I'll talk with you later."

Chapter 34

At two o'clock that afternoon, Brent walked into the front lobby of Graham Memorial and looked around. The scene was quite familiar. Visitors came and went by way of the various corridors, and a volunteer in a pink frock sat behind a large, circular information desk. Overhead speakers announced pages for doctors and technicians, and the air had the peculiar, antiseptic smell so unique to hospitals. Brent sighed. He loved this place.

Mitch sat reading a newspaper in a stuffed chair near the front windows. Their eyes met, and Brent walked over to the detective.

"Afternoon, Doc. How's everything?" Mitch said, folding the newspaper on his lap.

"Better than you'd believe, to tell the truth. Are you ready to take a walk around?"

"Sure. That's why I'm here." Mitch got up and dropped the newspaper on a small table beside the chair.

Brent hesitated. "We're sure to bump into a few people I know. I'll try to avoid stopping to talk, but if we do talk, I'll introduce you as my sister's husband from San Antonio. You're just here for a short visit."

"Right. What's my name?"

"How about Scott Anderson. I don't have a sister in San Antonio, so it doesn't matter."

"Check. Scott it is. Where'll we start?"

"Administration. There's someone there I hope you'll recognize."

The two men walked down a corridor to the right then took a left down a hall filled with administrative offices. Several of the administrators shared a common waiting room and secretarial staff about halfway down the hall. William Rudman's office was in this group.

Brent opened the door to the large reception area, and the two men went inside. Several desks were arranged around the room, and they all were occupied by secretaries working at their individual computer terminals. Mitch stopped by the door, and Brent went to a desk adjacent to a small sign that read "William Rudman -- Vice President, Internal Affairs". A secretary sat typing at the desk. He recognized her.

"Hello, Anita. How are you today?" He could sense his pulse quickening in anticipation of speaking with Rudman and perhaps witnessing a reaction on his part when he saw Mitch.

The secretary looked up from her work and smiled at him. "Oh, hello, Dr. Dalton. I'm fine, thanks. Can I help you with something?"

"Maybe so. I'd like to speak with Mr. Rudman, if he's available. I have a couple of questions about my office lease."

"I'm sorry. Mr. Rudman is out of town all this week. He's attending a big hospital administration meeting in Washington. Maybe Mr. Ross could help you."

Brent felt a wave of disappointment. He frowned. "No, I don't think so. This is something I need to see Mr. Rudman about. So he won't be back until Monday?"

"Yes, that's right. But he's pretty booked up with meetings and appointments for Monday. Can I have him give you a call?"

Brent shifted his weight. He didn't like the direction this was headed. "No, I don't think so. That is, I'm not sure where I'll be. It'll be simpler for me to call him."

Anita smiled again and turned back to her word processor. "Fine, I'll let him know you came by."

Brent had an idea. "Thanks, Anita. By the way, do you know when he left town?"

"Yes, on Saturday. I booked his flight to Washington myself. He had a Delta flight that left at ten thirty Saturday morning, and he'll be coming back Friday night, late. Why do you ask?"

"It's not important. Don't worry, I won't bother him at home." Brent walked toward the door, where Mitch waited, engrossed in a study of his fingernails. "Thanks again, Anita," Brent said over his shoulder as they left the office.

"Damn! What luck! Out of town all week," Brent cursed under his breath when the office door closed behind them.

"Maybe that's why Sheila only went out on Friday night." Mitch suggested. "She stayed home the rest of the weekend."

"Yeah, that's why I asked when he had left." Brent paused when they neared the main corridor again.

Mitch looked at his watch. "You still want to walk around some?"

"Might as well, as long as we're here."

The two men walked every corridor on every floor of the hospital, bumping into three people with whom Brent felt compelled to stop and talk. He had hoped to see Gary Morgan but didn't.

Later, they found themselves back near the front lobby. Brent was disappointed that they had been unsuccessful. He stuffed his hands into his pockets and sighed. "Mitch, have you seen anybody who even resembles our man? We've been walking these halls for almost an hour now."

The detective shook his head. "Nope, I'm afraid not. I'll recognize him if I see him. We haven't passed him in the hall. I'm sure of that."

Brent stopped walking. "What was he wearing when you followed him to the hospital?"

Mitch scratched his head and thought for a minute. "Street clothes. Shirt without a tie. Dark sport coat."

Brent frowned again and resumed walking. "Not much help there. Could be just about anybody. No clue as to where in the hospital he might've gone?"

"No. I told you he was nowhere in sight by the time I got to the front lobby. He had enough time to have gone anywhere."

Brent stopped and looked at his watch again. "There's no point in hanging out here any longer. Let's call it quits for today. At least we can beat the rush hour traffic if we leave now."

"That's fine. Tell you what, Doc. I'll come back a few times this week and walk around, keep my eyes open. Who knows? I might see the guy."

Brent shrugged and shook his head. "I doubt it. I think he's at a meeting in Washington. But it's worth a try. Let me know if you see him."

Mitch slapped him on the back as Brent started for the front door. "You can be sure I'll do that, Doc."

***

Although Brent still felt drained from the overnight ordeal in the bay the previous weekend, he was on a mental high as a result of his reunion with Nicole. Further, having canceled the sailing trip, he realized that most of his recent anguish had been due to their emotional separation.

And last, he had decided to remain in Houston and pursue a teaching position at one of the medical schools. He knew he had a lot to offer in the teaching arena as a result of his years of experience, and the anticipation of continuing to work in his chosen field gave him an enormous sense of peace. The one thing that prevented him from being content at this point, the thing that loomed larger than all his other thoughts, was the fact that he knew in his blood he carried a death sentence. It was like a time-bomb ticking inside him, and he wondered if he would ever know complete happiness again.

Days passed. Friday, Mitch called to tell Brent he had been back to the hospital several times but had not seen the man they wanted to find. He would resume his weekend vigil at Sheila's apartment that night and give Brent a call on Saturday.

Sheila's attorneys declined Todd's first offer, as he had predicted they would. Todd said he was encouraged, however, by the fact her attorneys continued to push for an expedited settlement. He said this indicated they would be inclined to accept a somewhat lower figure than if they had all the time in the world to drag this thing out in court. Todd recommended they sit back and let a few weeks pass before making another offer. If the plaintiff was sincere about wanting to settle this affair soon then maybe she would be ready to accept the next proposal.

***

Alone in her tiny apartment Friday evening, Sheila cleared the small table and rinsed a few dishes at the sink. Her place was near the home of her parents in Pasadena, and travel anywhere in the downtown Houston area was quick and easy.

When the telephone rang, she had just finished the dishes and had turned on the television set.

"Hello," she said into the receiver while hitting the mute button on the remote.

"Hi, Sweetheart. It's me. What's happening?"

"Sweetie! I was hoping you'd call. The phone's okay now. You were right -- it was tapped."

"Did the repairman show you how to check to see if it gets tapped again?"

"Yes, it's simple. And the phone is okay. I check it every day when I get home. Where have you been?"

"Busy at work. You know how that goes. How's the job?"

"Oh, all right I guess. I'll be glad when we get the settlement money and can get away from here."

"Yeah, me too. Are you planning to go out tonight?"

She glowed at the question. "Sure. It's Friday, isn't it?"

"I guess I should have known that without asking, right?" he said with a hint of sarcasm.

She ignored the question. "Can you meet me?"

He cleared his throat and didn't answer right away then said, "I don't think we should meet tonight. That same guy we first saw at the hotel followed me when we left the motel last weekend. I managed to lose him, but we're still being watched."

Sheila's mood darkened. "So how long does this have to go on? I'm sick and tired of having to hide!"

"Not much longer, Sweetheart. Dalton's attorney will come up with a decent offer soon then we'll be out'a here!"

Sheila sat on the side of her bed. "He offered half a million last week, and I turned it down, like you said to."

"Good girl. When he gets up to two million, that's when we take it and run."

"Are you sure he'll go that high?"

"Sure he will. They risk losing ten times that much if we go to court, and they won't take that kind of chance."

"Tell me again where we'll go and what we'll do. I love hearing you talk about it."

"Sure, Sweetheart. We'll start in Paris -- fly there first class and stay in the fanciest hotel in town. You can buy new clothes there, whatever you want. After we've seen Paris, we'll go to Spain and Italy and then Greece. You'll like it there. The statues and fountains are unbelievable."

"Yes!" she laughed. "It'll be so much fun! Where will we go after that?"

He chuckled. "Anywhere you like, Sweetheart. England, Switzerland, the orient -- you name it."

"Oh, Sweetie! I love hearing you talk about it. I just can't wait! Do you think it'll be much longer?"

"No, not much longer. Just a few weeks, at most. Then we'll be able to be together all the time, and it won't matter who sees us."

"Can you come over? I don't want to go out without you. We can just stay here -- maybe watch a movie and fool around a little. Sound like fun?"

"It sure does! And you know I want to see you more than anything, but it's too risky. That guy has your place staked out. Then it'd all be over. No money, no Paris, no nothin'."

"Okay, Sweetie, if you think so. But when can we see each other again?"

"I don't know for sure. Maybe not until after all the paperwork has been done with the settlement, and you have the money."

"It seems like this is taking forever," she whined. "I hope they offer more money soon. I'm so tired of all this waiting!"

"Yeah, me too. But it won't be much longer. Then we'll be free as birds on the wing!"

"Will you try to call me more often?"

"You bet, Sweetheart. I'll call you every day 'till we get that settlement."

"You said that before, and it's been a whole week since I've talked to you."

"I'm sorry. It's my work. And I wasn't sure if the phone was okay until I talked to you tonight." She noticed that he sounded annoyed. "I've just been real busy this week -- but I'll start calling every day. You'll see."

"Good. I get so lonesome here all by myself. I've watched television until I'm almost blind."

"It won't be much longer. You'll see. I gotta' go now, Sweetheart. I'll call you tomorrow."

"Oh, Honeybun, don't hang up so soon! You just called!" Now it was her turn to be annoyed.

"Sorry, Babe. I gotta' go now. Talk to you about the same time tomorrow. We'll talk about going to Europe again. Okay?"

"Oh, all right then, if you really have to go. I love you, Sweetie. Bye."

"Bye, Sweetheart. I love you too, and I'll be thinking about you."

***

Friday night passed with all the speed of oil paints drying for Mitch, sitting alone in a dark green rental Taurus just around the corner from Sheila's apartment. He wondered why Sheila had quit using her phone and considered the possibility that she might have had the tap removed. If he replaced it, she would find out, and that would put her more on guard than ever. Better to leave things as they were.

He replayed mental images of the man he had seen with Sheila on several occasions and tried to come up with something that might help them learn his identity, but it was of no use. He either would have to get a better photograph or the doctor would have to see the man himself.

***

Late Sunday night, Brent awoke with a start. It had been a week since he had the blood sent off from Bayside Hospital. Tomorrow, he should get the result.

Chapter 35

Brent awoke at daybreak Monday morning, as usual. He made plans for the day while sitting on a stool in the kitchen over a cup of hot coffee. He decided to call Dr. Brown first and discuss a faculty position with the Department of Surgery. He sipped the coffee and mused over the fact that he hadn't decided to get involved with full-time teaching earlier in his career. If he had, things would look a lot different now.

Nicole came downstairs a little later. She kissed him on the cheek then poured herself a cup of coffee. "Another cup?" she asked, taking a seat at the kitchen table.

He stretched and yawned. "No, thanks. I've had my limit. Busy day today?"

She settled into a chair near him and took her first sip. "About usual, I guess -- just the deskwork that always piles up. And it's the end of the month, so that means it's payroll time. What are your plans?"

He told her about his decision to call Dr. Brown and try to get a faculty appointment before the new academic year began the first of July. Her eyes lit up at the news.

"That's wonderful, Brent. I've felt all along that someday you would wind up teaching. It's just a shame it took so long to get you there." She reached across the table and put her hand on his.

He put his other hand on top of hers. "There's still a lot of time left. We have some good years ahead of us. You'll see."

Nicole smiled at him. "I know we do." She finished her coffee and put her cup on the counter. "I need to take a shower and get to work. Would you like anything for breakfast?"

"No, thanks. I'll eat a piece of fruit later." Brent's mind had already moved elsewhere. He planned to give Dr. Williams, the internist in Kemah, a call when Nicole left for work. There was such a small chance that his Western Blot would return negative, and he had not wanted to build Nicole's hopes about it. He hadn't told her he had asked to have it repeated last week before checking out of the hospital.

Nicole disappeared up the staircase, and Brent occupied his time reading the morning newspaper until she came back down a short while later.

"My, you look nice," he said when she appeared again. Nicole always looked great to him, even when she wasn't dressed up. But when she did dress up, she looked fantastic.

She threw her head back and did a little pirouette for his benefit then smiled. "Just work clothes, dear."

Then, looking at her watch, "Oh, my! Look at the time!" She rushed over and gave him another kiss, this time on the lips then picked up a small briefcase and headed for the door. "That'll have to hold you until I get home tonight."

He smiled and blew her a kiss. "Bye, Nikki. Be careful on the road."

When he heard Nicole drive out of the driveway, Brent went to the phone directory and looked up the number for Dr. Williams' office.

A pleasant female voice answered. "Dr. Williams' office, this is Marie. May I help you?"

"Marie, this is Dr. Brent Dalton. Is Dr. Williams in?"

"No, Doctor, his appointments begin at nine, so he should be here any minute now. Can I have him call you?"

"Yes, please. I'm calling to see if he has the result of a test I had run last week. He'll know what I'm looking for. Just have him call me when he gets in."

"I'll do that, Doctor. Does he have your number?"

Brent gave her his phone number and hung up.

He looked up the number for the Department of Surgery at the University of Texas and called the Chairman's office. Within a few minutes, he had made arrangements with the secretary to have an interview with the Chairman himself on Thursday afternoon. She requested that he fax a *Curriculum Vitae* for review before the interview. No problem. Brent, from long force of habit, kept an updated CV in his file at all times.

The phone wasn't yet back in the receiver when it rang, still in Brent's hand. He almost dropped it when he answered.

"Hello, Brent Dalton here."

"Dr. Dalton? Please hold for Dr. Williams." There was a brief pause then Paul Williams' voice on the other end. "Brent?"

"Yes -- thanks for returning my call. Sorry I didn't make it in to see you last week, but I'm doing just fine. No problems at all that I could relate to the hypothermia episode. I'm feeling great." *God, I sound like a nervous teenager calling for his first date -- slow down and get to the point.*

He cleared his throat. "I was wondering if you had gotten the result of my Western Blot back yet."

"The regular mail isn't here, so we called the lab and got them to FAX a copy of your report. I knew you were eager to get the result."

"I know there's not much hope that the result is any different than before, but I wanted to be sure." Brent felt a little lightheaded in anticipation hearing the test result. He knew this would be the last time he would have it run. There remained a small glimmer of hope that a mistake could have been made, and he would be told his result was negative.

"Brent, I'm going to make your day, maybe even your whole year. I'm not surprised that you're feeling fine --your Western Blot is negative!"

Brent's head spun, and he leaned on the kitchen counter for support. He couldn't believe what he had just heard. This must be a dream. "I'm sorry. Could you repeat that?"

"You're negative! I've been trying to call you, but your phone was busy. You don't have the HIV virus. Your test is negative!

Brent pulled a chair over from the table and sat down. He was speechless for a minute as he tried to comprehend what he had just heard. *This can't be real. I'm dreaming again.* He slapped himself on the cheek, but nothing changed.

"Negative? My test is negative?" His voice broke as he choked on words. "Could there be some other reason?"

"No! You're negative! You don't have the virus!"

Brent felt a sudden flood of emotion as the reality of the situation sank in. "Oh, my God! Paul, thank you so much! You'll never know what this means to me." A sudden beam of sunlight illuminated the kitchen, and he felt so lighthearted he thought he could float right out through the window and off into the sky! "Thank you, thank you, thank you!" He felt a knot forming in his throat and tears of joy welling in his eyes. His voice still breaking, he spoke again. "I need to call my wife."

"Of course, Brent. Let it sink in for a few minutes then call her."

A thought occurred to Brent as he prepared to hang up the phone. He cleared his throat, recovering from the news. "Paul, one quick question. How could this have happened? How could my other tests all have been positive and then turn negative?"

Williams didn't answer right away. "Hm-m, that's a tough one. I really don't have any explanation. It's not something that I've ever heard of before. One false positive maybe, but not several!"

"Thank you again, Paul. I need to call Nikki."

"Good-bye, Brent. You're more than welcome."

Brent hung up the phone and took a deep breath. Shafts of bright sunlight now beamed through the kitchen windows and lit up the entire room. He felt alive and energized. Jumping up from the chair, he raised his arms and shouted with joy. "I'm well! I'm well!"

He dialed Nicole's work number, and a secretary answered. "Home Health Agency. May I help you?"

"Hello, Millie. This is Dr. Dalton. Has Nicole gotten there yet?"

"No, she's not here yet. Can I have her call you when she gets in?"

"Yes -- on second thought, give her a message for me. Tell her that I've just gotten some fantastic news and need her to come home as soon as possible so I can share it with her."

"How exciting! I'll tell her just as soon as she gets here, Dr. Dalton."

"Thanks, Millie." Brent walked the length of the kitchen a couple of times, almost tripping over his own feet in his excitement and still finding the information he had just received too incredible to believe.

What should he do next, he wondered. The lawsuit would go out the window. After all, there was no way he could have given HIV to anyone if he wasn't infected himself. So there was no great urgency to notify Todd.

The first thing he would do, he decided, would be to go to the hospital and request an immediate reinstatement of his privileges. Then he would take steps to open his office again. That would require a visit with Bill Rudman. He gloated at the thought of confronting the man with the news that he was HIV negative and as healthy as a horse. And while he was at the hospital, he would talk to Al Martin and ask him how all this could have occurred. Al was an old friend. If anyone could explain what had happened, he could.

There remained many questions to be answered. Why had so many tests been equivocal then positive? How did his test result leak out so quickly to the sleazy tabloid? Could Rudman have been manipulating the test results somehow? That was a possibility he had never even considered, someone manipulating the test result. Who else could have done such a thing? Why would they have done it? If it were Rudman, and he and Sheila were lovers then the obvious motive would be the lawsuit.

He paced the kitchen and pounded his fist into his palm when he arrived at the conclusion that someone had manipulated his test result. But now, he had his life back again, and all he had to do was pick up the pieces and put them back together.

Brent knew things would never be the same. He had been tempered in the fire of this experience and now was a different person. The flame which once had been fueled by his desire for fame and fortune no longer burned. It had been extinguished like a candle thrown into a bucket of water. Maybe it wasn't too late to talk to Gary Morgan again. With a partner, he and Nicole would have time to rebuild their lives and enjoy a slower pace.

He heard Nicole's car pull into the driveway and went to the door to meet her. She ran inside when he opened it for her. "Brent, what has happened? Are you going back to work? Why did you want me to come home?"

He hugged her with all the love he felt bursting from his heart, relishing the warmth of her closeness. "Better than that, Nikki. Much better."

She pulled back from him. "What is it then?"

"I had another Western Blot run last week, and it's negative! Nikki, I don't have HIV!"

Her face paled, and she stared at him in silence for a minute. "Negative? You're okay?"

"Yes, I'm okay! I don't have HIV!" His face beamed with a broad smile. "I didn't mention the test to you because it was just routine, and I had no real hope that the result would be any different from the others. But it was!"

Nicole looked skeptical. "Oh, Brent -- are you sure? How can that be? Once you have the virus, you can never be free of it, can you?"

"That's just it, Nikki. I never had the virus. I think somebody altered my test results at Graham."

Nicole stood in the same spot by the garage door, her face still ashen from the unbelievable news she had just heard. Her lower lip trembled, and tears began to well in her eyes. "Brent, I want to believe this more than anything I've ever wanted in my entire life, but it just seems too incredible. Are you sure?"

"Yes! Yes! -- I'm negative! Everything is going to be all right. You can believe it."

Nicole burst into tears and fell into his arms. "This is too good to be true," she managed to say between sobs. "This is the happiest day of my life."

Then, like a switch had been flipped, Nicole began laughing. It was contagious. He also began laughing, and soon they were both hysterical, holding their sides and gasping for breath.

"I just can't believe it!" Nicole said, wiping her eyes with the back of her hand. "How did you find out?"

"I called Paul Williams' office right after you left. He wasn't in yet, but when he arrived and got the message to call me, he checked with the lab and got a phone report. Then he called me back."

Nicole looked serious. "You don't think there's any chance that there could have been a mistake, do you?"

"No, of course not!" Brent reflected for a minute. "But -- I wonder what would happen if I had another test run at Graham Memorial."

She looked at him, now with a puzzled look on her face. "Why do that?"

"So we can track the specimen and find out if someone has been manipulating the results."

Nicole went to the counter and began filling a coffee pot with water then quit before she had finished. She sat at the kitchen table. "Do you actually think someone altered your tests? Why would they do that?"

Brent sat near her. "So the Walters girl could sue me. I still think Bill Rudman is involved in all this. He has to be Sheila's boyfriend. That would explain everything!"

Nicole shook her head in disbelief. "Oh, Brent. Let's just get our lives back together. The suit will be dropped when it's known that you are negative. Why pursue it any further?"

"To keep it from happening to someone else, for one reason. And for another, I just want to know."

"But, how do you go about tracking a blood sample? If someone did change the reports, won't they know you're watching it this time?" She gasped and put her hand to her mouth in sudden shock. "What if you have it run at Graham and it comes back positive again? Would that mean someone tampered with the test or that you really do have the virus?"

Brent shook his head. "I'm convinced I don't have the virus, regardless of what any future tests at Graham show. But I'll need some help finding out why the earlier tests were reported positive." He rubbed his chin. "Al Martin will help, I'm sure. He's always been very concerned about me. I'll explain the situation to him and see what he thinks."

"Al Martin? Do I know him?"

"He's a pathologist. In charge of the lab. I've known him for years, and he's a good friend. If anybody would know how to track a lab specimen, it would be him."

Brent went to the telephone and began dialing a number.

"Who are you calling?"

"Martin."

"Right now? Why don't you think about this some more, Brent. This whole scenario scares me."

"I can't do anything about going back to work or reopening my office without announcing that I'm HIV negative. Once that news is out, there won't be a very good chance of finding out who messed with the previous test results." He paused, gazing out the back window while waiting for someone to answer his call. It was a nice view.

Another pleasant female voice answered. "Laboratory, may I help you?"

"Yes, this is Dr. Dalton. Could I speak with Dr. Martin, please."

"One moment, please. I'll see if he's in."

There was a pause, and Brent listened to the melancholy strains of Pete Fountain's "Sentimental Journey Home" while he waited. How appropriate.

The music clicked off. "Hello, this is Dr. Martin."

"Al, this is Brent Dalton. I've just received some wonderful news."

"That's great. What sort of news is it? Have you won a lottery somewhere?"

"Better than that! I'm HIV negative!"

Martin didn't respond right away. When he spoke, it was slow and deliberate. "That would be nice if it were possible. What leads you to think you're HIV negative? You've had several tests now that have tracked the course of your infection, and your Western Blot was definitely positive."

"I had another Western Blot done at a different lab, and it's negative! I just found out!"

Martin sighed. "Brent, I wouldn't get my hopes up right away. The test is probably a false negative. There could be any number of reasons for that. Maybe the other lab used an old reagent or something.

We need to have another one done here. I'll have it expedited so we can get the result overnight."

"Yes, I want to do that. But there's something else, Al. Is there any way you can oversee the test yourself and monitor the handling of the specimen?"

Nicole watched him with an intense stare when he made that last request. It appeared she did not feel secure with his plans.

Martin answered after a brief pause. "Yes, of course I can. But why do you want me to do that?"

"I'm suspicious that someone may have tampered with my test results."

The silence from the phone went on for such a long time that Brent thought he might have been disconnected, but Martin answered at last. "Tampered with the results? In my lab? Why on earth would someone do a thing like that? It's not possible!"

"Anything's possible. Especially when millions of dollars are hanging in the balance. Remember the lawsuit that was filed against me right after the news of my infection became public knowledge?"

"Yes, how could any of us forget? So you think that's a reason for someone to have tampered with your test results?"

"Yes, I do. Can you help me check it out?"

"Yes, of course, Brent. But I can assure you that you're barking up the wrong tree. This is a top-quality lab, and there's just no way your tests could have been tampered with."

"I'd like to come down there now, if it's all right with you."

"Come on down, and we'll talk some more." Martin sounded very concerned. "Oh, wait a minute. I just remembered I have a meeting in about fifteen minutes. Why don't we meet later, say for lunch. After we've talked, we'll repeat your test. I'll supervise it myself this time. And, Brent -- don't hang your hopes too high on that test you had done somewhere else. It has to be a false negative."

"We'll see. I'll come by around noon."

"I'll be in my office."

Chapter 36

Brent felt a certain degree of alarm at the suggestion that his last test result could be a false negative. He kept reminding himself that the lab for the hospital in Kemah was every bit as trustworthy as the one at Graham Memorial. Besides, Western Blot tests were sent off to a reference lab, probably the same one for both hospitals. He also knew, from the extensive reading he had done, that false negative test results were uncommon after an HIV infection had become established.

He didn't want to alarm Nicole by bringing up the possibility of a false negative test, so he explained that he was going to have another test run, as he had planned even before talking with the pathologist. That would allow the sample to be traced this time.

It was a little past eleven forty-five when Brent parked in the doctor's parking area outside the emergency room and entered the hospital through a side door. Martin's office, in the back part of the lab, was just a short distance down the corridor which ran between the ER and the main part of the hospital.

The lab was in a typical Monday morning flurry of activity. The central core had sorting and receiving areas, computer terminals, stacks and baskets of reports and other paperwork, and several printers, all of which were whirring like angry swarms of bees. Several side rooms adjoining the central core were the actual places where the work was done. Brent noticed one right away. It had a sign which read "serology". This would be the room where specimens for HIV tests were processed.

A hefty receptionist in a set of green scrubs sat behind the receptionist's desk inside the entrance to the lab. Brent stuck his moist palms in his pants pockets. He disliked the anxiety he could sense in the back of his mind. "Is Dr. Martin in?"

"Are you Dr. Dalton?"

"Yes, I am."

"Dr. Martin is expecting you. He had to run out for a few minutes and asked me to have you wait for him in his office." She stood up and started to come around the desk.

"That's all right. I know where his office is. I'll just have a seat and wait for him there. Thanks."

Brent walked into Martin's office and took a seat in one of the padded chairs in front of the pathologist's desk. The room was small, and the wall behind the desk was lined with books and journals. A couple of large, color prints hung on the wall opposite the desk, and the wall to his right was covered with the usual array of diplomas and certificates displayed in most doctor's offices. Another desk with a microscope and several cardboard folders holding colorful glass slides was on the left side of the office. A file cabinet stood in a back corner.

Feeling restless, Brent got up and went over to the certificates and began reading them. Martin's credentials were excellent: a graduate of an ivy-league medical school, with honors, and then did his residency at one of the largest universities in the northeast. He was board certified and belonged to numerous professional societies as well.

Brent looked around the office for pictures of Martin's family, but the only pictures in the room were the two prints on the wall, both depicting city scenes with grotesque, leaning buildings.

What am I doing here? Why do I think Al Martin is going to be of any help to me? Why is he so convinced that I do have the HIV virus? Brent paced back and forth in the small room. *Where the hell is Martin?*

Minutes went by. Moving away from the wall with the certificates, he noticed the bottom two drawers of a file cabinet standing open. He walked in that direction. The labels on the front of the drawers read "Personal". They were both empty.

The door to the office opened with a sharp snap, and the secretary in the green scrubs stuck her head into the room. "Would you like a cup of coffee? I'm sorry Dr. Martin isn't back yet. He should be here any minute."

Brent looked at his watch. He had been waiting in the office for twenty-five minutes. "No, thanks. I'll just wait awhile longer. Did he happen to say where he was going?"

"No, he didn't. But it must have been very important. He left in a big hurry with a stack of files in his arms." She closed the door and left Brent alone again.

He moved back to the large chair and sat down. Staring at the wall of books, he began to wonder about Martin. The pathologist had been at Graham for almost ten years, having come there right out of his residency training. He had always been competent enough but never seemed to have any close friends on the medical staff. Brent knew him only on a professional basis, but he had come to regard Martin as a friend because of the numerous occasions they talked at length about surgical specimens and their pathological significance. Martin had always been willing to spend as much time as Brent wanted in the discussions, and this was of enormous help to Brent when making decisions about treatment and prognostic discussions with his patients.

Brent had never met Martin's wife but understood he was married. He had no idea about whether or not they had any children.

The title of a book on one of the shelves caught his eye: *Living with HIV.* That was a strange book for a pathologist to have in his library. Resting next to the first book were several others on the subject of AIDS and the HIV virus. Why does Martin have so many books on HIV?

Like a light turning on, the picture of the man Mitch had photographed at the motel flashed into his mind. Medium build, medium height. Dark hair, combed back. It had to be Rudman, but something didn't look quite right. It was the hair! Rudman's hair was longer than the man in the photograph.

A dim light of recognition began to glow in Brent's mind. Of course! How stupid of him not to have realized it earlier! The man in the picture was Al Martin! He and Sheila were lovers! That's why he had called about her the night Brent was asked to see her in the ER. And how easy it would have been for him to have tampered with the test results!

Brent burst out of the room and went to the receptionist's desk. "Where does Dr. Martin live?"

Startled, the plump lady jumped back from the desk, almost falling over in the process. "Why, I have no idea! Why do you want to know?"

"Never mind. Do you have a phone book?"

Without taking her eyes off the impatient visitor, the receptionist reached under the desktop and pulled out a thick phone book. Brent grabbed it and turned to the "M's". There were several Martins, two of which had the first name of Alfred but with different middle initials. One had "MD" after his name. That had to be the Al Martin he wanted. The address was one on Holly Street in Bellaire, not far from where Brent himself lived. He was acquainted with the area.

Jotting the address on a scrap of paper, he dashed out of the laboratory and ran down the hall toward the doctor's parking lot. Time was of the essence! People in the hallway jumped in all directions and looked over their shoulders at the spectacle of him running in the hospital, but he didn't care. Martin was running away, and if Brent was ever going to get any answers about what had happened, it would have to be now!

Jogging into the parking area, Brent glimpsed a figure getting out of a vehicle near the exit. What luck! It was Gary Morgan.

"Gary!" Brent hailed, stopping to catch his breath. "Over here!"

Gary trotted over and clapped Brent on the back. "Hey, it's good to see you again! What's the big rush?"

"Can you come with me for a little while, Gary? I'll explain in the car, but right now we have to hurry!" Brent began jogging again, and Gary followed.

"What's going on, Brent? I'm supposed to help Dr. Wilson with a couple of hernias in just a few minutes."

Brent hit the electronic door lock on his key ring when they approached his Suburban, and they jumped in. He started the engine, threw the shift into reverse and tromped the accelerator.

"Wilson will be all right. This is important, Gary!" Brent zoomed out of the parking space, and his tires squealed all the way through the exit leading to the street.

Gary sat dumbfounded while Brent explained what had happened during the past few days, ending with the news about his negative HIV status.

The young surgeon burst into a wide smile when he heard the story. "Brent, that's fantastic!" he said clapping his hands together and bouncing in his seat like a child. "It's almost unbelievable! Now you can get back into practice, and we can work together—if the offer is still open."

Brent grinned without taking his eyes off the road. "You better believe the offer is still open! Now, more than ever!"

"But, Brent—where are we going in such a hurry?"

"I'm pretty sure I know why I was led to believe that I had HIV, Gary. It was a setup so that I could be sued for infecting the Walters girl."

"How could that happen?"

"I'm not sure I know how, but I'm almost positive I know who. And he's running away right now as we speak."

Gary appeared puzzled. "Who is it? Rudman?"

"No. Al Martin."

Chapter 37

Midday traffic had begun to increase, but Brent ignored speed limits as he and Gary Morgan raced after Martin. Brent prayed he wasn't too late as they sped down Main Street and turned right onto Bellaire Boulevard toward Martin's house. Assuming the pathologist had left his office right after Brent's call, he had nearly a three hour head start.

Thoughts raced through Brent's mind. What was the connection with the books on AIDS? Sheila has the virus. Maybe Martin has it too! But why had Martin tampered with Brent's test results? Was it just for the money?

Every stoplight seemed stuck on red, but they made slow progress toward Bellaire. Brent gripped the steering wheel with white knuckles as they turned south on Rice Avenue and sped down the street.

"Watch for Holly Street, Gary. On the left."

"How far down is it—does it cross Rice?"

"I think it runs east and west somewhere in the lower part of this subdivision, near Bellaire High School."

The school appeared in view on their right, and they watched the street names as they zipped by: Pine, and then Valerie. Gary pointed and shouted, "There it is! Holly Street!" The tires on the Suburban squealed as they rounded the corner and looked for street numbers.

They had traveled just a short distance when a speeding vehicle flashed past going in the opposite direction. Brent caught a glimpse of the figure behind the wheel of the black Lexus and recognized him without question. It was Martin!

"That's him, Gary! That was Al Martin in the black car!" As fast as he could, Brent pulled into the nearest driveway and turned around just in time to see the Lexus turn left onto Rice and disappear. Tires screaming, Brent floored the accelerator and sped after him.

The Lexus made another left onto Beechnut just south of the high school and raced toward the 610 west loop. Brent was forced to run a red light just after it changed from caution near Meyerland Plaza, causing two vehicles to slam on their brakes and honk their horns. Brent was oblivious to what happened. They charged up an entrance ramp to the Interstate a few car lengths behind the Lexus.

"Brent, do you want me to call the police on your car phone?"

Brent thought for a minute. "What would you say? That I want them to pull Martin over so I can question him?"

Gary chuckled. "Good point. But what are you going to do if you catch up with him?"

Brent glanced at him then squinted his eyes and spoke through clenched teeth. "I'm gonna give 'im a chance ta make my day!"

Gary howled and slapped the dash. "If that's supposed to be Clint Eastwood then I'm Daffy Duck!" They both laughed.

Brent became serious again. "I think he's getting away. I can't go much faster than this."

Martin darted in and out between cars seeking to increase his lead, and Brent knew that he must have been recognized when they passed. The secretary might even have called to warn him that someone was coming to the house. Brent glanced at the speedometer – eighty-five and climbing! If the police stopped him now, Martin would get away. He reached down and turned on his flashers. At least he would let it be known that something was wrong.

The black Lexus gained a little more distance after they raced around the curve below Braeswood Boulevard and headed east. The speedometer on the Suburban read eighty-five as they whipped in and out of traffic, and Brent gripped the wheel with a death grip. He knew if they passed a patrol car the chase would be over. The Lexus would get away, and he might never see Martin again.

Not two minutes later, flashing blue lights appeared in Brent's rearview mirror, and he saw cars pulling into the right lane to let the police get by. He gritted his teeth with determination and pressed the accelerator even harder. He had to catch the Lexus before the police caught up with him.

Gary glanced over his shoulder several times in rapid succession toward the flashing lights. "Brent, are you going to stop? This is getting serious!"

"I have my emergency blinkers on. They have to know something is wrong!"

There was a flash of blue to their right, and another police car pulled onto the Interstate ahead of them and sped off in pursuit of the Lexus!

"Ya-hoo! Go get 'im, Smoky!" Brent shouted.

Martin apparently saw the police car too. He changed lanes as if pulling over to the right then made a break toward an exit ramp. Another car blocked him from getting into the lane he needed, and he jammed on his brakes to pull in behind the other vehicle. He was almost even with the ramp when he made a hard right and slammed into a protective barricade of large, black rubber bumpers that shielded the ramp entrance.

Brent pulled onto the shoulder in front of the now-blocked ramp with a Texas State Trooper directly behind him. The trooper who chased the Lexus pulled up behind the wreck to shield traffic from the area. Martin sat in the driver's seat, slumped forward on the steering wheel. The front of the vehicle billowed steam from under the buckled hood.

"Step out of the vehicle and place your hands on top of the car, both of you," announced the trooper from a speaker behind Brent. "You on the passenger side, step around to the other side of the car."

"What a way to start a partnership," Gary Morgan mumbled, opening his door. They climbed out of the Suburban and placed their hands on the top, as instructed. The trooper sat in his patrol car for a minute, talking on the radio then walked over to the two men.

"Do you have an emergency, Sir? You were going pretty fast back there." He proceeded to pat them down then told them they could take their hands off the top of the car.

"Yes, I do -- or did," Brent replied. "I was following the Lexus that just wrecked. The driver's a criminal."

The trooper's interest freshened. "What kind of criminal?" he asked.

"He falsified some laboratory tests at a hospital where we work. We're doctors, all three of us. Would you mind if we check to see if he needs any assistance?"

The trooper hesitated a few seconds then waved his hand toward the Lexus. "Go ahead. EMS is on the way, so don't try to move him."

"Right."

Brent and Gary jogged over to the steaming Lexus. A trooper stood by the side of the open driver's door talking to Martin, who appeared dazed. The trooper reached across his lap and turned off the ignition switch, although the car engine was already dead. "Are you okay, Sir?"

Martin nodded his head. "I think so." There was a little blood trickling out of his nose, and he wiped it with his hand and stared at the bright red streak on his palm. "I'm --I'm not sure. I'm bleeding." Brent stepped up to the open door.

"Officer, I'm a surgeon. Mind if I check him?" The officer stepped back to let him get closer.

"Al, are you having any trouble breathing?"

The pathologist looked startled at seeing Brent then shook his head. "No." He hung his head and closed his eyes. Brent took his wrist and found a strong, full pulse. The seatbelt, which was still buckled across Martin's lap and torso, had worked well.

Brent leaned forward, his face close to Martin's. "Al, why did you do it?"

There was no immediate response. Martin shook his head side to side with his eyes closed then mumbled something unintelligible.

"What did you say, Al?"

Martin opened his eyes and stared straight ahead. "I said, 'I have AIDS.'"

Brent felt elated. His suspicions were confirmed! "You have AIDS?"

"Yes. I caught the virus doing an autopsy during my first year of residency. I cut myself with a knife and was afraid to be tested for several years. Then I developed some symptoms and found out I was HIV positive... had the virus all those years and didn't know it. That was four years ago, right after I started seeing Sheila on a regular basis."

"So, she caught the virus from you?"

Martin's head dropped again. "Yes, she caught it from me. She has some good years left, but it's just a matter of a short time for me."

"But why did you fake my test results?" Brent thought he knew the answer to that question even before Martin answered.

"I didn't fake them all. Didn't have to." The pathologist spoke in a low voice, looking straight ahead as though in a trance. He appeared to be glad to get this off his chest. "Your initial screening test was indeterminate. That's when it occurred to me."

"When what occurred to you?"

"That if you turned out to be HIV positive, we could blame Sheila's infection on you and collect from a lawsuit. It would have worked, too."

"Except that my Western Blot was negative, wasn't it?"

"Yes. When I saw the result, I realized how easy it would be for me to change it, so that's what I did. I called it indeterminate, because the lab follows up on all positives by repeating the test on the same sample. They would have caught it if I'd called it positive. Then I switched your serum sample for one of my own for the repeat test."

The two troopers huddled behind Brent, listening to the confession.

Brent continued. "Does Sheila know about this?"

"Not all of it." Martin sighed. He seemed anxious to tell everything. "She knows that she caught the virus from me. She thinks you have it too. She was willing to blame her infection on you so we could sue then run off together with the money."

A siren behind them caught Brent's attention for a second as an EMS vehicle pulled up and stopped. Two paramedics jumped out.

271

Brent shook his head. "This is unbelievable. To think of the misery you put Nicole and me through makes me sick. How could you do it, Al?"

Martin looked at him with a sneer. "It wasn't that difficult, under the circumstances."

One of the troopers took Brent by the arm and pulled him back. "That's enough for now, doctor. Let's let the paramedics take over."

Brent stepped back. The two troopers had heard it all. "I think we can let you off with a warning this time, Doc. I understood enough of what he said to know why you were chasing him. Just don't make a habit of driving like that."

"Thanks, officer." Brent and Gary Morgan walked back to the Suburban and drove toward Graham Memorial.

Brent felt vindicated, as though he had just awakened from a long, bad dream. He grinned at his future partner. "Well, Pilgrim, let's get back to the camp and saddle the horses! We've got work to do."

Epilog

Caribe heeled over at a steep angle and sliced through cool, choppy bay water. Almost six months had passed since Brent had caught Martin in his scheme to run away with Sheila. He had gotten his surgical privileges back within a couple of days, and Martin had lost his job and his medical license almost as fast.

Nicole, at the helm, looked radiant in her white shorts and knit shirt. Brent slackened the jib sheet a little then went over and stood behind her, putting his arms around her waist. She leaned into him and smiled. "Having fun?"

He kissed her neck, just behind the ear. "You better believe I am. How about you?"

"I had forgotten how good life can be. I've never been happier."

"Having a partner makes all the difference in the world, doesn't it? Gary is a real workhorse, and everyone likes him. He's a definite asset to the practice."

Nicole looked over her shoulder at him. "It's not just having a partner. It goes deeper than that. It's the way our lives have changed. We're spending time together and having fun, doing things -- smelling the roses."

Brent laughed. "That's true. But I know one person who's not going to be smelling roses for awhile."

"You mean Al Martin. Has his trial started?"

"No, but he's charged with attempted insurance fraud and a few lesser crimes. I don't think there's any doubt he'll be behind bars a few years."

"Do you think he has long to live?"

"No, I don't. He's been infected for several years now and looks terrible."

"It's sad, isn't it? I mean—that he ever even caught the virus in the first place. And then what he did to try to make his miserable life right."

"Yes, he messed up a lot of other people's lives, and came close to ruining ours."

Nicole frowned. "What about his poor wife?"

"I've never met her, but I understand that they had a marriage of convenience, so to speak."

"…convenience?"

"Yes, Martin married her while he was in medical school. He needed someone to cook and clean for him and hold down a job or two on the side in order to pay the rent and buy groceries."

"How sad. Does she have the virus too?"

"I don't know, but thank goodness, they never had any children."

Nicole studied his face for a minute. "How can you say that, Brent? Being childless is not a blessing."

Brent realized he had not made himself clear. "I meant, under the circumstances. You know, with her husband not loving her and being infected with HIV and everything. I know having children is a blessing under the usual circumstances."

Nicole leaned against the wheel and beamed at him. "Well, I'm glad to hear you say that, Dr. Dalton."

Brent was puzzled. "Why do you say that? You know we've always wanted children."

Nicole radiated happiness. "Well, maybe you'd better sit down, because I'm about to make your day, Papa."

"You, you don't mean…."

She threw her arms around his neck. "Yes, I found out yesterday! Next June, you're going to be a father!"

About the Author

Dr. Bill Booth is a graduate of LSU School of Medicine in New Orleans, where he also trained in general surgery. School and residency training were interrupted by a two year tour of duty in the Navy which included a year aboard the hospital ship *USS Sanctuary* in Vietnam.

Following residency training, Dr. Booth practiced general surgery first in a rural community in southeastern Missouri, then in Baton Rouge, Louisiana, where he retired in 2001.

Bill and Cherry, his wife of 45 years, have four adult children and five grandchildren. They now live in the mountains of north Georgia where he writes, ties flies, and plays golf. He practices medicine part-time at a free clinic in Jasper, Georgia.

Printed in the United States
90676LV00004B/1-99/A